C

D0099129

INEVITABLE
AND
ONLY

LISA ROSINSKY

INEVITABLE
AND
ONLY

BOYDS MILLS PRESS
AN IMPRINT OF HIGHLIGHTS
Honesdale, Pennsylvania

Boyds Mills Press
An Imprint of Highlights
815 Church Street
Honesdale, Pennsylvania 18431

Printed in the United States of America
ISBN: 978-1-62979-817-2 (print)
ISBN: 978-1-62979-921-6 (e-book)

Library of Congress Control Number: 2017937884

First edition
Design by Barbara Grzeslo
The text of this book is set in Aldus.

10 9 8 7 6 5 4 3 2 1

For my mom,
who read this one in the right order

CHAPTER ONE

After three and a half weeks of waiting—or really, fifteen years, nine months, and the slowest three and a half weeks ever—there it was. I dropped the junk mail and bills onto the hall table and picked out the long envelope with a rectangular bump, stamped with the words "Official Documents Enclosed, Do Not Bend."

"Dad!" I shrieked, running into the kitchen and flapping the envelope in his face.

"Error. Error. Cannot. Read. Moving. Object," he said in Malfunctioning Robot Voice, taking a block of tofu out of the fridge.

I waved the envelope again. "It says 'Department of Motor Vehicles,' Dad, guess what it is!"

"Speeding ticket?" he suggested, unwrapping the tofu.

I rolled my eyes. "It's addressed to *me*, not Mom." I don't know how my mom manages to get so many speeding tickets—she drives, like, less than ten miles a day.

"Mmm, fermented soy juice," he said, switching to his Gollum impression, as he drained the block of tofu in the sink. "Fermented sssssssoy juicccccce."

Dad's tofu scramble isn't bad, if you ask me. Mom grumbles, but if she's not home while Dad's cooking, then how can she expect to be served whatever she wants? When we go out to dinner she likes to order fancy stuff like brussels sprouts salad with truffle oil or chickpea fritters with date compote. But that's just on special occasions like birthdays, or to celebrate when Josh

7

wins a cello competition. Most nights, Dad cooks, and it's usually something like tofu scramble or black bean burgers or Quinoa Surprise.

"Dad, *focus*!" I said. "It's my learner's permit!" I ripped open the envelope and pulled out the laminated card triumphantly. "See?"

He pushed his glasses down his nose and looked at the card over them, preparing his snottiest British accent. I know the telltale signs. Martin Chuzzlewit Voice, he calls it. I think he just likes saying *Martin Chuzzlewit*. "Why, yes, indeed, it does seem that the state of Maryland is permitting you to learn. But to learn what, is the question? To learn the fine art of helping your father steam a spot of broccoli?"

I took the head of broccoli he held out and began breaking off bits and tossing them into the steamer. "Can we go out tonight? Please? Just to drive around the ShopRite parking lot. I won't go over ten miles per hour. I promise."

Dad pursed his lips and pretended to consider, but I thought I saw a smile starting to crack through.

"Eight miles per hour! Six!"

"We'll go right after dinner," he said, in his normal voice, which I've always thought sounds just like the weatherman's from the news and traffic report Mom listens to every morning in the car. Deep and resonant and, well, radio-like.

"Yes!" I shouted, dropping the last of the broccoli into the steamer. Josh had wandered into the kitchen, and he jumped at the noise and started to back away. But I caught him and lifted him off the floor, spinning him around in a circle, even though he's almost as tall as me now. "Yesyesyesyesyes!" I said, spinning the other way.

"Put me down, please," he said patiently. My little brother inherited all the patience in this family.

I put him down because he was really too heavy to spin anyway. "Did you hear me? I'm going to learn how to drive!" I waved my permit over my head.

"Can I have real cheese on my scramble?" he asked Dad, ignoring me.

Dad took a block of cheddar out of the fridge and set it down on the counter beside the tub of Daiya cheese. "Just remember you might turn into a baby cow one of these days, and don't say I didn't warn you. Which one do you want, Cadie?"

I sighed. "I'll have the fake cheese."

My parents have been vegetarians since they were in college—they met while peeling potatoes in their campus co-op kitchen—but Dad's recently "jumped on the vegan bandwagon," as Mom puts it. Usually while wrinkling her nose at the soy creamer or cashew butter Dad's plunked in front of her on the table. Secretly, I think almond milk belongs inside an almond, not in a bowl of cereal, but officially I side with Dad on this one. As with most things.

Mom came home just before eight, and I had the table set, the water glasses filled, and the salad dished out onto four plates so we could start dinner as quickly as possible. At eight thirty on the dot, Dad pushed back his chair and announced, "Cadie and I are going out for a driving lesson, if the other half of the family would be so good as to take dishwasher duty tonight."

Mom nodded absentmindedly, then processed what Dad had just said—I practically saw the wheels turning. Her head snapped around to me. "A driving lesson? Already?"

I held up my permit, which I'd tucked carefully into my sweatshirt pocket. Mom took the card and examined it. Then she sighed.

"*Dios mío.* My little girl. You're growing up too fast."

Something twisted in my stomach a little, and for a moment I wished I'd asked Mom to take me for my first lesson. Maybe it would've helped close the gap that had been widening between us for the past, oh, decade and a half.

But then she rubbed her eyes and said, "Go ahead, you two. Thanks for taking her, Ross. I'm beat. Could hardly keep my eyes open on the way home myself."

"Tut, tut. Not a very good example to set for our new driver here," Dad said, dropping a kiss on my mother's head. "You'd better rest up tonight, milady. Pamper thyself."

You'd have to know my dad's voices as well as I do to have recognized the barb in his tone.

To me, he said, "'Tis hatch'd and shall be so!" and I grinned, because it was a quote from *The Taming of the Shrew*, which we'd seen back in April at the Shakespeare Theatre in Washington, DC. Last week we'd gone to *Much Ado About Nothing*. Dad was thrilled that I'd signed up for drama class this year—I finally had room in my schedule for electives. He'd started collecting secondhand pocket editions of all the Shakespeare plays for me whenever he had extra copies at the bookshop.

I scooped up the car keys from the blue bowl on the counter, tossed them to Dad, and danced to the door.

Dad got into the driver's seat of our ancient Honda Accord and reached over to unlock the passenger's side door for me. Once upon a time, the car was some shade of red. But the roof had been painted blue, the hood was now purple, and the bumpers

10

were green. The doors were still their original color but had faded to a pinkish brick red and had been covered with little white stars, which is why Dad dubbed it the Commie Comet. He and Mom had plastered it in so many bumper stickers—which said things like ARMS ARE FOR HUGGING and EVERY MOTHER IS A WORKING WOMAN and QUESTION CONSUMPTION and JESUS WAS A LIBERAL—you could barely see the color of the car underneath anyway.

That was one thing that made me think maybe there was still hope we could get the old Mom back: she didn't insist on painting over all the stickers when she got the job at Fern Grove Friends School. She bought herself a wardrobe of business suits and high heels, cut off her long hair, and started wearing makeup, but she kept driving the Commie Comet just the way it was. Then again, most of the other cars in the parking lot at Friends look similar to ours. Of all the academic jobs out there, managing a Quaker school must be the crunchiest.

Dad drove up Elm Avenue to the ShopRite at the corner of University Parkway. This late at night, the parking lot was deserted, just as I'd known it would be. We pulled into a spot in the middle of the lot, under a flickering streetlight, and Dad turned the ignition off and unbuckled his seat belt.

"*All right*, he said, albeit dubiously." Dad loves to narrate himself, especially when it involves using adverbs. "Have at it, youngster."

I flew around to the driver's side and waited for him to get out (have I mentioned that patience isn't my strong suit?), then slid into the driver's seat, scooted it forward so I could reach the pedals, and adjusted the mirrors. I touched the steering wheel, the gearshift. Dad buckled himself into the passenger seat and said (in his normal Weatherman Voice, which meant that he was more nervous than he was letting on), "I'd suggest we begin by turning on the car."

We drove around that parking lot for close to an hour. Very slowly. I learned how to ease off the gas pedal and transfer my foot to the brake without jerking the car. How to check all my mirrors before changing into an imaginary left lane, an imaginary right lane. How to twist the wheel ever so slightly to a position that would make the car turn in a graceful wide circle, not a tight corkscrew.

"Do you want to drive home?" Dad asked, finally. "There's no traffic on Elm this time of night. I'm fine with it if you are."

This is one of the many things I love about my dad. He trusts me. Trusts that I know how to make good decisions.

"Yes!" I said, pumping my fist.

"Mirrors," Dad reminded me, as I turned out of the parking lot.

I kept the speedometer needle at 10 as the car bumped along Elm. It's a hilly road, cresting slightly at every cross street and then rolling down a gentle slope to the next one. We passed 39th Street, then 38th.

"Now, as you reach the top of a hill," Dad said, "you always want to slow down slightly. You never know what might be coming up the other side."

We rolled downhill from 38th and I pressed the brake lightly to keep the needle at 10, then transitioned my foot over to the gas pedal to climb the next hill.

"Like right now," Dad said, "you want to ease off the gas right about—"

Something blurred across the road as I reached 37th Street.

THUNK.

I stomped on the brake and screamed.

Dad shot out of the car and I sat there, frozen, my foot glued to the brake, until he banged on my window.

"Put it in park!" he was yelling. I shifted the gear into park, then he yanked the door open. "Let me back it up."

So I stood on the sidewalk while my father rolled the car off the cat I had just run over.

I couldn't look away. Where the front tire had been, there was a dark pile of fur with a darker pool of liquid forming around it. It was glistening faintly in the light from the nearest streetlamp, but it wasn't moving. Not a twitch. I was sobbing and screaming and I didn't realize what I was saying at first, until I'd said it over and over again, and finally Dad put his hands on my shoulders and said, "Yes, Cadie, honey, I know you're a vegetarian. Cadie, Cadie, take a deep breath."

He crouched to examine the situation, then took his phone out of his pocket and made a quick call. After he hung up, he walked over to me, his face pale, and put his arms around me. "Sweetie. You were driving entirely responsibly. It was an accident." Weatherman Voice. Serious Dad.

"But I'm a vegetarian," I sobbed again, as if I didn't know any other words in the English language.

"Good people can hurt things without meaning to," he said. "It happens all the time. Shh, Cadie, breathe. Breathe with me."

He started counting inhales and exhales and I breathed with his counting until I calmed down enough to stop hyperventilating. Then we waited for Animal Control to come, and when they arrived they examined the body and told us there was nothing they could do: the cat had no collar or tags; it was probably a stray.

But they scooped it into a bag so they could take it back to the lab and look for a microchip, and then Dad said he'd drive the car home. We could see our house from where we'd stopped, so I said I'd walk the three blocks down Elm Avenue. Dad gave me another hug, then nodded.

I cried while I walked, and when I opened the front door, Mom was waiting to give me a hug, too.

"Dad told me what happened, *querida*. Don't cry. It could've happened to anyone. At least you're okay."

But I didn't want to be comforted out of my misery. I'd killed an innocent living being and I deserved to suffer.

"And it sounded like the cat was very old, anyway," Mom said, stroking my hair.

I pulled back and gave her my best look of disgust, then stalked upstairs to my room. When I curled up on my bed, I felt something poke me in the ribs, and pulled my learner's permit out of my sweatshirt pocket. I tossed it under my desk, rolled over to face the wall, and closed my eyes.

I heard footsteps coming up the stairs a while later, but I kept my eyes closed when the door creaked open. The footsteps paused at the doorway, then continued into my room, and I felt my mattress sink down. I opened one eye a crack to see Dad perched on the edge of my bed.

He didn't say anything for a few minutes, just sat there. I squeezed my eyes shut again. Finally, he spoke.

"Cadie, my Cadiest," he said quietly. "What can I do?"

I just shook my head. How could I say it out loud? I, Acadia Rose Greenfield, was a murderer. At the age of fifteen. With my eyes closed, I saw one image burned into my retinas: Animal Control lifting that little body off the road, its matted fur glowing midnight black in the beam of their headlights. My stomach twisted and all I wanted was to vomit it out, to purge myself of the horrible memory. To go back in time before it had ever happened and fix it somehow. But there are some mistakes you just can't undo.

"Dad?" I whispered. "If crossing paths with a black cat is supposed to be bad luck, what kind of luck is it if you *kill* one?"

Dad didn't say that was stupid or superstitious. He didn't try to comfort me or convince me I was overreacting or try to make me feel better. He knew it wouldn't do any good. Dad knows me inside and out, because we're the same that way—when we're upset or angry, we just have to ride it out.

"I don't know," he said at last. "But I know how much you're hurting. Do you want me to sit here with you awhile longer?"

I nodded and reached out my hand, and he held it. And he must have stayed there until I fell asleep, because when I woke up the next morning, I didn't remember him letting go or leaving.

• • •

The next day Mom whisked Josh off to the Peabody Preparatory for his cello lesson after school. I had art club, and then I took the bus down to Mt. Vernon to the bookshop. I couldn't wait to tell Dad my news.

I got off the bus a few blocks early so I wouldn't have to transfer and walked the rest of the way. I love walking through Mt. Vernon, especially in early September when the leaves are starting to turn. Baltimore is grimy, lots of it is falling apart, but it's also a city full of brightly colored row houses, old churches, little monuments tucked away in odd corners.

Fine Print Books inhabits one of those painted row houses, a musty three-story structure approximately the same shape and size as our house. (You might wonder whether that tells you that our house is small, or the bookshop is huge. Let me give you a hint: used bookstores don't make enough money to be huge.) Dad hides there among the stacks all day, while my mother runs meetings and draws up budgets, and my brother practices cello to become the next Yo-Yo Ma.

And me? I convinced Mom to stop my violin lessons when I was ten, when it was already clear that five-year-old Josh was a cello prodigy. To my surprise, she agreed without too much arguing—I think because the extra money they saved on my lessons went to buy Josh a decent half-size cello—and I was allowed to amuse myself however I wanted to while Josh was herded off to Peabody for lessons. While he practiced for an hour in the morning before school, I slept in. During his two hours of practice in the evening, I joined clubs I never stuck with for more than a few months.

But I'd never been as excited about any of those clubs as I was about drama class. I started walking faster just thinking about it. Dad was going to flip when I told him about the winter play.

Fine Print has at least one resident cat per floor at all times. Dad says that "all true bookshops have feline familiar spirits." He says it's a principle of physics, like magnetism. Cats are naturally drawn to a place filled with armchairs and people sitting in them with books on their laps.

Today, when I walked in the door, Grendel—a huge tabby who spends all day sleeping in the window display—rubbed against my legs, and a lump of tears rose in my throat. What if that black cat had been someone's pet? Someone's feline familiar? What if it used to sit in someone's lap and make it impossible for them to turn the pages of their book, like Grendel does?

16

Cassandra heard the jingle of the bells against the door and looked up, put on her perfectly round, gold-rimmed glasses, and said, "Well, well, Grendel, look what you've gone and drug in from the cold." (It was seventy-three degrees outside.) Cassandra is my father's assistant. She's a grad student in medieval history at Goucher College, and she dresses like she's forgotten what century she actually lives in. Either that, or she does all her shopping at the Renaissance Festival.

Today she had her waist-length cherry-red hair braided and wound around her head in coronets, and she was wearing a crimson skirt with knee-high black combat boots and a billowy white blouse. Oh, how I lusted after those boots.

"Grendel, see if Ross is upstairs, and tell him that his daughter is here."

Cassandra never speaks to humans. She directs all her comments to whichever cat is nearest. If none of the cats are around, she simply doesn't answer you. This makes her a less-than-ideal bookshop assistant, as I've pointed out to Dad many times. He always sighs and tells me that he understands how hard it is to find work in grad school, and he appreciates her valuable literary expertise. Dad is a very nice guy.

I wondered what Cassandra would think of me if she knew what I'd done. The thought made me shudder, and I swallowed hard, ducked my head, and scurried upstairs to find Dad myself.

He was in his office on the second floor. The room had once been a bedroom with an adjoining bath. Now he kept books piled up in the claw-foot bathtub, and filing cabinets lined the walls, topped with even more books. His desk was cluttered with random things like quill pens, bottles of ink, some dead plants. Two more bookstore cats, Hieronymus and Bosch, were curled up in a basket near the door. They looked up when I entered, but I had to say "Dad!" twice before he lifted his eyes from his paperwork and noticed that I was standing in the doorway.

"Cadie!" he said. "To what do I owe this pleasure, *meine Tochter*?"

I crossed the small room and kissed him on the top of his curly mop of hair, tugging his ponytail. "Still sorting through the Goethe?"

"The complete works, my dear," he said, in his best Sleazy Car Salesman Voice. "Thirteen leather-bound, kissably intact volumes."

"Ew, Dad. No one wants to kiss dead cows."

"From 1902, did I mention?"

"Let's see," I mused, squinting into the distance and pretending to search my memory. "I believe you may have said something about it. At dinner two weeks ago? The day you bid on the set? Every five minutes since then?"

Dad stopped shuffling his papers and grinned at me. "So, to what *do* I owe this pleasure?"

"They announced the winter play in Meeting today!"

Dad looked at the books piled on his desk. "*Faust*?"

"No, and stop thinking about cow skin." I cleared my throat. "Ahem. Dramatic pause."

"Dramatic pause," Dad agreed. "So? What is it?"

I did a little flourish with one hand. "*Much Ado About Nothing*!"

"Well, how about that!" Weatherman Voice, because he was too excited to be anything but genuine.

I grinned back. "I know, right? It's like it was meant to be, after we just saw it last week!"

18

Dad laughed. "Well, Watson, as a former professor-in-training, I'd have to say that no, it's probably not a coincidence—I'd bet your teachers planned it this way, so they can tie in a field trip to the Shakespeare Theatre. At any rate, that means you're already one step ahead of the game. As your mother would say." He stood and pushed his chair back, scattering Hieronymus and Bosch. "When are the auditions?"

"Next Monday."

"Less than a week! 'Love alters not with his brief hours and weeks,'" Dad cried. Shakespearean Tragic Voice, one of my favorites, because it usually signaled the onset of a one-man mimed sword fight, ending in grisly death.

Today, though, Dad sat back down and said, "I have a bit more work to do. Are you meeting Mom and Josh at Peabody?" Mom was concerned that Josh's teacher wasn't pushing him hard enough, so she'd started observing his lessons.

"I guess so." I checked my watch. "His lesson is probably just about over."

"'Parting is such sweet sorrow,'" Dad droned in Bored Student Voice.

"Oh come on, Dad, you can do better than that." I picked up my backpack from where I'd dropped it by the door. "See you in a bit?"

He nodded. "I should be home in an hour or so."

"I'll start dinner."

"Thanks, well-trained offspring."

I headed downstairs, waved to Cassandra (who didn't wave back, shocker), and stepped out onto the sidewalk. Peabody Conservatory, where Josh took lessons in the Preparatory division, was just a couple blocks from the bookstore. I passed the Washington Monument, surrounded by cobblestones—it's a smaller replica of the famous one in DC—and climbed the marble steps to the conservatory entrance.

As I sat down on a bench, I caught my reflection in the glass door. I wished I looked like Dad, but Josh was the one who had inherited the curly strawberry-blond hair, the freckles, the blue eyes. My skin was a warm bronze, even in winter, like Mom's. I had her round nose, her thick eyebrows, and my hair was the same shade of espresso as hers. Although I'd done my best to change that: strands of pink, powder blue, and violet whipped across my face in the breeze.

That's one of the great things about hippie parents and Quaker school. No one cares if you dye your hair crazy colors, or if you show up in red Converse sneakers and a mustard-yellow hoodie dress printed with the words *Always be yourself. Unless you can be a unicorn. Then always be a unicorn.* I was one of the tamer dressers at Fern Grove, actually. I inspected my outfit in the window. I still wasn't sure how I felt about the fabric pulling tight over my chest and waist like that, but I didn't have any choice. Mom was wide-hipped and curvy, too. I pulled the hood up over my head and scowled at my reflection.

"Acadia!"

Mom was waving to me from across the street, where Josh was loading his cello into the back seat of the Honda. There was barely room for all three of us plus the instrument. But I knew we couldn't afford a bigger car.

Josh folded himself in under the cello in the back, and I climbed into the passenger seat, trying not to think about what this car had so recently rolled over. What *I* had so recently rolled over.

"How was your lesson?" I asked, twisting around to look at Josh.

"Fine."

Josh had never been a kid of many words. In fact, up until someone put a cello in his hands, we were slightly worried about him. Once he started preschool, Mom and Dad noticed that he didn't seem to take much interest in other kids, or in the things other kids liked—Play-Doh, make-believe, kicking a ball around. Or else he'd pick one activity and concentrate super hard on it, long past the time when other kids had gotten bored and drifted away.

But it turned out he was just storing up all those words so they could come out of his fingertips when he drew a bow across the strings of his cello. He started lessons at five, and he was winning competitions in the Prep by his sixth birthday. At seven, he began competing regionally. Now, at ten, he was studying with Olga Menshikov, the best teacher in the Prep, playing repertoire usually assigned to sixteen-year-olds, and it was clear he was on a conservatory track.

Mom's full-time job was school, and her other full-time job was Josh.

Which was fine by me. I had Dad, and we were a perfect pair.

CHAPTER TWO

When we got home, I sliced vegetables for a stir-fry, then curled up on the couch with my pocket edition of *Much Ado About Nothing* (a gift from Dad) and started reading from the beginning. The very beginning—page i, not page 1—the part with the introduction and preface and cast of characters. It was slow going.

Dad came home a while later and dumped his satchel on the coffee table. I held up my book; he gave me a thumbs-up.

"Veg is prepped," I said.

"Hallelujah!" He blew me a kiss, then breezed into the kitchen.

I realized I'd been reading the same paragraph over and over for the last fifteen minutes. I sighed. Maybe I should skip the introduction stuff and just read the play.

ACT I
SCENE I. *Before LEONATO'S house.*

Enter LEONATO, governor of Messina, HERO his daughter, and BEATRICE his niece, with a MESSENGER.

LEONATO
I learn in this letter that Don Pedro of Aragon comes this night to Messina.

MESSENGER
He is very near by this: he was not three leagues off
when I left him.

I jumped when Dad's phone rang inside his satchel. His ringtone
was the opening notes to Beethoven's Fifth Symphony. *Dum-
dum-dum-dummmmm. Dum-dum-dum-dummmmm.*

"Dad!" I yelled without moving. "Your phone!"

Pans rattled in the kitchen. He came in, fished his phone out
of the satchel, and looked at the number, then lifted an eyebrow
and took it back to the kitchen before answering. I heard the buzz
of his voice faintly, but couldn't make out what he was saying. I
was feeling too lazy to follow him and eavesdrop.

Twenty minutes later, my stomach rumbled. I yawned, stuck
a bookmark in *Much Ado*, and wandered into the kitchen to see if
dinner was ever going to happen.

The vegetables I'd sliced were sitting on the cutting board
untouched. Dad was leaning against the counter, still talking
quietly on the phone. He said, "If Elizabeth is ready, then we are."

He noticed me and waved an arm, shooing me away.

Huh?

I wondered who Dad was talking to. He isn't really a phone
guy. No matter who's on the other end, he finishes calls after just
a few minutes. He's good at making up excuses, like, "What's that
smell? Oh, dinner's burning!" Or once, with Awful Aunt Marge,
"What's that smell? Oh, the outhouse is overflowing!" (Awful
Aunt Marge, who thinks we're "a bunch of dirty hippies," did
not call him again for a long time.) He says he misses the days of
letter writing and express carrier pigeon, that the communication

center of his brain doesn't work as well in real time.

I, however, living in the twenty-first century, went upstairs to my room, dug into my backpack, and grabbed my own phone to call Raven. I was grumpy and hungry and Dad was being weird and secretive. Plus Raven and I hadn't gotten a chance to talk after school, with me rushing off to art club, and I still hadn't told her about my horrendous first driving lesson.

"Hey," I said, when she answered. "You're going to think I'm a terrible person and I hope you don't hate me forever because I think I'm going to hate myself forever already."

"Uhhh," she said. "Okay?"

I told her what had happened, all the gory details. "They never found a microchip, it was a stray. Someone from Animal Control called and told us. Is that worse? It never even had a loving home!"

"Tragic," Raven agreed.

"I feel like my soul will never be clean again," I said.

"You don't believe in souls," she pointed out.

"But it's like I've been marked. 'Cat-killer.' And I *love* cats."

"Well, I guess you could spend the best years of your prime caring for stray cats," she said. "Wearing cat-lady clothes. That seems like a fitting punishment."

"My prime? When's that?"

"Probably right now," she admitted.

"Ugh, I hope this isn't my prime. I think you have to know how to drive a car without murdering innocent animals to be considered 'in your prime.'"

"Stop saying *murder*, Cadie. You're being melodramatic."

"I know, but I'm so good at it."

"You are. Also, it was an accident. You have to stop beating

24

yourself up about it. You're going to get back on the horse, right?"

"Horses, sure. Behind the wheel, nope. Never."

"Never is a long time to be walking everywhere."

"Then I'll have great legs."

"While you're running around looking for stray cats to feed? With no Farhan to appreciate them?"

"*Raven!*"

"That reminds me," she said. "The Fall Ball is in a month. Are you going to ask him to go with you?"

I squeaked. "*Me* ask *him*? That would require bravery. Lots of it."

"Oh, come on. I'm going to ask Max."

"You and Max have been dating all summer! That doesn't count. The me-and-Farhan thing is way more complicated. Since there *is* no me-and-Farhan thing." But now I was grinning. Raven always managed to cheer me up, sooner or later.

Then Josh knocked on my door and told me that Mom and Dad needed us to come downstairs.

. . .

Mom, sitting tight-lipped and red-eyed on the living room couch. Dad, looking sick, perched on the edge of the piano bench. I noticed right away that he was sitting as far from Mom as possible.

"Acadia, Joshua," she said. "Your father has something to tell you."

"Okay . . . ," I said. "What's going on? Dad?" I heard my voice rising. "Is everyone all right?"

Josh stood next to me, saying nothing.

"Just have a seat," Dad said. In a voice I'd never heard him use before. Thinner than Weatherman, sadder than Shakespearean Tragic.

25

Josh and I sat, squished together on the ottoman.

"Kids . . ." Dad crossed then uncrossed his legs, smoothed his hands down his pants. "Everyone makes mistakes."

Mom bit her lip and clenched her fists so tightly her knuckles started turning white. "Oh, that's an understatement," she muttered.

"Melissa, please." Dad paused. "Are you sure you don't want to—process this some more, before we tell them?"

Mom just glared at him, and he sighed. "Kids," he said again, and I pinpointed it. The voice. Not a Voice at all, I mean. Just a voice, lowercase *v*. Dad never talked like that. Only normal people talked like that. Everyone else.

"Get to the point, Ross," Mom hissed. I'd never seen her this upset, either. Not even when Josh fell off the back porch and we thought his arm was broken.

"Kids," Dad said a third time. "You have—a sister."

I gasped. "Mom's having a baby?"

Mom glared at Dad. "Wouldn't that be the simple way. Nice and easy. But no, your father went and took care of that without—"

"Melissa, I'll explain."

"Well then, get to the point already, because I, for one, am getting tired of sitting here listening to you fumble." Mom was practically spitting.

Dad shifted on the piano bench, stood, clasped his hands behind his head. Turned to look out the window, and addressed his next words to the street. "It turns out you have a half sister." He paused again.

"I don't understand," I ventured, when it felt like the silence had grown thick enough that a hatchet wouldn't make a dent.

Mom swore, and I felt Josh stiffen next to me. "Ross found out he has another daughter," she snapped. "Somewhere in Ohio, of all places. And apparently this woman—the *mother*—has finally gotten around to letting him know. *If* she's even telling the truth." She muttered something else in Spanish that made Dad's eyebrows jump.

Okay, Mom occasionally swore, but she hardly ever swore in Spanish—only when she had exhausted the level of fury she could convey in English. And she always referred to him as "Dad" in front of us, not "Ross," unless she had forgotten we were in the room. Which was odd, because she was still addressing us. Not Dad.

"Melissa," Dad started, "I have no reason to believe she's lying. And can you please try not to—not in front of the kids—"

"Not to what?" Mom shouted, her eyes narrowed. "Not to *what*, Ross?"

Dad sighed. "Are we done here?" he asked, so quietly I barely heard him.

"Are we done here, he wants to know," Mom reported, staring at a point somewhere just over my head. "As if we could file this one away in a neat little 'Completed' folder and move on now."

I stood up. "Dad. What's she talking about?"

He turned and looked at me, then Josh. "It's true. I'm so sorry—I know this is tough to understand. When you're older—"

"Not when they're older, Ross, right now!" Mom finally turned her gaze to Dad. "This is going to affect them right now. This is affecting *our family right now*, you selfish *asshole*." And to my horror, Mom burst into tears.

Dad's face crumpled. He moved toward her, but Mom stood up and slapped him, hard, across the face. Then she turned and walked out the front door.

. . .

Dad went upstairs and didn't come back down, so I finally ordered dinner in for me and Josh.

"I *know* what it means," Josh said when I tried to explain it to him over the kung pao shrimp (nonvegetarian rebel food) that neither of us were hungry enough to eat. "I'm not a *baby*."

Then he stomped up to his room, slammed the door, and turned on a Shostakovich symphony at top volume. You know, normal ten-year-old boy music. I wasn't sure if he really did understand, but I didn't feel like talking about it, either.

After Josh went upstairs, though, Dad came back down and sat on the couch across from me while I wordlessly pushed shrimp around with chopsticks. He didn't even notice that it wasn't tofu. Then he told me more details.

She was the same age as me. A few months older, in fact.

"Your mother and I were so young," he said, still in that thin, sad voice that made him sound like someone else. "Things were rocky that first year we were married. And it was different then— when we were living at Ahimsa House. In theory, it was okay for us to—but I wasn't honest about it with your mother, that was the problem. I mean, clearly, there was more than one problem."

"Too much information," I muttered.

Dad sighed. "Cadie, I'm not denying it. I screwed up. Big-time."

I had no idea what to say to that.

Oh, and her name was Elizabeth Marie.

Elizabeth Marie?

No one in my family had a name like that. Ross Greenfield, Melissa Laredo-Levy. Colorful names. Names steeped in history, in stories. Elizabeth Marie? How much preppier can you get? Not like Acadia Rose, or Joshua Tree. Those names say, "Hi, I was conceived in a national park by free-spirited parents who lived with seventeen other people in an intentional community." Otherwise known as a giant purple house in Takoma Park with a composting toilet out back and a telescope on the roof. Back before my mother went MIA—excuse me, became Dr. Laredo-Levy, Head of School at Fern Grove Friends School—and my father went ABD (all but dissertation) and decided to "fritter away his talent" (Mom's words, of course) selling used books.

"I'm not asking you to understand, Cadie. My head's still spinning, too. But can you at least forgive me?" I could feel Dad's eyes on me, but I stared at the shrimp, at their pink question-mark curlicues.

"It was a long time ago, and I've changed since then," he said, trying again. "But this changes nothing about us—about me and you. I promise that. Do you believe me?"

I couldn't stand it—this version of Dad whose voice I didn't recognize, who was doing and saying things that made no sense. None of this felt real. I still couldn't make myself look at him and I couldn't figure out if I wanted to cry or punch something. Dad was watching me, waiting for a response.

Instead, I went up to my room and slammed the door, too. It wasn't loud enough the first time, so I opened it and slammed it again, feeling like I was even younger than Josh.

CHAPTER THREE

The next morning, Dad was gone.

There was a note on the kitchen table: *Staying at the bookshop for a few days. I love you all.*

I couldn't believe he just left like that. Yes, I'd pushed him away. But I didn't want him to *let* me push him away so easily.

Or maybe it wasn't me. Maybe Mom kicked him out.

Chinese takeout boxes still littered the coffee table and the piano bench, but Mom didn't mention him or anything that had happened the night before. I didn't want to go to school but I couldn't figure out what to say to her. *Umm, can I stay home since our family's falling apart?* Josh was up as usual, practicing scales and arpeggios for an hour before breakfast. I ate a chocolate s'mores Pop-Tart (forbidden breakfast food), just to see if Mom would notice (she didn't), grabbed my backpack, and slouched to the car.

Mom had thrown her briefcase and about a zillion piles of paperwork all over the passenger seat, which was weird because she was usually super organized, so I slid into the back next to Josh, feeling like a little kid. She drove even more quickly than usual, stomping on the brakes at intersections, and I cringed every time I saw a squirrel dart toward the road. I was never going to be able to get behind the wheel again. I was scarred for life.

Speaking of scarred for life, I couldn't figure out how Josh could act so normal. Not that he ever showed much emotion of any sort. But still—I was a mess, my hair unbrushed, my limbs stuffed into baggy jeans and a wrinkly old sweatshirt. I had my headphones on and Ani DiFranco at top volume (also to see if Mom would notice, because she's normally very concerned about our hearing). This kid, on the other hand, sat quietly in the back seat with his hands folded, his clothes neat and tidy, his hair combed, staring straight ahead.

Staring straight ahead. With big glassy eyes that kept fluttering shut.

I took my headphones off and put an arm around him. He looked at me, startled.

"I didn't sleep much last night," I said quietly, so Mom wouldn't overhear. "Did you?"

He hesitated, then shook his head. After another moment, he leaned against my shoulder.

I hate crying. So I didn't do it. But some tears might have fallen on Josh's hair, from somewhere.

When we got to school, Mom dropped us off by the front door before going to park in the faculty lot. As we got out of the car, she jumped out and gave us each a quick hug and kiss.

"Have a good day, kiddos," she said, too brightly, then hesitated. "I know this is—a strange day. Remember, I'm up in the front office if you need anything. Anytime."

In my head, I grudgingly gave her a few points. She looked ten times worse than me—I was sure she hadn't slept at all—and she hardly ever said things like, "Have a good day, kiddos."

Josh and I parted ways inside the front doors. I turned right, toward the high school lockers, and he went left, to his fifth-grade classroom. I stumbled through classes all day, avoiding anyone I knew (which takes serious skill, when your whole grade has only eighty-nine kids), and tried my best not to think about Dad. Impossible, of course. I ducked into the bathroom between class periods, brushing my hair or messing with eyeliner until the bell rang. Twice during the day, I convinced myself it had all been a bad dream. Then I'd remember the note on the breakfast table, and the Pop-Tart would rumble unhappily in my stomach. No one had remembered to pack lunches, and I didn't have any money, so I went to the bathroom during my lunch period and spent even more time on my eyeliner. I hoped Josh had a friend who would share a sandwich with him.

The only thing that remotely redeemed the day was drama class, which was in a separate building behind the school. We called it the Shed, even though it was big enough to hold a theater. There was a tiny classroom, but it didn't look like we were ever going to use it. Mr. Goodfellow—I mean, Robin (he told us to call him by his first name, which made the whole class fall in love with him immediately)—said we may as well get used to being on stage.

Even though school had started the week before, Robin had been in New York for the final week of a play he'd directed, so this was our first class with him. We sat in the audience seats and he passed out an FAQ sheet, then perched on the edge of the stage and shuffled papers while we read it and filled it out.

Five facts about me:

1. Yes, my name really is Robin Goodfellow, like Puck in *A Midsummer Night's Dream*. I changed it legally when I was eighteen. Do not try this at home.

2. I believe in the One Bard, William Shakespeare, poet and playwright and actor supreme, hallowed be His

name—and when you are in my theater, you will respect my beliefs. Do not take the Bard's name in vain.

3. My dream come true would be playing Hedwig in *Hedwig and the Angry Inch*. As I cannot sing worth beans, however, I am resigned to a life of Hamlets, Algernon Moncrieffs, and Septimus Hodges.

4. If you don't know who those people are, you'll soon learn. Actually, if you don't know who Hamlet is, I don't know what you're doing in my class. But welcome all the same!

5. That last one wasn't really a fact about me, so here are three more for good measure: I grew up in Idaho, I have four younger sisters, and my favorite disgusting food is scrambled eggs with ketchup and mustard.

Now, tell me five facts about yourself:
1.
2.
3.
4.
5.

I stared at those five blank spaces. Then I wrote:

1. I was named after Acadia National Park in Maine.

I started to write "My dad owns a bookshop" on the next line, but I got as far as "My dad," then crossed it out. Instead, I wrote, "My brother plays the cello." Lame. These were supposed to be facts about me, not about my family. I crossed that out, too. Now there wasn't much room left on line 2, so I thought for a few minutes before squeezing in, "I also love Shakespeare."

Robin clapped his hands. "Aaaand that's time, people! You can take these home and finish them for tomorrow, if you're not done yet."

He gathered us on the stage and had us sit cross-legged in a circle. We began by "centering" ourselves with five minutes of meditation, which was possibly the longest five minutes in the history of the universe. My feet fell asleep, then my hands. Even my lower back fell asleep. Finally Robin rang a little bell to signal that we were all centered, and announced that we were going to start with something called Meisner repetitions.

"This exercise was developed to help the actor get out of his or her own head," he said, pacing at the front of the stage and slapping the sides of his head.

Perfect, I thought, and the dark cloud over my own head lifted slightly in anticipation.

Robin had short, spiky gray hair, but he didn't look old enough for gray hair—I wondered if he dyed it to try to appear older. He had the kind of sculpted face you see on Hollywood actors and his skin looked like leather, as if he'd spent too much time out in the sun. He was extremely thin, with ropy muscles that stood out starkly on his arms and even his hands, which he gestured with constantly. He smoked out in the parking lot between classes— you could smell it on him as soon as you stepped into the room. And he was wearing three little silver hoops in both ears, tight black jeans, a tight black turtleneck, and Doc Martens.

Did I mention that the whole class fell in love with him in the first ten minutes?

Anyway, the Meisner exercise. The repetitions were just

that: we worked with a partner, repeating one simple phrase back and forth to each other over and over, responding to the way our partner said it or something about their body language.

"The phrase can be a simple observation, or something meaningless. For example," Robin said, "you could say, *You look so sad today*, or *How are you?* or even *I love you*."

The class giggled nervously.

"When you have a given line, you don't have to worry about what to say—only *how* to say it. Be spontaneous! Respond to what you're given, people! Respond truly to each other as human beings, not as actors, or however you think an actor *should* act." He thumped the Meisner book he was holding. "Don't try to be an actor. I am here to teach you how to *respond*, not how to act."

Then he paired us up, and we got started.

My partner was Sam Shotwell, a junior, who I was surprised to see in this class. Sam was a jock—or that's what I'd always thought. Dad liked to say, *Jocks have feelings, too. They just express them differently than we do—by throwing small projectiles at each other and running in circles.*

Dad.

I swallowed and pushed the thought away.

"You look so sad today," Sam said.

I jumped and felt my face flush before I remembered what we were doing. "Let's try a different one," I said quickly.

Sam shrugged. "Okay. What do you want to use?"

But Robin had already stopped beside us. "No, no, that was very good!" he said. "Keep it up. Cadie?"

I looked at Sam's ear and said, "You look so sad today."

Robin waved his arms. "Time out. Cadie, *listen* to the way Sam says it, then *respond*. Sam, again."

Sam took a deep breath, then let it out slowly as he said, "You look so sad today." The breathy way he said it sounded like he was truly concerned. Not just a student repeating a line in drama class.

I narrowed my eyes. "*You* look so sad today."

Robin wagged his head happily, pressed one hand to his lips, and gestured toward Sam.

"You look so sad today?" Sam questioned.

"You look *so* sad today," I confirmed.

Sam quirked an eyebrow at me and winked. "You look so *saaad* today," he said, managing to make it sound suggestive.

I fluttered my eyelashes and said each word separately, a hand on my hip. "You. Look. So. Sad. Today . . ."

"Whew!" Robin interjected, unable to contain himself. "People, this is *excellent* work. Keep it up, keep it up!" He clapped one hand on Sam's shoulder and the other on mine, then moved on to the next group.

My pulse was racing from the adrenaline, and I felt myself blush again. "Okay. Should we try another phrase?"

Sam grinned. "I love you."

Who knew drama class would be flirting class?

And who knew that Sam Shotwell was *cute*?

Of course, none of this changed the fact that Farhan Mazandarani was my one true love.

Which was what me and Raven had called him for almost a decade now. Farhan and I had barely ever spoken to each other, but what did that matter? In fact, it was part of the romance. Raven used to call him Afar-han, because she said I pined for him from afar (I know, very funny, hardy-har). I'd started at Fern Grove in second grade, which made me a perpetual newcomer—most kids attended kindergarten through the twelfth grade. "Lifers," they were called. Raven was a lifer, but Farhan was a newcomer like me. He started in second grade, too, when his family moved here from Iran. I instantly fell in love with everything about him: his dark curly hair, his accent (which was mostly gone now). His chubbiness, which made me feel less self-conscious about not being skinny like Raven.

Or Sam Shotwell, who wasn't exactly skinny; more like— toned. Buff. Fit. As I left the Shed after class, I wondered if we'd ever do exercises that involved touching each other. I'd heard about lots of touchy-feely stuff from upperclassmen who'd taken drama before—trust circles, contact improv, stuff like that.

"Cadie!" I turned the corner to my locker, and there was Raven, waiting for me. Her curly red hair cascading down her back, her tight acid-washed jeans paired with chunky apple-green high-heels. Raven tended to look like she was dressed for a magazine photo shoot. "Where have you *been* all day? I kept trying to catch up with you but you were, like, *running* between all your classes. And I couldn't find you at lunch."

"Oh, sorry," I said, trying to cram my books into my already-overcrowded locker. Trying to push away thoughts of last night.

You have to learn how to compartmentalize, Mom always said when I got upset or too emotional about something.

I pictured a little compartment labeled *Dad* and tried to shove my tangled mess of thoughts in there, slam the lid, and—

"Cadie?" Raven looked worried. "You're making this face like you're in pain. Are you feeling okay?"

"Fine! Just had the best class of my life, in fact. Drama with Mr. Goodfellow. I mean, Robin. He wants us to call him by his first name." I chattered away about Meisner repetitions while we walked to our next class. "In what *universe* can a teenage guy say 'I love you' to a female classmate with a straight face?"

Raven slapped both hands over her mouth. "Sam Shotwell did *not* tell you he loved you."

"He did! It was part of the exercise. I swear, actors are so much more highly evolved than the average high schooler."

Raven laughed. "I wish I was in this class with you. Except I'm terrified of being on stage."

"It really did feel like the Drama Shed was its own little world, separate from school," I said, "where jocks are allowed to have feelings and people can forget their problems for a while." I blew out a deep breath. "I guess that's the point of acting, right? To be someone else."

I must've said it too wistfully. Raven studied my face. "Cadie, are you sure you're all right? What's going on?"

But I wasn't ready to tell her yet. If I said it out loud, then it would really be true.

CHAPTER FOUR

I didn't go to the bookshop after school. Josh was already waiting outside Mom's office when I got there. Mom emerged a few minutes later, carrying a huge stack of paperwork, dark circles under her eyes. She tried to smile when she saw us, but only managed it with half of her mouth. Something in my chest twisted a little.

"Hey," I said, "can we stop at the ShopRite on the way home? I'll make dinner tonight."

She looked at me, surprised. "All right, then. What are you planning to make?"

She sounded dubious, as if she didn't believe I knew how to cook, as if she wouldn't like whatever I made. As if I hadn't helped Dad make dinner enough times that I could imitate any of his recipes. But thinking about Dad made the twist in my chest tighten, so I swallowed my sarcastic answer and said, "Whatever you want. You place the order, I'll be the chef."

Mom lifted a hand to rub her eyes. "My contacts are drying out," she explained.

Mom doesn't cry, either. One of the very few things we have in common.

When we stopped at the grocery store, Mom said she wanted comfort food, something warm and filling. I wished I knew how to make vegetarian paella and chocolate-dipped churros, the special treats my *abuelita* made for us whenever we visited Mom's parents down in Florida. But that wasn't what I was craving, anyhow. So I sent Mom to get flour and sugar while Josh and I filled the cart with cottage cheese, eggs, apples, and raisins. Ingredients for Cottage Cheese Contraption—one of the holdovers from our days at Ahimsa House. Everyone took turns cooking, so some nights we had gourmet Indian stir-fry or fancy Italian pasta dishes, and other nights we had unidentifiable casseroles made with cream of mushroom soup from a can.

Or Cottage Cheese Contraption, invented by an old woman everyone called Granny. She'd been a housewife in Arkansas for fifty years, and when her husband died, she packed all her essential belongings into one suitcase, sold everything else, and took off on a road trip across the country. A year later, she landed in Takoma Park, at Ahimsa House. She'd lived there ever since, grandmothering every lost and lonely kid who came through.

Josh was two when we left Ahimsa House, too young to remember anything about it. But he loved hearing stories about the people who lived there. About the days when Dad was a grad student in Renaissance literature and drama at Georgetown, when Mom served chai lattes at the Sunflower Café and played jazz piano at fancy DC nightclubs on the weekends. I'd shown Josh pictures of Mom in a tiny black dress at one of her gigs, a choker of pearls around her throat. She was unrecognizable, her eyes outlined in smoky makeup, her long hair loose down her back, a white rose tucked behind her ear.

Before Josh was born we took a lot of vacations—camping trips to Sugarloaf or the Catoctin Mountains. Mom and Dad had once promised each other that someday they'd hike the entire Appalachian Trail. I had hazy memories from those vacations: campfires, marshmallows, getting dunked in freezing-cold streams by way of having a bath, the thrill of peeing in the woods.

When I was almost five, Dad got invited to present a paper at a Christopher Marlowe conference in California, so he took Mom and me with him—"his girls," he called us—and we spent a weekend camping in Joshua Tree National Park. What I remember about that trip was that I had my own tent for the first time, a pink-and-purple-and-orange tie-dyed tent that someone from Ahimsa House had lent us. I was so proud of that tent, of sleeping in it all by myself.

A month later, Mom found out she was pregnant.

Dad dropped out of school to find a job, and Mom picked up the last semester of doctoral work she'd never finished at the University of Maryland after she and Dad eloped. I remember watching her walk across the stage in a funny cap, her gown pulled tight over her gigantic belly, holding a scroll that she read to me later: *Doctor of Musical Arts.* Two weeks later, I had a baby brother.

After a couple years of teaching at Montgomery Community College, Mom found her job at Fern Grove, and we left Ahimsa House for our very own row house on 34th Street in Hampden. Three tiny bedrooms plus a bathroom upstairs, living room and kitchen downstairs, and a semi-finished basement. There wasn't room for four people and Mom's piano, plus all of Dad's books, so Mom said either Dad had to figure out what to do with the books, or they had to go.

We weren't used to hearing Mom talk like that, but she was supporting the family now, as she kept reminding us. So Dad found Fine Print Books, which was going out of business, and got a good deal on the place. He sold off some of their rare and antique stock, moved in his own collections, and settled in.

I started school at Fern Grove, driving in with Mom every day, and Josh spent his first year in Baltimore crawling around the bookstore, making book towers and playing with the cats and generally getting in Dad's way. This was long before Dad hired Cassandra, who probably would've dealt with baby Josh by leaving out bowls of water and cat food.

When Josh was five, he discovered the cello. It happened at the Baltimore Symphony Orchestra. Mom was excited because it was an all-Haydn program—the "Farewell" Symphony and a cello concerto. Mom's always said, *Haydn is the underappreciated Einstein of the music world.* Whenever she was upset or stressed in those days, she sat down at the piano and took out her big tattered book of Haydn sonatas, held together with a rubber band, loose pages sticking out everywhere. Now she hardly ever has time to play the piano, and all her music sits neatly stacked in milk crates along the wall.

I remember the "Farewell" Symphony, how at the end the musicians all got up, one by one, switched off their stand lights, and walked off into the wings, until there were just two lonely violinists still playing by themselves. And I remember the cello soloist, his wild curly hair flopping all over the place like a lion's mane while he played, the way he made the cello sound like it was singing. But mostly I remember Josh, sitting there with his lips parted, as if he were getting ready to take a bite of ice cream but forgot what he was doing and froze in place. When it was over and the cellist took his final bow and left the stage, Josh burst into tears and wailed, "Make the cello man come back!" Mom and Dad were shocked. Josh barely ever complained or whined or asked for anything. The next day, Mom signed him up for cello lessons at the Prep.

Thinking about all this while I unpacked the Cottage Cheese

Contraption ingredients on the kitchen counter, I had an idea. "Josh, why don't you play me some cooking music?"

Dad always used to tell me to play "cooking music" on my violin when I wanted to help him with dinner but was too young to be much use. I suspect it was also a sneaky way of getting me to practice, even for only ten or fifteen minutes. I never had the discipline Josh seemed to be born with.

Josh had wilted a little when we walked into the empty house, but brightened up at my suggestion. He ran upstairs and came down slowly, carrying his cello with both hands, his rock stop slung over one shoulder. He settled himself on one of the chairs at the kitchen table and started playing movements from the Bach cello suites from memory.

I cracked eggs, stirred cottage cheese and flour and sugar together, chopped apples, tossed in raisins, and fried it all into a delicious hot mush, while Josh "talked" to me. That's how I thought of it—this was Josh's way of saying the things he didn't know how to express in words. He played the slow, mournful Sarabande from the second suite, and I heard his confusion about everything between Mom and Dad: *What are we supposed to do now? What should we say to Mom? What else is Dad hiding? How else is he going to confuse us and disappoint us and let us down? Do we even really know him?*

Or maybe those were my own confusing thoughts.

But just when my eyes were starting to burn, Josh moved on to the Courante from the first suite, in a major key instead of a minor one, full of little trills and ornaments and musical jokes. *Cheer up, Cadie,* I heard. *I'm here and Mom's here and somehow things are going to be all right.*

I knew the names of those two movements because he played them often enough that I'd learned to recognize them from the rest of the endless Bach he was always practicing. He'd worked on the first suite last year, and he was tackling the second suite this year. Each suite was six movements long. I liked their symmetry, like six short scenes in each long act of a play.

Mom came downstairs in her pajamas and slippers, and I scooped big helpings into bowls, handed her a spoon, and joined her at the table. Josh stopped playing to eat with us, and then he went back to his cello. I scooted my chair closer to Mom's and rested my head on her shoulder to listen. She put an arm around me and stroked my hair. "Thanks for cooking, *mija*," she murmured.

It still didn't feel right, the three of us home, cooking, eating, playing music, without Dad. Not talking about what had happened. What would happen next. In fact, it was weird that Mom wasn't trying to talk about any of it at all; that was how she dealt with problems—by analyzing or consoling or encouraging or convincing. By taking charge. Usually I was the one who just wanted to sulk it out in silence. Well, me and Dad. We were both like that.

I sighed. I didn't want to think about Dad, how we were alike. Or maybe not. How could I be sure I was similar to someone I didn't really know—and did that mean there were parts of *myself* I barely knew, too? The warm, rich meal, so comforting a few minutes before, now felt like a heavy lump in my stomach.

· · ·

By Friday, I couldn't stand it anymore. I broke down and went to see Dad.

I didn't tell Mom I was going, just said I didn't need a ride home. But I could tell she knew. She looked relieved, actually. She almost said something, then changed her mind and simply nodded.

When I got to Fine Print, Cassandra was nowhere to be seen. I dropped my backpack by the desk and went upstairs.

I hadn't known what to expect, and Dad looked in better shape than I'd imagined. But it still broke my heart to see him sitting at his desk, his shirt all wrinkly as if he'd slept in it, his face stubbly, his ponytail greasy. He was so engrossed in what he was reading, he didn't hear me come in.

"Dad, have you even taken a bath all week?"

He looked up, startled. "Of course I have!"

"Have you taken more than *one* bath?"

"Err." He looked sheepish. "Well, once I dried out the tub and put all the books back in, I figured I probably wouldn't be here much longer, so it didn't seem worth it to . . ." He jumped up, as if he'd just realized who he was talking to. "*Cadie!*"

I grinned and met him halfway. We slammed into each other for a hug.

"Dad, please come home," I mumbled into his chest. "We need you. No one else knows how to make tofu scramble." I couldn't say *I miss you* without the threat of shedding tears, which was definitely not on the agenda.

"He heaved a sigh," he said, doing just that. A little glow kindled in my chest, melting away some of my doubts from last night. *Everything will be okay. He's still Dad. Still his same old self.*

"Here," he said, "come sit down."

I plunked myself into the overstuffed armchair next to his desk.

"I've spent some time talking to Elizabeth this week," he said, and the glow in my chest fizzled out, just like that. "And to—her mother. Sunshine."

"*Sunshine?*" I echoed. "That's really her name?"

"She'd been very ill," he said, as if he hadn't heard me. "The hospital called this morning to tell me she passed away last night." He rubbed his eyes. "She was in a lot of pain at the end. It was—a mercy, really."

I barely knew what to say. "Did you even know she was sick?"

He shook his head. "Not until she got in touch with me to tell me about Elizabeth. That's why she got in touch. Why she went through the whole process with the lawyer, naming me as legal guardian. She said she wouldn't have done it otherwise— she never intended to disrupt my life." His voice caught on the end of that sentence.

"Dad," I said sharply. "Did you *love* this woman?"

He looked at me unhappily. "What would be more horrible, Cadie? If I said yes, or if I said no? Look, it was all a long time ago—"

"Sixteen years," I interrupted. I could feel my palms starting to sweat and my face heating up. I clenched my fists.

"And now I have to deal with the consequences. There is a grieving young woman in this situation who no longer has a family. She needs a home, and I am going to give her one."

I felt light-headed, as if someone had just sucked all the air out of the room. "She's going to come live with us, in our house?"

Dad nodded. "I'm taking the train to Ohio this weekend to help Elizabeth pack her things and take care of business with her

46

house. I spoke to your mother last night. While she's not exactly enthusiastic, she agrees that it's the right thing to do."

"You talked to *Mom* about this already? When were you planning to tell me and Josh? If I hadn't come over here today, then what—this girl would've just shown up at our door?"

Dad frowned. "Acadia Rose, you do not speak to me like that, and she's not 'this girl'—"

But I'd heard enough. I flounced down the stairs, grabbed my backpack, and shoved the door open. The bell jangled loudly, as if I'd punched it.

CHAPTER FIVE

I called Raven and Micayla as soon as I got home from the bookstore.

"Mom!" I hollered. "I'm going out."

"Where?" she yelled back, from her bedroom.

"The Charmery. With Raven and Micayla."

"Fine." She didn't even say *Don't ruin your appetite for dinner*, which meant she still wasn't her usual self. Not that saying it would matter. I never feel like eating Mom's cooking, appetite or not.

I pulled on my Jackson Pollock jeans, the ones Micayla made for me. She always wore paint-spattered clothing—overalls, mostly—and I loved the way she looked. Her clothes were paint-spattered from wearing them while actually painting, not because she'd bought them that way.

Micayla and Raven were already sitting at a window table, waiting for me, when I walked into the Charmery—it was only a few blocks from my house, so I knew they must've really hurried. I felt tears prickling up and quickly squeezed my eyes shut. God, I was such a leaky faucet these days.

When I opened my eyes, my friends were standing in front of me.

"Girl, what are you doing? Making a wish?" Micayla asked, grinning. "Well, ta-da, here we are!"

Raven gave me a sharp look, though, and I could tell she knew why I was all squinty-eyed. Have I mentioned that I *never* cry? "Let's get this girl a double scoop," she said, leading me to the ice cream counter.

I ordered an Old Bay Caramel–Berger Cookies & Cream combo in a cup. Raven got two scoops of Thai Tea with sprinkles. Micayla chose something called Chinese Food & a Movie, which turned out to be buttered-popcorn–flavored ice cream with chocolate-covered fortune cookie pieces.

"Totally gross, and yet totally delicious," she reported. We passed each cup to the right until we'd tasted everyone else's ice cream.

Raven and Micayla both looked exhausted. Micayla was a junior, and she spent all her free time studying for the SAT and working on her college portfolio and being the president of the Black Student Council. She wanted to study art therapy and teach art to kids with learning disabilities. Raven spent Wednesday afternoons tutoring middle schoolers in Waverly, and Saturday mornings she helped plant and harvest vegetables at the community garden in Remington. In her nonexistent free time, between debate team and student government and getting straight As in all her classes, she had her nose buried in biographies of women like Malala Yousafzai and Hillary Clinton. It was hard sometimes to watch my two best friends planning to change the world while I sat around taking up space and feeling like I wasn't particularly good at anything.

And yet, they were both here.

My ice cream started turning into a sticky brown-gray puddle as I stirred it with my spoon.

"So," Micayla said, "do you want to talk about it?"

49

"About what?" I mumbled.

"Oh, come on," Raven said. "You called us and said it was an ice cream emergency. We came running."

"I know. You guys are the best," I said.

"So?" Micayla prompted.

"I don't even know where to start."

"Well, start *somewhere*," Raven said. "You're killing me!"

"Okay, okay." It was going to sound melodramatic no matter how I said it. "My dad . . . found out that he has another kid. A daughter. My age. Her mother just died and she's coming to live with us."

Silence.

Then Micayla whistled, and Raven clapped a hand on my arm. "Cadie. Shut. Up."

I nodded. My ears were ringing, as if hearing my own voice utter all those words had done some sort of permanent damage. My tongue felt glued to the roof of my mouth, which was suddenly very dry. As if the words had scorched me from the inside out.

"Wow." Raven blew out a long breath. "*Shit.* Who knew your dad was such a player?"

"Raven!" said Micayla.

Dad? A player?

Raven saw the look on my face. "Oh god, Cadie, I'm sorry. Me and my big mouth."

Micayla shot Raven a dirty look, then turned to me. "Honey, how's your mom doing?"

I shook my head. What if I could invent a head motion for every word in the English language and never have to speak again?

I could see Raven thinking over what I'd said. "If she's

your age . . . ," she said slowly. "That means your mom and dad were already married."

I nodded again.

"Sweet mother Mary," said Micayla. "I'm not sure two scoops is enough for this situation."

I held my stomach, which was rumbling ominously, and groaned. Raven and Micayla scooted closer on either side of me and put their arms around me.

"This shoulder's here," Micayla said, "no matter what happens. You hear me?"

"Second that," said Raven. "Plus, you can always come sleep over at my house if things get too weird."

I looped my arms under theirs, so the three of us were linked together. Luckily we were facing the window, not the rest of the shop. I was sure everyone else was staring at us. Despite that, and the way I seemed to have lost my powers of speech, and the fact that I was kind of lactose intolerant and ice cream was always a terrible decision . . . I felt a little better.

CHAPTER SIX

Dad came home Friday night. I'd been expecting a big blow-up, Act Two of the scene in the living room on Tuesday. But he was just there when I came home from the Charmery, quietly making Missing Tuna Casserole for dinner. In a fat green glass vase on the table, there was a giant bouquet of pink and white lilies, Mom's favorites. She acted as if they'd materialized there all by themselves. Normally I loved their scent, but tonight it seemed to clog up all the air in the room.

No one ate much or said much at dinner, but at least we all ate together. Mom has always been big on "family meals." Dad would be happy to eat on the couch while reading a book, but *Mealtime is our chance to talk to each other like human beings,* Mom always says. Tonight, though, they sat at opposite ends of the table with the lilies between them like a pink-and-white buffer and pretty much ignored each other. I wasn't hungry after all that ice cream, and I've never been too fond of Missing Tuna anything. Josh ate quickly, then went up to his room to do homework. (For crying out loud, what kind of ten-year-old does his homework on a *Friday night*?) The strains of a Shostakovich string quartet filtered down through the kitchen ceiling a few minutes later, which wasn't good. Josh only listened to Shostakovich when he was really upset.

I pushed back my chair and said I was going to go check on Josh, but Dad held out a hand.

"Cadie. Just a minute. Mom and I have to talk to you."

What now?

"We discussed this with Josh while you were out, and he's fine with it." Dad paused. "We want you to know that any decisions we make going forward are your decisions, too." I noticed how many times he was using the word "we," as if stressing that he and Mom were still a team. I wondered who he was trying to convince. Mom hadn't made eye contact with him once.

Now, though, she rolled her eyes and interrupted him, as if trying to get this conversation over with more quickly. "The problem is," she said, addressing me, "we don't have another bedroom. For Elizabeth." It was the first time I'd heard Mom say her name, and it didn't sound quite right coming out of her mouth. As if she were pronouncing a word in a new language that she didn't know very well. As if she wasn't quite sure where to place the accent. Or the girl herself, apparently.

Dad nodded. "So Mom and I had an idea—we could move into your room, and you and Elizabeth could share the master bedroom."

My jaw literally dropped. "You want me to share a room with her? With a girl I've never even *met*?"

Dad continued as if I hadn't said anything. "In the long term, we'll finish the basement and make another bedroom down there. But we can't afford to do that right now, and obviously there's not enough time, anyway." He glanced at Mom for a moment, then back at me. "And Cadie . . . try not to think of her as just 'a girl.' I know this will take time. But remember, she's your sister."

"My half sister, who I've never met," I mumbled. *Who I didn't know existed until this week.*

53

"Anyway, Josh said it's fine with him, but of course it doesn't really affect him. You're the one who gets to say whether it's all right or not."

I hated the way Dad was acting like I even had a choice.

I shrugged. "Like you said. Where else is she going to sleep?" Then I stomped upstairs and discovered that Mom and Dad had already moved some of their furniture out into the hallway. So it had been decided without me, no matter what they were pretending.

I went into my room—my *old* room—and grabbed an armful of clothes, then hung them dead center in Mom and Dad's gigantic closet. At least I could set up the room the way I wanted it before Elizabeth showed up.

Mom came up to help me, while Dad spread out papers all over the kitchen table and made a lot of phone calls to lawyers. We spent the rest of the evening moving stuff, and by midnight, we had all my furniture relocated into the master bedroom. Most of Mom and Dad's furniture wouldn't fit into my old room, so we left their bookshelves and vanity table in my new room, and carted their rocking chair down to the basement. Mom packed up their summer clothes to store in the basement as well, since my old closet was tiny.

We left the queen-sized bed in the master bedroom, because Mom said they were ordering a new bed for Elizabeth and we could wait to move all the beds around until it arrived on Monday. She said they'd be fine squeezing onto my twin bed in the meantime. But when I came downstairs in the middle of the night for a glass of water, Dad was sleeping on the couch.

· · ·

Dad left early on Saturday morning for Ohio, before I woke up. There was a note in the middle of the kitchen table: *See you Monday night, plus one!* Mom threw out the lilies—they'd already started to rot—but she didn't touch the note, so we ate around it all weekend, like it was a weird centerpiece.

I spent Saturday rearranging the new room, trying to get it to feel like my own space. Hanging up stuff on the walls helped— two paintings Micayla had given me for my birthday last year, a drab landscape of a Scottish moor and a sickeningly picturesque English cottage. She'd found them in an antique shop on The Avenue, then doctored them by adding a yeti to one and Darth Vader to the other. The yeti was emerging from the gloom of the moor, holding up a cell phone like he was trying to find service, and Darth Vader sat cross-legged in the yard of the cottage, making a daisy chain. Micayla had done such a good job matching the color palettes that it looked like they'd been created that way originally.

I also had a giant signed poster of Regina Spektor. Raven and I each bought one when we went to see her at Georgetown University last year—Mom drove us down to the Glenmont metro and we all rode into the city together, but then she dropped us off at the auditorium and went shopping in Georgetown. So it was basically our first unchaperoned concert. Raven wore lipstick and a miniskirt with fishnets for the occasion. We didn't meet any cute guys, though, and Raven complained she was freezing all night. We ended up sitting next to an old Israeli couple who nodded their heads quietly to the music the whole time and smiled at us a lot.

I covered the wood floor with a big rag rug I found rolled up in the basement when we were carrying down boxes of summer clothes. It was something we'd brought with us when we moved to Baltimore, a farewell gift from everyone at Ahimsa House. I showed it to Mom, and she sighed and said, "Well, that brings back a lot of memories." But she didn't say any more about it, so I carried it upstairs. Maybe Mom thought we'd left that life behind, but clearly it had caught up with us.

Saturday night, I slept over at Raven's. I didn't want to sleep in that gigantic bed again, in a room that wasn't really mine. We stayed up until four in the morning. First we tried to figure out how to make mix tapes using a tape deck Raven had rescued from Hampden Junque on The Avenue. "So romantic," Raven said. "I'm totally making a mix tape for Max."

"But Max probably doesn't have a way to listen to tapes," I pointed out.

"Irrelevant," she said. "He'll know what it means."

Then we took out Raven's nail polish collection and painted each of our toenails a different color, just to see what they all looked like. Plus, when we were seven years old we'd made a solemn vow never to paint all our toenails the same color. That was what other girls did. Not us. At the time, this seemed very important.

Finally we watched *Pulp Fiction*. The dialogue was awesome, but I had to cover my eyes at least once in almost every scene. Raven, on the other hand, loved gore.

"If you like this, you've got to see *Kill Bill*," she kept saying.

"My parents would kill *me* if they found out I was watching this. They hate blood-and-guts movies."

"Which makes it all the more enjoyable," Raven said crisply. "If someone's going to ruin your little-lamb innocence, I, as your best friend, certainly deserve the honor." Raven lived with her mom and grandmother, whom she called by their first names, Renata and Ruby, and who didn't care much about what she did. She said it was partially an only child thing, and partially a "sisterhood of women" thing. Not that Dad was strict with me, either. But Mom seemed to make up new rules every year. Every month. The older I got, the more rules there were.

"Isn't it supposed to work the other way? More freedom as you get more mature?" I complained to Dad once, after the first time Raven and I dyed my hair—green and purple streaks. Mom was *not* pleased, and proceeded to lay down a dozen new rules for what I was or wasn't allowed to do. But Dad said, "She just hates to see you growing up so fast."

Raven and I slept until noon on Sunday, and then her grandmother Ruby made us raspberry waffles and coffee. Neither of us really liked coffee, but Raven said that was a sisterhood thing, too, so we stirred in lots of sugar and cream and sipped it to be polite. Afterward we felt super energetic and zoomed around the house in our pajamas like little kids, cracking ourselves up about nothing in particular. When we crashed, we curled up in her room, listening to music and procrastinating on our weekend homework. The whole day was exactly what I needed.

But the weekend finally came to an end, and I spent Sunday night tossing and turning in the middle of that big bed in the master bedroom, thinking about what the next day would bring. Trying to picture Elizabeth here in our house. Realizing that I had no idea what she even looked like. Would she look like Dad? The thought made my stomach churn. I'd always been Dad's girl— we just fundamentally *got* each other, on this very basic level. But we don't look alike at all. I mean, Dad's white, so technically I'm half white too, but I don't look it. I've spent my whole life with strangers not believing me and Josh are siblings, asking me "So where are you from, sweetie?" when they see me and Josh and Dad together, as if they assume I'm adopted. A registrar at Peabody even asked Mom once where Josh's mother was. When Mom realized the registrar thought she was Josh's nanny, because her skin is darker than his, I could almost see the steam billowing out of her ears.

What if Elizabeth was a music prodigy too, like Josh? Or really good at something else? I was used to being less talented than Josh, but what if I was truly the only untalented Greenfield kid out of, like, the bunch? Did three count as a "bunch"? And then, what would it be like to have another girl my age around all the time—a *sister*? What if she was skinnier, prettier, smarter, cooler than me? I'd always been the oldest, the only daughter. Even when I felt weird or out of place at school, at home I was the big sister, the only girl—Dad's girl, his Cadiest. That's who I *was*.

Except now maybe I wasn't, because my family wasn't the same family anymore.

I yanked a pillow over my face and breathed in the starched scent of the fabric, pressed it against my closed eyelids until I saw stars. But there was no way to stifle that voice on repeat inside my head.

Not the same family anymore. Not at all.

. . .

Monday morning, my alarm rang what felt like two seconds after I'd pulled that pillow over my face. I woke up sweaty, parched, nauseated. Then I remembered what bed I was in, and why, and felt even worse. *Focus, Cadie,* I told myself. *Get up. Get dressed.*

One thing at a time. Bleary-eyed, I yanked a sweatshirt over my head.

At least Mondays mean drama class. The weight in my stomach lightened a little. I went to the bathroom and splashed cold water on my face, which helped too. Then I brushed my hair and changed into a short purple-and-white striped skirt, a stretchy burgundy sweater, yellow tights, and brown boots. Putting together a cute outfit always made me feel a little better about life. We'd been practicing Meisner repetitions and other partner exercises all last week, and although I hadn't been paired with Sam Shotwell after that first day, there was always hope.

But of course, Farhan was still my one true love—which Raven reminded me as we plunked down our lunch trays at our usual corner table, where we had the best vantage point for people watching.

"Tickets are on sale today," she said, adding pickles to her burger.

"Tickets?" I repeated groggily. All the hours I hadn't slept over the weekend were weighing down my eyelids like little sandbags. I picked at my PB&J.

"So have you asked Afar-han yet? Please don't tell me he's still unaware of your existence."

"Of course he's aware of my existence," I snapped. "We've been friends since we were, like, eight years old."

"A *friend* is different from a *Fall Ball date*. And don't grouch at me, you're the one who insisted on watching *Pulp Fiction* twice."

"Did we? I must've slept through the second time."

"You didn't. You were repeating all of Uma Thurman's lines

59

along with her. I swear, your memory is freakish. If I could memorize stuff that quickly, my GPA would be through the roof."

I grinned. "'Why do we feel it's necessary to yak about bullshit in order to be comfortable?'"

Raven narrowed her eyes at me for a moment before she realized I was quoting one of Uma Thurman's lines from the movie. "Case in point. Now, I refuse to speak to you again until you have marched up to Farhan Mazandarani and asked him to the Fall Ball. Ready, set, go." She took a giant bite of her burger and gave me a no-nonsense glare while she chewed.

Well, she was right. What did I have to lose? At least I could take one little piece of my life into my own hands. And maybe approaching Farhan would distract me from thinking about what was happening—who was arriving—tonight. Smother one anxiety with another. Or, maybe I'd wind up in the hospital with heart palpitations. At this rate, I'd have ulcers before I even graduated.

I skulked by Farhan's locker before the bell, trying to look nonchalant. Luckily, he was alone when he turned the corner.

"Hey, Cadie." He started spinning the knob on his locker.

I looked down at my boots. "Hey, do you want to go to the Fall Ball? With me, I mean. If you don't, it's okay, or if you already have plans or something, I mean, I don't really go to dances anyway—"

"Yeah, sure!" The enthusiasm in his voice surprised me, and I looked up.

Bad move. His dark shiny curls fell over his ears and forehead in an adorable mop. He tossed his head to get his hair out of his eyes and smiled at me. Did he *realize* that was total movie star behavior?

"Great! Awesome!" I blurted. "So I'll go pick up tickets after my next class, unless you want to, I mean, not that you have to pay for mine, I can definitely pay for my own ticket, I'm definitely a feminist, you know?" That was definitely the most words I'd ever spoken to Farhan.

He was still smiling at me. "Um, I'm not really sure what you just said."

"Oh." I took a deep breath. "Sorry."

"I have study hall next period, so I can go get us tickets. Okay?"

"Sure!" I nodded vigorously and willed my mouth to stay shut.

"Okay, see ya later then." And he slung his backpack over one shoulder (*adorable*), turned, and walked away.

Just like that, I had my very first date.

. . .

Drama was next. I made it out to the Shed somehow, although all I wanted to do was find Raven and tell her everything that had just happened. The sky was a perfect September blue; the maples at the edge of campus were just starting to hint at their fall plans. And I had a date. With Farhan Mazandarani. Who I'd had a real (sort of?) conversation with for the first time ever. Who had smiled at me and tossed the hair out of his eyes even after I verbally vomited all over him.

Gross. I reminded my brain never to use that phrase again.

I pushed open the door to the Shed and my stomach contracted.

Auditions.

I'd completely forgotten, even though Robin had reminded us on Friday.

"Class, let's center," he called, already perched in lotus pose on the stage. "We've got a lot to get through today. Those of you who would like to try out for *Much Ado About Nothing* will be doing so during this period, while any other would-be thespians not in this class will be auditioning after school. We begin rehearsals next week. Before you sign up for an audition slot, please take one of these handouts and make sure you can commit to our schedule." He waved a sheaf of papers. "Shakespeare is a rigorous lifestyle, people. This is not an extracurricular for the faint of heart. If you're only hoping to pad your college application, please waste another teacher's time."

Someone was crabby today.

And I hadn't prepared for this audition at all. My bookmark was still very close to the beginning of my pocket *Much Ado*.

Well, I'd just have to try to remember something about the characters from seeing the play with Dad at the Shakespeare Theatre in DC, and wing it. At least my reactions would be authentic today—Meisner would approve.

After we centered, Robin split us up into two groups. Those who weren't auditioning—only four of the sixteen students in the class—took copies of *The Crucible* to the small classroom behind the theater and started a read-through. We'd be working on scenes from that play next week.

The rest of us were given "sides," photocopies of the scenes we'd be reading for the audition.

"Come downstage to read, stay upstage while you're waiting your turn," he instructed, hopping off the edge of the stage and perching on the armrest in the first row of seats.

Half of us milled slowly to the back of the stage, and the rest stayed at the front, everyone surreptitiously glancing around to see if anyone knew what we were supposed to do.

Robin clapped his hands. "Downstage means closer to me. Stage directions are from the perspective of the actor, people. Stage left—*your* left. And downstage got its name from the early days of theater, when the stage actually tilted slightly downward toward the audience. Capeesh?"

He called the first pair forward and they began to read a Beatrice-Benedick scene, but he stopped them almost immediately.

"You're both moving around too much. No moving around for now, unless it feels absolutely necessary. We'll work on blocking and stage directions later. For today, just read."

He stopped the next pair and repeated the same direction. "For the love of the Bard, people, the most colorful stage direction Shakespeare ever wrote in *any* of his plays was 'Exit, pursued by a bear.' Unless a *bear* is *pursuing* you at this moment, *stay still.*"

I could tell the others were starting to get nervous. Shuffling their pages, shifting their weight from one foot to the other. I took a deep breath and tried to listen to the pair who were currently auditioning—Sam Shotwell and Rina Crane, a junior who'd been in drama the previous year and was totally rocking her audition, flinging her arms and tossing her head to emphasize the emotion she was putting into the words. Actually, she looked totally ridiculous. Trying way too hard.

I started shifting my weight from one foot to the other, too.

Then Robin called my name. I crossed to the front of the stage—I mean, downstage—and faced my partner, Zephyr Daniels. He was a senior who'd taken drama before as well, and he'd had the lead in the winter play last year. His gangly frame disappeared into an oversized brown leather coat, a shade or two lighter than his skin, and his hair stuck up all over his head in little twists. He was staring down at his pages, his shoulders hunched, mouthing words silently.

I read the first lines: "I wonder that you will still be talking, Signor Benedick: nobody marks you."

Zephyr finally looked up at me. I was momentarily stunned by the brightness of his eyes—they were honey-colored, almost amber. He narrowed them, then threw back his head and laughed, and I jumped. "What, my dear Lady Disdain? Are you yet living?" He spat the words at me, rude, mocking.

I stood up a little straighter and matched his tone, shooting my next lines at him like little arrows. We went back and forth like that, and then he started to circle me like a wrestler sizing up an opponent. I expected Robin to yell "Stop moving!" again, but he kept quiet, so I moved away from Zephyr as I said my next lines, as if keeping a large round table between us. I had to, if I didn't want him to crash into me.

"God keep your ladyship still in that mind! So some gentleman or other shall 'scape a predestinate scratched face." He reached out suddenly and swiped at my face. I pulled back instinctively.

"Scratching could not make it worse, an 'twere such a face as yours were." I jabbed a finger at his nose.

"Well, you are a rare parrot-teacher." That laugh again.

"A bird of my tongue is better than a beast of yours." I was really mad now at the way Zephyr was getting into my space, that mocking tone of voice, the way he was forcing me to speak more quickly to keep up with him.

But then he slowed down suddenly, drawing out his words to make the speed at which I'd been talking sound even more absurd. "I would my horse had the speed of your tongue, and

64

so good a continuer. But keep your way, in God's name; I have done."

That was the end of the page. We stared at each other, both breathing hard.

Robin clapped his hands together twice and said, "Next!" and Zephyr jumped off the edge of the stage and headed for the classroom. I lingered, though, and watched the next few auditions. Robin barked instructions at everyone else—"Stop moving!" or "Speak up!" or "What's that? You're mumbling! Mumble not in the house of the Bard, people!" But he hadn't said a word to Zephyr and me.

Robin gathered everyone at the end of class and announced that audition results would be posted the next morning right after Meeting.

"We are going to read great swaths of Shakespeare this year," he said. "So even if you don't land a role in the play, you'll be practicing scenes in class all semester. Thank you all for your fine work today. Go home, do your reading, we'll start in on *The Crucible* tomorrow."

Great swaths of Shakespeare. It sounded like something Dad would say.

And just like that, I was back in the real world. Where tonight, I would be meeting my half sister for the first time.

CHAPTER SEVEN

By 7:45, Dad hadn't called yet. Their train was due in at 7:15; he was supposed to call when they arrived at Penn Station, and Mom was going to pick them up.

"Trains always run late," Mom grumbled. She kept straightening things that didn't need to be straightened—a Klimt print on the wall, the fifth chair we'd added to the table. It didn't match the others, of course—it was just a folding chair.

Mostly to distract her, I said, "Mom, I asked Farhan Mazandarani to go to the Fall Ball with me. He said yes."

Mom's head swung around slowly like a brontosaurus's. She stared at me. "Farhan Mazan . . . ?"

"Yeah, you remember, the boy who snorted ice cream through a straw at my ninth birthday party?"

Mom raised her eyebrows.

"He's way beyond that now, I swear."

"Acadia, I didn't realize you were going to the Fall Ball."

"You promised I could go this year! Remember?"

"Well, yes. But we'll need to discuss who you're going with, and what the driving arrangements will be, and whether you'll—"

Then we heard keys in the lock, the front door swung open, and there they were.

"Hello, hello, hello!" Dad said.

Mom started to say something, but Dad cut her off. "We splurged on a cab! Didn't want to make you come all the way out to get us."

I could tell Mom was furious at being blindsided by the change in plans, at being confronted by Elizabeth's sudden presence in the house without having time to prepare herself. At Dad, who *never* spent money on cabs, and who was holding a fresh bouquet of lilies, purple this time. We were probably all going to hate the scent of lilies for the rest of our lives. But Mom bustled forward and grabbed a few suitcases, set them down in the living room, then returned to give Elizabeth a hug.

"It's so good to meet you, dear. We're all so happy to have you here."

Mom was speaking in a high-pitched, tight voice, and she always called us Spanish pet names—I'd never heard her call someone "dear" before. Unless maybe you counted the fawn at the Maryland State Fair petting zoo, which was, objectively, a deer.

Elizabeth, standing on the welcome mat, smiled hesitantly at us. "I've heard a lot about you." She was pale and had dark circles under her eyes, but she had done her best to cover it up with a tasteful amount of makeup.

I tried to take her in at a quick glance without staring. She was picking nervously at the sleeve of her navy blue cardigan, half-buttoned over a white blouse. Her whole outfit, down to the argyle socks and brown loafers, said *100% Genuine Prep School*. She even had pearls in her earlobes and a delicate gold necklace. And she did not appear to be wearing *any* of those items ironically.

And she was so . . . white. My fears from the night before had come true. Elizabeth had strawberry-blond hair, like Dad's and Josh's but a lot longer. With Dad's freckles, too. Just like I'd imagined.

I realized I'd failed at the whole not-staring thing.

I snuck a peek at Dad, standing behind Elizabeth with his hands on her shoulders. But he wasn't looking down at her, or even at Mom. He was looking straight at me. He had a too-wide smile pasted on, but his eyes were searching. I could almost hear him thinking at me: *Cadie, please be nice. Be friendly. Be welcoming. Be my Cadiest.*

I thought back at him: *Nice and welcoming to your secret other daughter? Who looks just like you? Who you've probably already given a nickname to on your long bonding train ride? Who looks completely perfect and I don't even know her yet but I already hate her?*

"Dinner's almost ready," said Mom crisply, interrupting my internal dialogue. Dad gave her a questioning look. "And by dinner, I mean takeout. I'm so sorry, Elizabeth, Ross is really the cook in this house. I didn't want your first meal here to be one of my sad attempts. But our local Thai restaurant is excellent."

"Takeout's fine," Elizabeth said politely.

"Great!" Mom beamed. "I'll just run out and pick it up, then. No sense in paying extra for delivery, the place is just around the corner." She couldn't have moved toward the door more quickly if the snapping hounds of hell had been at her heels. Elizabeth leaped out of her way, and Dad laughed. His laugh sounded like a word we didn't know in some other language. We all turned and looked at him.

"Cadie," he said, in Jovial Suggestion Voice, "why don't you help Elizabeth move her things upstairs? You can give her a tour of the house while we're waiting for Mom."

And so I trudged upstairs with a duffel bag over each arm and showed Elizabeth the room we were going to share, now complete with a new twin bed against the far wall. My old bed was under one of the windows. I had to admit that that was one advantage of this bedroom—the two big windows that looked out over the street.

The duffel bags weighed a *ton*. "Did you bring rocks or something?" I said, dropping them on the floor with a thump. The words sounded much ruder than I'd meant them to be, as soon as they were out of my mouth. I bit my lip.

"No, those are books," she said, as if I'd asked nicely. "And—there are a few more downstairs."

Hmm. Good thing we had an extra bookshelf we could bring up from the basement.

Elizabeth complimented everything: Micayla's paintings on the walls, the rag rug, the patchwork quilts on the beds. But she had a wide-eyed rabbit look on her face the whole time, as if she was still considering whether or not to bolt. I showed her my old room, which was completely filled by the queen bed, with about two feet of space around the edges. I didn't tell her that my parents had given up their room for us, but I think she figured it out.

When I showed her Josh's room, with his cello and music stand set up in the corner, she said, "I'm looking forward to hearing your brother play. Ross told me how good he is."

Ross? At least she wasn't going to call him *Dad*, or at least not right away. That would make things feel even weirder. I wondered what she'd call Mom. Then I remembered that she didn't have a mom anymore, and I felt bad for feeling good about the Ross/Dad thing. Sheesh.

"I guess Josh is your brother, too," I mumbled, and she shot me a startled look.

"Oh. Um. I guess he is."

The rest of the tour didn't take long. I showed her the half-finished basement, filled with our old couch and a mishmash of boxes and other random items like a baby stroller, a gigantic dollhouse, and an exercise bike Dad had found at the Goodwill and used exactly once, before it occurred to him that he already had a real bike that he enjoyed using to actually ride places.

I showed her the back deck and our tiny backyard, with its one tree and view of the alley. "Stray cat central," I said. "Don't get any ideas, though. My mom won't allow anything that would shed in the house."

Elizabeth nodded. "I've never had a pet, either."

"Oh, we've had plenty of pets. Fish, mostly, but once we had a snake. It was supposed to be Josh's snake but he was terrified of it, so I took care of it. *It* was a *she*. Rosie. She was really sweet." I was doing my babbling thing again, like I'd done with Farhan that afternoon. I pressed my lips together and noticed Elizabeth was staring at me in alarm.

"You don't still have the snake, do you?"

Oh, for crying out loud. "No, she died years ago. I don't think it's very good for snakes to keep them in little tanks."

Elizabeth let out a sigh of relief. "That's too bad. I'm terrified of snakes, too, though. Just like your little brother."

I could tell she was trying to make me smile, so I refrained from reminding her again that he was her little brother, too. After all, I wasn't going to force her to share anything about my family if she didn't want to.

"Girls!" Mom called. "Food's here!"

And that's when the Great Shocker happened.

We were sitting around the table, passing out cardboard

boxes and chopsticks, the lilies staring at us from the kitchen counter because there wasn't room on the table. I'd gotten stuck with the folding chair. Mom said, "Does everyone have what they want? There's some more orange bean curd over here," and Dad said, "I've got the tofu pad Thai." (I noticed Mom had ordered a separate pad Thai with beef, for Elizabeth.) We all filled our plates. Elizabeth hesitated, so Dad said, "Well, let's dig in!"

But she kept fiddling with the charm on her necklace. "Do you—I'd like to, if you don't mind—we usually say grace before we eat." *We?* She seemed to catch her usage of the plural pronoun at the same time, and bit her lip. And then I realized what the tiny necklace charm was. It was a gold crucifix.

Dad and Mom, for the first time in a week, looked like a team again—because they had the exact same stunned look on their faces, as if Elizabeth had just told them she was pregnant. Or the proud owner of a unicorn. Or pregnant with a unicorn.

"We're Jewish," Mom offered. As if this somehow answered Elizabeth's implied question.

"Jew-*ish*," Dad clarified. "You know, the atheist kind. We don't do synagogue or any of that stuff, we don't believe in God. But we sure are glad She created latkes and hamantaschen." He grinned, but Elizabeth just stared at him.

I used to be embarrassed about trying to explain this to teachers who pointedly wished me "Happy Hanukkah" while doling out red-and-green plates and napkins at Christmas parties, or to friends who wanted to know in eighth grade why I was the only Jewish kid at school who wasn't having a bat mitzvah.

Mom was still gazing at Elizabeth like they used to stare at me, and suddenly I wanted to put my hand under her chin and snap her mouth shut.

"Of course we can say grace," I said, grabbing Josh's hand on my right and Mom's on my left. "Elizabeth, would you like to lead us off?"

The only time I remember ever saying grace was at Ahimsa House, where we used to join hands before meals sometimes and sing, while a man named Dancer played along on his guitar. But Elizabeth didn't sing. She bowed her head, clasping her hands together under her chin.

"Bless us, O Lord, and these your gifts, which we are about to receive from your bounty. Through Christ, our Lord. Amen."

Dad and I had bowed our heads, too, but out of the corner of my eye I saw Josh, his brow furrowed, looking around the table as if he wasn't sure who these people were. And Mom was staring at Elizabeth as if she'd sprouted horns. Or angel wings.

"Amen!" I said loudly, releasing Mom's and Josh's hands, and picked up my chopsticks. "And *l'chaim*, and all that," I added, trying to break the tension.

Dad reached across the table and patted Elizabeth's hand. "That was lovely, just lovely. We're excited to learn more about your traditions, sweetie. *L'chaim* indeed!"

Mom smiled weakly and echoed, "*L'chaim*." Then she left the table to pour herself a glass of wine.

. . .

That night, as we lay in our separate beds, I tried to figure out what to say. I couldn't ask her about her mother, of course. And I didn't think she'd want to talk about her school, her friends, her old life in Ohio. "So," I said, "do you go by Liz? Lizzie? Beth?"

"No, just Elizabeth."

There was an awkward silence.

When Josh had gone up to his room to practice after dinner, Elizabeth had asked if she could come and listen. Josh brought his cello downstairs instead, and Elizabeth and Dad sat on the couch together and listened for an hour or so while Mom and I worked—homework for me and paperwork for her—at the kitchen table. *Do you think she goes to church, too?* Mom had whispered. *Probably*, I whispered back, and Mom grimaced. *We have to make her feel at home*, I hissed, angry that I was being forced to pick sides between Mom and Elizabeth here. I didn't want to be on either of their sides. I wanted to be back on Dad's side. The old Dad, the one who had two children, Acadia Rose and Joshua Tree, the Dad who—

"Do you play any instruments?" Elizabeth asked, saving me from spiraling further into that memory.

"I used to. I played the violin. But I wasn't anywhere near as good as Josh, so I quit." I sighed. "What about you?"

"Clarinet. I play in the band—I mean, if there's a band at your school?"

"Yeah. We have a few bands. Jazz band, marching band, wind ensemble." Elizabeth didn't respond, so I tried to think of something else to say. "Um, our school is very big on the arts."

There was a soft knock on our door.

"Girls? Can I come in?" It was Dad.

He flicked on the light and took a few steps into our room, hesitated, then sat down on the edge of Elizabeth's bed.

Not mine.

"Just wanted to say good night," he said softly. "To my two girls." He paused, but neither of us said anything, so he kept going. "I know this is a lot of changes all at once, and maybe you

73

haven't even processed everything you're going through right now. But Elizabeth, I want you to know that we're all here for you. Whatever you need. We are your family, and we love you. How are you doing so far?"

I noticed how many times he said *we* again. Putting words in my mouth, speaking for me, without even asking me how *I* was doing.

"I'm okay, thanks," she said, just as quietly. I started to feel like I was eavesdropping on a private conversation in my own room, for the love of God. (I mean, for the love of Zeus and Hera and all their children. I'd have to learn how to stop taking God's name in vain around Elizabeth.)

"Okay?" Dad repeated. "Well, I guess that's better than 'not okay.' But it's also okay if you're not okay—okay?"

I could tell he was trying to get her to laugh, and maybe she smiled, but I'd already rolled over to stare at the wall.

Elizabeth's bed creaked as Dad stood up, and then I felt my mattress sink as he sat on the edge of my bed. He squeezed my feet. "You too, Cadie. How are you feeling? Do you want to talk?"

I closed my eyes. "Can you just let me go to sleep?"

Dad let go of my feet, and my words hung in the air for a tense moment. Then he whispered, "Of course," and got up to turn out the light.

After Dad left, neither of us spoke again. I stared at the ceiling for what felt like hours, my stomach twisted in knots, watching shadows from the streetlight playing across the ceiling. I wondered if Elizabeth was already asleep, but after a while I heard soft sniffling coming from her side of the room.

If I were spending my first night in a new house, with a new

family, less than a week after my mom died, I'm sure I'd cry, too—
except I didn't do crying if I could possibly help it. And when I
did, I usually wanted people to pretend it wasn't happening. So
I rolled over and convinced myself I hadn't heard anything. But
the moonlight was brighter on this side of the house than I was
used to, and it took me a long time to fall asleep.

CHAPTER EIGHT

Mom and Dad had suggested that Elizabeth take a week or so to "adjust to her new situation" before starting school. Mom offered (somewhat feebly, I thought) a back-to-school shopping trip, and Dad said he'd take her down to DC to see the sights—the White House and all the monuments, the Smithsonian Institution, the National Zoo, the Kennedy Center. But Elizabeth had declined (politely, of course), saying that she didn't want to have to worry about making up schoolwork. I could tell Mom was relieved, but Dad seemed disappointed.

So the next morning, we all squeezed into the Honda and rode to school together—Dad, too. He'd insisted on leaving the bookshop in Cassandra's capable paws for a few hours in order to come help Elizabeth "get settled at school." There really wasn't much for him to do. As soon as we got there, Elizabeth went to the front office with Mom and handed in all her paperwork. Then they gave her a locker assignment and a class schedule and turned her loose. Mom said, "Well, that's that, I've got a meeting in four minutes, you know where to find me if you need me, oh and Cadie, don't forget Josh has a double lesson today after school," and disappeared into her office. But Dad hovered, reminding me again to show Elizabeth the ropes and help her find her classrooms.

"Dad. I *know*," I said. "You don't need to stick around. She's going to be fine."

Dad hesitated, then held out his arms. I saw the relief that softened his face when Elizabeth stepped forward for a hug. "If you need anything at all, you have my cell number," he murmured into her ear, and she nodded. The hug went on long enough that I started to feel awkward standing there, so I pretended to look through my school bag for something.

"*Dad*," I said. "We're going to be late."

"Right," he said, and made a motion as if reaching to pull me into the hug too, but I ignored him.

Dad sighed. He let go of Elizabeth and stood there, looking from one of us to the other and back again. He smiled. "My girls. You really do look like sisters." I stared at him. What was he seeing? Elizabeth and I looked nothing alike. We *were* nothing alike.

He turned twice to wave at us as he walked down the hall. I didn't wave back.

Elizabeth clutched her schedule and shifted her bag to her other arm. She didn't carry a backpack—she'd piled all her notebooks into a beige L.L.Bean tote bag. It looked much more chic than my ratty orange backpack, which had song lyrics scribbled all over it in multicolored Sharpie markers.

The tote bag had a monogram: E.M.J. I snuck a peek at the top of her schedule. *Elizabeth Marie Jennings*. So she had her mother's last name. At least we didn't have to share a name, too.

She saw me glancing at her schedule and held it out, so I took a good look and saw that we wouldn't be sharing many classes, either. Which made sense. Elizabeth was a junior. She was only six months older than me, but that put her a grade ahead. She'd gone to Catholic school in Ohio, and she seemed nervous about Friends. She'd asked me twice that morning, while we were getting dressed, if I was sure there wasn't any sort of uniform or dress code. When she'd seen my outfit—tight black jeans with patched knees, purple ankle boots, and a blue-and-green sweater with multicolored buttons sewn all over it—she'd said, "You're wearing that to *school*?"

I'd muttered, "Yes, Mom," and then immediately felt terrible. I tried to cover it up with a laugh, which only made things worse. Her freckly face reddened as if I'd slapped her, although she tried to hide it by going quickly to the vanity mirror across the room and brushing her hair. Her shoulders slumped. It looked like she was trying to retract herself into her own body. The only sound was Josh, practicing minor scales down the hall. Slowly. Very slowly.

"Hey," I said, "I'm sorry. I'm always a grump in the mornings. But I do the best French braids on the planet. Want me to do your hair?"

"I always wished my mom knew how to braid hair, but she was terrible at it." Elizabeth spoke so softly I could barely hear her, and for a moment I almost wondered if I'd imagined the words—until she turned and sat primly on the edge of her bed. I knelt behind her and began crisscrossing strands of that long strawberry-blond hair. Dad's hair.

"It's gorgeous," I told her.

She actually smiled—a tiny one, but I saw it in the mirror. "Thanks. I really like your highlights. Did your parents freak out about them?"

"Not really," I lied. "Okay, just a little bit. But at least they're not permanent. Mom said the hair dye was fine but I'm not allowed to pierce anything except my ears until I'm eighteen."

Her eyes widened. "Would you *want* to pierce something else?"

I shrugged. "Maybe. I like eyebrow rings. And lip rings. A belly button ring sounds too painful, plus what if it gets caught on your shirt or something and you rip it out?"

"*Ouch.*"

"Exactly." I wrapped a hair tie around the end of her braid and slid off the bed to examine my handiwork from the front. "Oh, it looks great! But wait—can I try something else? We have ten more minutes till we have to go, and I never get to practice on anyone." Raven never let me play with her curls.

She checked her watch. "Sure."

I undid the braid, brushed her hair out again, and clipped half of it on top of her head. Then I French-braided the rest from the nape of her neck up to the crown of her head, braided a few strands back from her temples, and gathered all that hair into a neatly coiled bun. I stepped back to evaluate.

Elizabeth looked in the mirror and gasped. "Wow. I have Renaissance Festival hair! I love it. Thanks, Acadia."

"That was fun," I said. "And it's Cadie."

She smiled at me this time, and I smiled back. "I've always wanted a sister," she said.

I couldn't truthfully say the same, so I was glad that at that moment Mom called up the stairs, "Girls! Time to go!" and we headed off to school.

. . .

The first thing I did once Dad finally left, of course, was to check the bulletin board outside the cafeteria. But audition results weren't up yet.

I filled in Elizabeth about Meeting as we waited in the crowd of students milling around outside the cafeteria.

"Quakers call their service 'Meeting for Worship,' but it's

not about worshipping in the sense of priests and prayerbooks," I said, then quickly added, "not that you aren't welcome to worship, of course. Worshipping is fine. But I mostly think of it as, like, a chance to clear my head. People can stand up and speak, if they feel moved, but you definitely don't have to."

"Speak about what?"

"Anything that's on your mind. Deep thoughts. Spiritual stuff. Current events. Whatever."

Elizabeth was looking at me as if I'd just announced that we were going to sacrifice a goat and dance around a bonfire.

I sighed. "I'm sure it's really different from Catholic school. But it's not so bad. And we only do this on Tuesdays."

I imagined a little speech bubble over Elizabeth's head: *So God doesn't exist the rest of the week?* But all she said was, "It sounds interesting."

"The other days, we have electives. I'm doing yoga." I checked Elizabeth's schedule. "Oh, you're signed up for Student-Led Readings. Mom taught that last year. All the students take turns picking something for the class to read that they think is—" (I made air-quotes with my fingers and imitated Mom's voice) "—'intriguing, instructive, or incendiary.'"

Elizabeth was biting her lip and looking nervous.

"You can probably get excused from Meeting if you really don't like it," I said. "Everyone's very flexible around here."

"Is it all the yoga?" she said, and it took me a second to realize she was trying to make a joke. "You know, *flexible*."

I grinned at her to show I got it.

Elizabeth sat quietly next to me through Meeting. After a few minutes of silence, Kieri Cantor stood and said her older sister's baby was due any day now, and asked us to hold her in the Light. I closed my eyes and pictured Kieri and her sister and a new baby, surrounded by a warm, protective glow. Then Josiah Sampson stood to talk about how the president was creating our generation's Vietnam by sending troops to the Middle East. Manny Sampson (his twin brother) rose to say that Vietnam was totally different, dude. He sat and we all absorbed that for a little while. A minute or two later, Heron Lang got up and said she'd noticed some street art on an abandoned building that morning on her way to school, and it made her think about how even broken-down things can be reborn. We sat in silence after that until we closed Meeting by shaking hands with our neighbors.

"I thought Quakers were pacifists?" Elizabeth said as we left the cafeteria. "That was a lot of war-talk for a prayer meeting."

"Well, it's supposed to be a time for quiet contemplation, not political arguments, but I guess pacifists get more upset about violence than most people. Plus, we're not all Quakers. Even though I think I'm more Quaker than Jewish at this point."

At that moment, I saw a crowd clustered around the bulletin board, and I bolted for it.

As I looked up at the board, an ache hit the spot right between my eyebrows. That feeling I got, once in a while, when I knew something was going to happen right before it did. Like the time Dad and I went to outdoor Shakespeare last summer, and we entered the basket raffle at intermission. Right before they drew the winning slip of paper out of the basket, I got that ache in the center of my forehead, and then I heard, "And the winners are . . . Ross and Acadia Greenfield!"

There it was. At the top of the board, the first two lines of text under the heading MUCH ADO ABOUT NOTHING CAST:

Benedick—Zephyr Daniels
Beatrice—Acadia Greenfield

. . .

Elizabeth had counseling during the last period of the day, so I waited for her outside the guidance office. She emerged with red, puffy eyes, and looked embarrassed when she saw me there, so I bent down to my backpack and pretended to reshuffle my books and papers. "Josh has a double cello lesson at Peabody today," I said. "He's preparing for a big competition in December. So Mom drove him there, and we'll take the bus home."

We walked down the hall in silence. I wanted to ask her how her first day had gone, but I wasn't sure if she felt like talking. And what could I expect her to say, anyway? *Yeah, I love your hippie school, where you call the teachers by their first names and talk about war and graffiti at your prayer meetings. Oh, and the fact that my mom just died? No big deal.*

As we walked past the cafeteria, I remembered that I hadn't read the rest of the cast list that morning. I paused to scan it. At a school this small, most of the names were familiar, even if I didn't know anyone else in the cast very well. Then I saw "Micayla Cooper" at the bottom, under "Costumes & Scenery." At least I'd have a friend to go to rehearsals with. And thank the gods Micayla had her license, so she could drive us.

"Hey, Acadia! It's you!" Elizabeth pointed at the top of the list.

"Cadie, but yeah," I mumbled, blushing, and started walking again. She must've thought I'd stopped just to point it out to her.

Elizabeth ran a few steps to catch up to me. "I didn't know you were into drama. That's so cool."

"Well, this is my first time being *in* a play, but my dad and I go to a lot of theater. Mostly Shakespeare. He's really into Shakespeare. And Marlowe. Did you know he was doing his PhD on the friendship and rivalry between Marlowe and Shakespeare?"

The bus pulled up, and I thought I'd better stop myself before I blabbered nervously the entire way to Fine Print. We sat in opposite seats near the front, and the doors hissed shut. "Oh, by the way. I was thinking we'd stop by Dad's bookshop. Unless you want to go straight home, of course."

"No, no!" Elizabeth actually looked excited. "I definitely want to see the bookshop. He told me about it on the ride from Ohio."

"It's the best secondhand bookstore in Baltimore." I didn't mention that Dad had been living in exile there until a few days ago.

When we reached Fine Print, I pushed the door open and walked in, and the bell tinkled behind us. Elizabeth looked around in awe. "I still can't believe your dad owns a *bookshop*." As if she was saying, "I can't believe your dad owns *the Vatican*."

I had to bite my tongue, but in my head I yelled, *He's your dad, too, remember?*

She said, "I mean, this is like my dream come true. I can't believe this is your life! Do you hang out here a lot? I'd love to hang out here. Can we read anything we want?"

I hadn't heard her say that many words at the same time since she'd arrived.

Dad came down the stairs at the same moment that

Cassandra emerged from the stacks, holding Bosch in one arm and half a dozen volumes of Dickens balanced in the other.

"Cassandra," said Dad, "this is my other daughter. Elizabeth." He put an arm around each of us.

Cassandra's eyebrows shot up, and for once she looked directly at another human being. She studied Elizabeth from her head to her toes. I knew what she was seeing: the strawberry-blond hair, the freckles, the red-rimmed blue eyes. I didn't know if Dad had told her what was going on or not, but she certainly seemed surprised. Of course, it was entirely possible that he *had* told her, and she just hadn't deemed it important enough to remember. Since it didn't involve books, the bubonic plague, or felines.

"I'm pleased to make your acquaintance," she said finally, and I shot a look at Dad, who was doing his best to keep a straight face and not meet my eyes.

Cassandra set the books down on the front desk and returned to the back room for more—still carrying Bosch—and I turned to Elizabeth. "She spoke to you!" I said. "That can only mean one thing. You're actually a *cat*."

Dad lost it, doubling over with laughter. Elizabeth grinned at us and shook her head. "She seems like a perfectly nice woman."

"Shhh!" Dad hissed, trying to catch his breath. "She's coming back."

He made a break for the stairs, and we followed him up to his office.

It felt weird to hear Dad crack up, when I . . . couldn't remember the last time I'd laughed like that. Not since he'd told us about Elizabeth. How could he be so happy, so relaxed? It seemed easy for him. *One daughter, two daughters—whatever. No big deal.*

84

"Do you mind if I go look around?" Elizabeth asked, her eyes shining with anticipation. "I *love* books."

I remembered the duffel bags I'd hauled upstairs last night.

Dad's whole face lit up. "Yes, absolutely, pick out whatever you'd like! Anything in the shop. Take it home, read it, bring it back only if you don't think you'll read it again."

Elizabeth looked like she'd just been handed a million bucks.

I like to read, too. Mostly mysteries and fantasy. Even some sci-fi. But I've never been into the dusty classics stacked up on all three floors (on the shelves, in the aisles, on the footstools) of Fine Print. Dickens, Dostoyevsky, Dickinson—authors I only read in school when I have to. Sure, I like books. But I looked at Dad's face as he watched Elizabeth disappear into the shop, and I saw that I didn't like books *enough*.

I pushed that thought as far down as I could, to a place where it roiled angrily in my stomach, and took a deep breath. If Dad could pretend nothing was wrong, then I could, too. "So Dad, I, um . . . I have good news."

"Oh?" he said, drawing out the word. Dramatic Pause Voice. Just like the laughing downstairs, it was weird to hear Dad doing voices as if nothing had changed.

"Guess," I said.

He pretended to ponder. "You and Raven have decided to join a convent."

I raised an eyebrow, not dignifying that with a response.

"Well, Mom told me about the Fall Ball, and I do think we need to discuss some ground rules—"

"*Dad.*" I was in no mood for Responsible Parent Voice. "They posted *Much Ado* results."

He did a double take. "Much *adid* they?"

I ignored that terrible joke and waited.

"Well???" he said, drawing question marks in the air with his finger.

"Beatrice!" I exploded. I couldn't help it. I was too excited to keep pretending I didn't care. "I'm going to play Beatrice!"

Dad did a little caper around the room—I kid you not, my father knows how to caper—before scooping me into an enormous hug. "Acadia Rose Greenfield's big debut!" he said, too genuinely happy to do any voice except his own. "My little thespian! When do rehearsals start? Do you need help running your lines? When's opening night?"

At first I went rigid against the hug, but after a moment, I felt that chilly place in my stomach soften. I let Dad prattle on, interrupting one question with another, telling me over and over how proud he was. Not even noticing my silence. Maybe it didn't matter after all if he had two daughters instead of one. Maybe, eventually, we could go back to the way things had always been.

Except I knew it wasn't possible, not really. From now on, I had to share him with a sister. A stranger with blond hair and preppy clothes, who walked around on tiptoes so she wouldn't spill the heavy, heavy load of grief she was carrying. And what if Dad had more secrets, more parts of his life that I'd never known about? How could I ever trust him again?

"Okay, chill out," I said, pulling away without making eye contact. "I just thought you'd want to know." I picked up my bag and left the office, even though I could practically feel his hurt radiating toward me across the room.

The future was a stack of unread books. Dad had pulled out the book at the very bottom, and now the whole stack was about to topple over.

CHAPTER NINE

Things were tense at home that whole week. Dad kept bringing Mom bouquets of flowers, and even a giant box of her favorite dark chocolate coconut truffles one night, as if he could buy his way out of trouble. And he was still sleeping on the couch, although he tried to get up early and move the pillows and blankets so Josh and Elizabeth and I wouldn't figure it out. But every night when I got up to go to the bathroom or get a glass of water, there he was—tucked in neatly and snoring away.

Elizabeth took forever in the bathroom in the mornings, and her showers used up all the hot water. I started showering at night just so I wouldn't have to get up ridiculously early to sneak in a shower before her. I noticed that Mom did, too, although she didn't say anything about it. Or at least not to us.

Meals began with grace, then limped along without it. (Ha—Dad would've enjoyed that line, but I wasn't in the mood to tell him jokes.) Mom avoided talking to Dad, and tried overly hard to be nice to Elizabeth. Josh was silent. I tried to make conversation, but Dad kept turning everything I said into a question for Elizabeth, who gave one- or two-word answers.

On Thursday night, Dad asked about her progress with the stack of books she'd borrowed from Fine Print, and Elizabeth finally smiled. They started discussing a book of Edgar Allan Poe stories. I squirmed on the stupid folding chair I kept getting stuck with—I didn't want to complain about it and sound whiny, but it did make my butt go numb.

"Did you know that Poe's grave is here in Baltimore?" Dad asked.

Elizabeth's (perfectly sculpted) eyebrows shot up. "No way!" (Side note: Have I mentioned the amount of plucking I have to do every week in order to see out from under the caterpillars on *my* forehead?)

"We'll plan a visit," said Dad. "How about this weekend?"

Dad used to take Josh and me to Poe's grave on Halloween every year. Now we'd have to share that tradition with Elizabeth, too. I pushed my food around on my plate. Poe's grave was stupid, anyhow. I was getting too old for that nonsense.

"Can I be excused?" I asked. Mom nodded, and I went upstairs. First I packed my overnight bag. Then I called Raven. The Woodbury sisterhood had no rules about sleepovers on school nights.

"It's not fair," I complained from the back seat on the ride to Raven's house. She and Ruby had driven over to pick me up, and I was out the door before Mom could protest—or maybe Mom just didn't want to start a fight in front of Elizabeth. "How are you so good at driving already? You've only had your permit a month longer than I have."

"Well, I didn't quit after my first lesson," Raven said, executing a perfect lane change.

"She's driving about ten miles under the speed limit," her grandmother pointed out.

Raven took one hand off the wheel to swat at her, and Ruby clucked her tongue. "Both hands on the wheel, young lady."

"But you drive with your knees sometimes and *no* hands on the wheel!"

"That is *not* true." Now Ruby swatted at Raven's arm, and

Raven immediately shrieked, "You can't hit me! I'm driving!"
Ruby laughed and her curls bounced. She had wild long hair
just like Raven's, only silver-white.

"Where's Renata tonight, anyway?" Raven asked as we
pulled up in front of their house.

Ruby sighed. "Working late." Renata was a medical
researcher at Johns Hopkins. She ran her own lab and often got
stuck finishing up experiments or helping the interns with their
projects late at night.

Ruby and I held our collective breath while Raven parallel-
parked, but she did it perfectly. We applauded for her.

As we walked up to the house, Ruby said, "And Cadie, I hear
that you're going out with a nice young man? To the Fall Ball?"

"Oh, he's just a friend." I felt myself blush and was glad it
was dark.

Raven elbowed me so hard I almost fell over. "She's been
crushing on him since before the dawn of time."

"Well, I think that's lovely, dear." Ruby smiled at me. "Let
me know if I can help with your dress for the dance. I'm doing
Raven's, of course."

Ruby was an expert seamstress, and she loved to rework
vintage gowns into dresses for Raven.

"That would be amazing!" I said.

"We'll go shopping this weekend. Let me just see what I'll
need . . ." Ruby disappeared down the hallway into her sewing
room, and Raven and I went upstairs.

"So? How is it?" Raven always cut straight to the chase.

I sprawled out on her thick white carpet, covered my face with
my arms, and groaned. "It's *so awkward.* I told you she's Catholic,

right? So we pray before meals now, and I think someone's going to have to take her to church on Sundays. She practically had a heart attack after Tuesday's Meeting."

"How's the Ice Queen dealing with the new princess in the house?" The Ice Queen was Mom, of course.

"She's trying so hard it hurts to watch. She and Dad are barely talking to each other. Dad sleeps on the couch but thinks he's hiding it. Mom walks around with this smile that pops up on her face whenever she sees Elizabeth, like she has an on/off button. I have no idea how Elizabeth's feeling because she barely talks. Like Josh. Except about books; she and Dad are really bonding over books. So, woohoo for them."

Raven made a sympathetic noise.

"And I hate wondering what other secrets Dad has lurking in his past. All I want is for everything to be okay with him again, but it's always at the back of my mind now—he *cheated* on Mom. Right before she got pregnant with me. I mean, that's messed up, right? And no one's talking about it. No one's mentioning Elizabeth's mom at all."

"Well, do you think Elizabeth wants to talk about it?"

"Probably not. She barely knows us. It must be like living in a foreign country. She's in counseling at school, but I figure sooner or later she's going to have a meltdown if she keeps it all bottled up."

"Very gritty. Very reality TV."

"Gee, thanks."

"I have no idea what I'd do if Max cheated on me," she mused.

"Yeah, let's talk about Max. I'm sick of thinking about my family. How are things with Max?"

90

"Max . . . is amazing." Raven closed her eyes and smiled. "Max, Max, Max."

I tried to imagine saying Farhan's name over and over just for the fun of it. Right now I was still working on being able to choke it out just once.

"Farhan was waiting at my locker today after lunch," I said.

"What!" Raven said. "Details!"

"Well, there's not much to tell. When I saw him there, my face kind of froze." In fact, my mouth had refused to open but my vocal cords hadn't gotten the memo and tried to say, "Hey, Farhan." The result was that I'd garbled wordlessly with my lips pressed together. Part of my nonexistent soul had shriveled.

"Hi," he'd said, holding up an envelope. "Here's your ticket."

I'd managed to unglue my mouth. "Thanks! Wow, it's, um, a nice ticket!"

Farhan had laughed. "You're funny, Cadie."

I loved the way he said my name. He said it so . . . sweetly. I made sure to emphasize that part to Raven.

"That was your entire interaction?" she said in disbelief. "Cadie. You have *got* to pull it together. Okay. Pretend we're at the Fall Ball, and I'm Farhan. What do you say?"

"Um. Will you dance with me?"

"*No.* Of course he's going to dance with you. He's your *date.*"

"So what am I supposed to say?"

"Small talk. Friend talk. Whatever kind of talk you want! Just because he's a boy, he's not *not* a normal person you can talk to."

"Raven. That made no sense."

"Look, I got pretty tongue-tied on my first date with Max, too. But you just have to relax. Remember that he already thinks you're cute, funny, smart, nice, whatever. You don't have to convince him."

"That's easy for you to say. You really are cute, funny, smart, and nice."

"I'm not nice," Raven said, offended.

"True. But you're cute."

"And smart! And funny!"

I pretended to consider it. "Ehhh."

Raven grabbed a pillow off the bed and clobbered me.

· · ·

Friday after school, Dad came home early and took me and Elizabeth out for a driving lesson before it got dark. She'd just received her Maryland learner's permit in the mail. Mine had taken weeks to arrive, but apparently if you already had a permit from the state of Ohio and you were Elizabeth Marie Jennings, red tape magically vanished before you. Not that I was pissed or anything.

"We may as well do driving lessons together," Dad said. "It'll save time. And you can learn from each other's mistakes. Right?"

"Lesson one: Cadie demonstrates roadkill," I muttered.

Elizabeth shot me a sympathetic look. I guess Dad had already filled her in about my disaster of a first lesson. By now I could almost think about it without that lump rising in my throat, but I still didn't want to get behind the wheel. I suspected this was Dad's other motive: if he combined our lessons, I'd watch Elizabeth and see that learning to drive wasn't so bad after all.

"So your, ah, your mom had a Corolla," Dad said to Elizabeth. I guess he knew because he'd helped her sell it to pay the medical bills. "That's not too different from our car. It should handle very similarly."

There was an awkward silence. It was the first time I'd heard anyone address Elizabeth directly about her mother.

"We call our car the Commie Comet," I offered, to break the silence.

It worked. Elizabeth looked startled, then laughed—quietly, of course. "Makes sense," she said. "All the bumper stickers."

"Hey, now!" Dad said. "We are progressives in this household, not Communists, although there's nothing necessarily wrong with Communists. My parents were fine examples. But the 'Commie' part of that name refers to the color of the car, not its political leanings or those of its occupants."

Dad was kind of babbling, the way I did when I got nervous. I wondered what Elizabeth thought about our political leanings. I assumed she was pretty conservative, what with the Catholic school and the argyle sweaters. She didn't respond to Dad's comment, though.

We spent the evening driving around the ShopRite parking lot again. Elizabeth didn't have much more experience than I did, because her mom had been too sick for the past few months to teach her. But she was definitely catching on faster than I was. Dad had me park in five different spots, then he had Elizabeth try it. I parked sloppily over the white lines or at a skewed angle each time. Elizabeth nailed them all after the first one.

"Are you ready to try a little road driving?" Dad asked finally. "We can just go up and down Elm a few times, nice and slow."

"*Dad*," I said. "I am not driving down Elm. No way."

"Chestnut, then," he said. "We can take 34th Street over and practice left turns."

"Sure," Elizabeth said.

So she drove around the block twice, practicing left turns and complete stops at stop signs, and then we switched seats and I drove around the block.

My hands were trembling on the wheel the whole time, but I managed to keep my foot steady, and I mostly stayed in my lane. Luckily no one else was trying to drive around that particular block, because I kept the speedometer needle at a daredevil 5 mph. At least no wildlife darted out in front of my tires.

"Good, Cadie," Dad said. "You have to work on checking all your mirrors, but you're getting the hang of it. Want to try once more around the block?"

I shook my head. "I'm tired. Let's go home."

"Okay. Good work for one night." Dad twisted around to face Elizabeth in the back seat. "And *you*, missy. You're a natural! I think you'll be ready for three-point turns next time."

I'd never heard him use Proud Dad Voice for anyone except me and Josh.

Which made sense, since he'd never had any kids except me and Josh. Before.

"I think I'll just walk," I said, getting out of the car. I slammed the door shut, shoved my hands deep into my pockets, and started down the sidewalk in the dark.

. . .

Saturday morning, Raven and I had a date to go shopping with her mom and grandmother for our Fall Ball dresses. Mom was already out of the house—she'd gone in to her office at school to catch up on work (or so she said)—and Dad was preparing to take Elizabeth out for a grand tour of Baltimore. Josh was going along, too, and he actually seemed excited.

"I'm going to show her all around Peabody," he told me, scraping his cereal bowl. We were finishing breakfast while Elizabeth showered. "The practice rooms, the dance studios, Friedberg Hall, and the Harry Potter library." Peabody has two libraries: an ugly functional one and a fairy-tale-gorgeous one, six stories high. The main room is a giant marble-floored atrium lit by hanging lamps and a skylight, with gilded cast-iron columns. Every floor opens to a balcony over the main atrium, hemmed in by an intricate scrollwork railing that runs around all four walls. Some of the Prep kids call it the Harry Potter library. Mom calls it the Chapel, because people really do get married there.

"And then the Meyerhoff," Josh was saying. "We might even get rush tickets for the symphony tonight!"

I smiled at him. "That's great. By the way, that second Bach suite you've been practicing all week sounds fantastic."

Josh said nothing.

"Are you nervous about the competition?"

"Nah."

"Well. That's good."

He nodded, then got up to put his bowl in the sink.

I grabbed the hem of his shirt as he walked by. "Hey. What did I say?"

"Nothing."

"But you clammed up. You were all excited, and then I mentioned the Bach and you stopped talking."

"I'm supposed to be practicing Popper's Hungarian Rhapsody for the competition. Not Bach."

"Oh. Well, do you already know the Hungarian Rhapsody?"

"No. But I'll learn it. It'll be fine." Suddenly he was red in the face. He twisted away from my grip and ran upstairs.

95

I followed him up to his room, but as I passed the bathroom, the door opened and Elizabeth came out in her bathrobe, and crashed into me.

"Oops, sorry," she said, just as the doorbell rang.

"I'll get that," I said.

I heard Josh start practicing arpeggios at breakneck speed as I ran back down the stairs and opened the door. Raven was on the step, and Ruby and Renata waved at me from the car.

"Leaving!" I yelled, grabbing my bag from a hook, and banged the door shut behind me.

"Hey," Raven said as we buckled ourselves into the back seat. "You don't think we should've invited Elizabeth, too?"

"Nah, she's taking a tour of Baltimore with Dad and Josh today. I don't even think she's going to the Fall Ball." But my stomach sank. I hadn't thought to ask Elizabeth about the dance at all.

Renata looked back at us from the passenger seat. "Who's Elizabeth?"

"My secret illegitimate half sister," I said, and Renata's eyes widened. "It's a long story. She just moved here. And she's probably not going to the Fall Ball because she's practically a nun."

I felt a little bad about making fun of Elizabeth, especially after not inviting her on our shopping trip. But then I remembered Proud Dad Voice from the night before and didn't feel quite so bad. After all, she had Dad for the day. And I didn't. Not that I couldn't have gone with them, if I'd wanted to, but I didn't, because I had better things to do, and—oh my god. I pressed "stop" on that loop in my head before it got out of control.

Renata had a million questions, and I told her all the details as we drove.

"Oh, that poor girl," she kept murmuring. "Oh, your poor mother."

I didn't mention how much I hated sharing a room, or how much my stomach hurt when I thought about Dad sleeping on the couch every night, or how Elizabeth was a natural at driving and perfect at pretty much everything else. All of that would've sounded like complaining. Plus it might've made my eyes water.

We were going up to the thrift stores in Roland Park first, because that's where all the rich people live, so the castoffs are more exciting. Then we'd circle back down York Road, and finally hit The Avenue in Hampden. I love shopping with the Woodburys. Ruby has a knack for finding treasures and bargains, and Renata is a big fan of ice cream pit stops at the Charmery.

By the end of the day, we'd found a slinky teal flapper-style dress for Raven that looked drop-dead gorgeous with her red hair and green eyes, and a strapless cream-colored A-line for me that Ruby promised would look stunning once she sewed scraps of black lace and multicolored beads all over it.

Raven, Renata, and I had squeezed into one tiny dressing room in Charm City Consignment, our fourth stop of the day.

I tugged at the top of the dress, staring at myself in the mirror. "I don't know how I feel about a strapless dress."

"Well, you've got the boobs for it," Raven said.

"I wish I *didn't* have them," I said. "They're heavy, you know. And all my clothes are getting tight."

"And I wish you'd share," Raven grumped, pressing her hands to her own flat chest.

Renata sighed, turning to look at the back of a mostly back-less black cocktail dress she was trying on. Her skin was just as pale as Raven's, and she was bony-thin. "You got that from me, dear, I'm sorry." To me, she said, "I'm sure Ruby can sew on a pair of straps, if that would make you more comfortable. But Raven's right. It looks lovely on you."

Ruby was waiting outside the dressing room. "Well, let's see!" she called, and I opened the door to show her the dress.

"Fits you like a glove," she declared. "We'll take it."

She insisted on buying the dress for me. "I consider it an art project," she said, waving my wallet away. "It's what keeps me young."

We stopped for dinner at Tamber's, an Indian fusion restaurant, which means that in addition to chana masala, saag paneer, and naan, they also serve burgers, fries, and milk shakes. Classic Baltimore.

Ruby took my dress home with her to start working on it— "Only three weeks till the dance!"—so I was empty-handed when I walked in the door.

Which was why I couldn't drop anything when Mom, who was sitting on the couch, looked up from her laptop and said, "Oh, good. Cadie. I'm so glad you're home. Your dad can't take off any more time from the bookshop, and Olga wants me to bring Josh in for an extra lesson on his competition piece, so can you take Elizabeth to church tomorrow morning?"

CHAPTER TEN

Elizabeth didn't seem thrilled about the arrangement either, but Mom was adamant that she wouldn't have Elizabeth wandering around town on her own.

"You can walk to Saints Philip and James over on North Charles. It's only a mile," she said. "And you can stop at the 7-Eleven and pick up milk on your way home."

"Baby cow juice," I muttered, even though I knew Mom hated it when Dad said that. She said it was disgusting and rude to those who preferred to drink "milk as nature intended it, not as vegans invented it."

"You don't have to stay for the service if you don't want to," Mom reminded me, under her breath, while she packed lunch for her and Josh, and I waited for Elizabeth to come downstairs. "Go sit in the sculpture garden while she's at Mass, or the Daily Grind. Just make sure she gets there and back in one piece."

Elizabeth came into the kitchen then, wearing her church clothes: khaki slacks, loafers, a black cardigan over a silky blue top. I looked down at my ripped jeans and sweatshirt, then ran back upstairs and changed into leggings, a skirt, and a button-down denim shirt. It had patches sewn all over it but at least it was clean. Then I swiped a brush through my hair and fished out a pair of black flats from under my bed. They were too small. I ditched them and grabbed my boots.

It was a nice day for a walk, although even 11:00 ("late Mass") was too early for anything on a Sunday morning, in my opinion. We walked down 34th Street to Keswick, then turned left on 33rd and cut across the Johns Hopkins undergrad campus to North Charles Street.

"Cadie," said Elizabeth tentatively, as if she still wasn't sure about using my nickname.

"Yeah?"

"I'm just—I'm curious about something, but I don't want to be rude." She paused.

"Okay . . ." I prompted. "Shoot."

"Well, I know you're not religious at all. I mean, you said you're more Quaker than anything. But do you still observe any Jewish customs?"

I sighed. "I never had a bat mitzvah or anything, if that's what you mean. We don't go to synagogue or Hebrew school. My mom's family moved from Spain to DC when she was nine and she never felt like she fit in with the kids in their new synagogue community. After her bat mitzvah, she finally refused to do any more religious stuff at all."

It was so weird to think of Mom rebelling against her parents. My mind wandered briefly, trying to picture Mom as a teenager.

"So . . . what about Ross's family?"

"Well, Dad grew up in New York with Communist parents, Grandma Ruth and Grandpa Morris, who thought religion was 'the opiate of the masses.' So he had no problem with raising us nonreligious." I wondered if this was awkward for Elizabeth, hearing about grandparents she'd never met—people she'd never known existed. "Mom's parents didn't like it and there used to be a big argument every year about whether they could take us to High Holy Day services at their synagogue in DC, but now they live in Florida, and they're too far away to do anything about it."

We'd finally reached the church. Saints Philip and James was a big marble cathedral just south of the Baltimore Museum of Art. We climbed the steps and I hesitated outside the door.

"I probably shouldn't stay," I said. "I was thinking about waiting for you over at the Daily Grind."

"Oh, that's fine," Elizabeth said. "I can meet you there when Mass is over."

I still didn't turn away, though. I was curious about Mass. I'd never been to one before. And it seemed that lots of Johns Hopkins students went to services here. Lots of male Hopkins students. Cute ones.

"It's fine if you want to stay," Elizabeth said. "You don't have to be baptized or confirmed or anything to go to Mass. No one checks your Catholic ID card."

"You have a Catholic ID card?"

Elizabeth raised her eyebrows and did not deign to answer. I gave her points for sarcasm.

"Well," I said, "I don't know any of the prayers, or what to do, or—"

"It's no big deal. I'll show you how to follow along with the readings, and you can just stand up and sit down when everyone else does." She grinned at me. "I guess you could say it's really not that different from Meeting."

She was totally wrong about that.

The priest stood up in a little pulpit that was sort of attached to the wall, like a gravy boat on the side of a big ship. I couldn't stop staring at all the gold leaf on the walls, the greenish marble columns, the stained glass, the polished brass of the enormous pipe organ. Most of the service went over my head; it was in English, not in Latin, but the echo in that enormous marble space blurred the priest's words like melted butter. It was a complex choreography, with standing and sitting and kneeling and sitting again. There was calling and responding in an order that I didn't understand, and the responses sounded like slight variations on the same one or two phrases. At the end of the whole thing, everyone turned and shook hands with the people around them and said, "Peace be with you." That part was all right with me, but I felt like a bit of an imposter saying it.

Then everyone lined up in the aisles and began a slow procession to the front for Communion. I stood uncertainly next to Elizabeth.

"You don't have to go up with me," she whispered, "but if you do, just cross your arms over your chest, and he'll give you a blessing instead of the Host."

I wasn't sure if I wanted a blessing, but it seemed rude to exit the line at that point, so I waited my turn and then stood in front of the priest with my arms folded across my chest. He bowed his head and made the sign of the cross over me, and mumbled some words. Then I turned and saw Elizabeth beckoning to me, and we went back to our pew.

I thought that was the end, but there were more prayers, and then finally the whole thing was over.

"So what did he think when I went up there with my arms folded?" I asked, as we walked out the door. "Do other people do that sometimes?"

"Oh, only if you haven't taken your first Communion yet, or if you're not Catholic, or if you're . . . indisposed to receive Communion."

"What does that mean?"

"Oh, just, you know. If you've committed a mortal sin."

"A *mortal sin?*" I repeated. "What the hell kind of sin is that?"

Elizabeth looked around quickly, and I wondered if swearing on the steps of the church might itself be a mortal sin.

She said, "Like if you're, you know, living with someone you're not married to, or if you've had, um, impure thoughts."

"*Elizabeth!*"

"Don't worry about it," she said quickly. "The priest wasn't judging you, I promise."

"Well, couldn't I have worn a sign or something? Like, an 'I'm not Catholic' sign? So he'd know I'm not a mortal sinner? Not that wearing an 'I'm not Catholic' sign is a great idea, in fact it's super offensive, but—"

"It's really not a big deal," she interrupted. "You're also not supposed to take Communion if you've forgotten to fast since the night before. So it's not just, you know. Sexual stuff."

"Great," I grumbled.

"Well, you don't have to come back next week, I know the way now. I won't get lost."

"There were some parts I liked," I admitted. "I liked some of the stuff he was saying about pacifism during the speech."

"The homily?"

"Is that what it's called? The part where he talked about our responsibilities to our neighbors."

"Yeah, that was the homily. It's different every week. This priest was a lot more liberal than our priest back in Ohio."

"I didn't know there was such a thing as a liberal priest."

"Oh, lots of Catholics are Democrats."

"Well, right," I said, pretending I knew that.

"And the new pope is practically a Communist."

I snuck a peek to make sure she was joking, and saw that she was grinning at me again. Elizabeth seemed to be in a much better mood today. She seemed—lighter somehow, as if she'd set down a hefty backpack she'd been carrying.

"You seem happier," I said, without thinking.

Her smile fell, and she shrugged. "I felt closer to Mom this morning, during Mass, than I have—in a long time."

I took a deep breath. "I'm really sorry. About your mom."

"Thanks."

We walked in silence for a few moments.

"I'm sure this is really, really hard for you," I tried again. "Coming here, living with a whole family you've never known. It's hard for all of us. But I'm sure it's way harder for you, with . . ." I trailed off, not wanting to say "with your mom dying."

"I didn't think I'd get along with Ross at all," Elizabeth said, catching me by surprise. "I was sure I'd hate him, actually. Because my mom never talked about him when I was little. I knew that she'd gotten pregnant and left without telling him, but I always thought that he'd come looking for us, that he'd find us someday. I know now that he didn't know I existed, but . . . that was hard for me to understand when I was younger."

I couldn't think of anything to say to that.

"And those days in the hospital, with my mom—at the end— that was pretty horrible. Talking to Ross on the phone for the first time during all that—I hated it. I didn't want to talk to him. I wanted to hate him. But then we talked a lot more, while we were cleaning out the apartment, on the train coming down here, and—it was like we'd always known each other. And just hadn't seen each other in a long, long time. I don't know." She looked at me, and I was shocked to see tears rolling down her face. Her voice wasn't wobbly at all. "It's like he really is my long-lost dad.

And somehow that makes it a little bit easier that Mom is—" But there her voice broke, and she didn't finish her sentence.

Instead, she pulled something out of her pocket. Two some-things. A pack of cigarettes and a lighter.

My mouth must've dropped open, because she glanced at me quickly, then looked away. "I don't care what you think about me," she said, lighting up. "I kind of picked it up when everything was happening. I'll quit. Soon." She took a deep drag, then blew out a long stream of smoke. "But if you could please not tell . . ."

"Yeah," I said, still stunned. "Yeah, of course."

We sat on the curb outside the 7-Eleven while she smoked and stared off into the distance. I didn't ask her for a cigarette and she didn't offer one. Not that I wanted one, anyway. I mean, I'd never smoked before. But Elizabeth, a smoker? That was the last thing I would've ever suspected about her.

"Cadie," she said finally, "thanks for coming with me. You don't have to come back next week. I mean it. But thanks for coming today. This would've been—really hard to do alone."

"I have to come back next week," I said. "I have to explain to the priest that I am not a mortal sinner. Thanks to your incomplete, incompetent instructions."

She laughed a little and stubbed out the cigarette on the pavement, then fished in her pocket for a handkerchief. She had an actual handkerchief. She wiped her eyes and blew her nose, and then we went home. I didn't realize till we walked in the door that we'd forgotten to buy the milk.

· · ·

Monday after school was our first *Much Ado* read-through.

"Gather round, people, and our revels shall begin!" Robin announced.

We sat cross-legged on the stage, as usual. There were twelve of us, plus Robin, as well as Micayla and Heron Lang, who were doing costumes and set design. Two guys wearing all black skulked near the back of the theater until Robin yelled, "Techies! That means you, too!" and they reluctantly emerged from the shadows.

"Now, people, tonight and tomorrow night's read-throughs will be the only rehearsals we'll have where we're all gathered together like this. Until tech week, of course. After tomorrow night, we'll rehearse scene by scene, and you only have to show up for scenes you're in." He handed out a thick schedule packet. "Let me amend that. Please show up fifteen minutes *before* your scene is scheduled. If you show up *at* the time you're scheduled, you're late."

We did five minutes of centering, then five minutes of stretches and vocal warm-ups. Which meant yodeling, humming, reciting vowels, and saying things like "The big black bug bit the big black bear" with as much enunciation as possible.

"Micayla, Heron, Troy, Davis—you'll meet with Peg now to get started on concepts. I'll have a separate meeting with you on Wednesday."

Peg, the art teacher, waved from the front row of seats, where she'd been listening to our vocal warm-ups with a smile. She had a shock of canary-yellow hair that stood straight out from her head, like duck fluff, and full-color tattoo sleeves on both arms. Peg was awesome.

The tech and design crew jumped off the stage and went into the classroom to work. Meanwhile, Robin was handing out scripts. I slipped my pocket *Much Ado* into my backpack, hoping no one had noticed that I'd brought it along. I thought we'd have to bring our own copies. Robin noticed, though, and nodded at me. "Great edition, Acadia. Definitely read the introduction; it'll help you understand the background of the play." A warm little light sparked in my chest. Even if I hadn't actually *read* the introduction yet, at least I was doing something right.

Then we started in on the reading.

It was a halting, stumbling read-through. People forgot what characters they were playing, missed lines, mispronounced words all over the place. None of the jokes were funny. None of the verse flowed like music, the way it had on stage at the theater in DC.

And yet. Some of the lines sounded like more than just words on a page, written four hundred years ago. Not everyone's lines. Mostly Zephyr's. He was sitting across the circle from me, hunched in his leather jacket, but I was hyperaware of every word he spoke. It was as if everyone else was reading from the dictionary but Zephyr was just talking. He made his lines sound casual, as if he wasn't waiting for a cue but actually listening to what the person was saying to him, and coming up with a response on the spot—only his response happened to be in Shakespearean English. I couldn't figure out how he was doing it; if anything, it was something he *wasn't* doing that everyone else was. Trying too hard, maybe?

Most of the cast was also in my drama class. Sam Shotwell was Don John, the villain—I tried not to make eye contact with him or stare when he was reading, but he definitely caught me looking at him once and grinned, which turned the thermostat on my face up to about a zillion degrees. Rina Crane was a good choice for Dogberry, the main comic relief character, because Shakespearean fools had to be so over-the-top; still, I thought she was overacting most of her lines. A sophomore named Tori Lopez was playing Claudio, the other main male character besides Benedick, and Priya Pashari was Hero, Beatrice's cousin and Claudio's love interest.

When Kieri Cantor complained about getting cast as Leonato, Hero's father, Robin told us that back in Shakespeare's day there was lots of gender-bending on stage, since only men were allowed to be actors. "I like to even the scores now when I can," he said. "Kieri, you and Tori and Rina will be our banner bearers." Besides, we all knew that there was a shortage of guys in the drama department.

"Good work, people," Robin announced after the second act. "We'll pick up with Act Three tomorrow night."

I met Micayla outside the Shed and we went out to her car, a beat-up Ford station wagon that she'd spray-painted with wild loops of color. "As long as it fits all my canvases in the back," she said, "I don't give a rat's ass if it *is* a granny car." Half-finished paintings were also stacked in the back seat.

Heron Lang, the other costumer and set designer, came with us.

"Mind if I drop off Heron, too?" asked Micayla. "She's just around the corner from you, in Remington."

"Not at all. Want shotgun?" I said to Heron.

"Nah," she said, "I'll snuggle with the artwork in the back." She winked at me.

I didn't know Heron very well, but I really liked her. She spoke up in Meeting a lot, usually about current events or something political. She was the president of the Social Justice Club, which I'd joined for a few months last year. Her hair had been purple then, but this year it was back to its natural black and cut super short, pixie style. She had industrial bars through her ears, a pierced eyebrow, a nose ring, and a stud just below her bottom lip. It wasn't overwhelming, though. Her face looked right that way. She was wearing a plaid flannel shirt and cargo pants tucked into work boots spattered with paint and, oddly, what looked like dried egg yolk. I loved that Micayla and her friends seemed to be constantly covered in art supplies, as if they could never stop making art long enough to clean up properly.

Just as we were about to pull out of the parking lot, someone came running toward the car.

"Cadie, wait up!" It was Elizabeth. I rolled down my window. "I'm sorry," she panted (I thought, *Smoker!*). "I had debate team and then I had to talk to the guidance counselor—about having my records sent over from my old school—some paperwork got lost in the shuffle somewhere—and Melissa said I could get a ride with you after rehearsal—hi, I'm Elizabeth"—this to Micayla— "would you mind taking me home?"

"Hop in, honey," said Micayla.

"Micayla, Heron, this is my—this is Elizabeth," I said. "She's new here. She's, um, my sister."

Micayla already knew the story, of course, but Elizabeth didn't know that, and I didn't want her to think I'd been talking about her. Heron looked confused, but she didn't ask any questions, thank the gods. She only said, "Welcome to Fern Grove," and scooted over to make room for Elizabeth on the seat next to her. "Sorry," she added, "there's not much room back here."

"So," Micayla said, pulling out of the parking lot, "I saw Zephyr got the lead. He's really talented—he's been in the school play every year. Bit of a loner, though. Odd duck."

"He *is* really good," I said, and then for some reason, I wanted to change the subject. "You've done sets and costumes before, right?"

She nodded. "Past two years. And what about you, Liz?" she called into the back seat. "You into any extracurriculars besides, what was it, debate team?"

"She doesn't like being called Liz," I whispered, but Elizabeth heard me and said, "Oh, that's fine, whatever. And no, so far, I'm just on debate. I did that plus math club and track at my old school, though."

Heron whistled. "Underachiever, huh?"

Elizabeth laughed a little, sounding embarrassed.

"Anyway," I said, "are you guys going to the Fall Ball? Raven and I just bought our dresses this weekend."

"Yeah, I guess so," said Micayla. "Troy asked if I wanted to go as friends. He's kind of *meh*, but it's fine with me as long as he doesn't expect me to dance with him the whole time."

"Micayla!" I said.

"Well, it's the truth," she said. "I was planning to ask Davis, but he's already going with Rina."

"Are you serious?" I asked. "Is *everyone* in drama dating each other?"

"Oh, totally," said Heron. "It's incestuous. Wait and see."

I thought about Sam Shotwell, his grin when he caught me watching him during the reading. What was wrong with me, anyway? *You're going out with Farhan!* I scolded myself in my head, and then immediately: *Am I going out with Farhan?* Was a date to a dance the same as "going out" with someone?

"Boys. Don't pay 'em much attention," Micayla was saying, as we pulled up at my house, "and they'll come after you in flocks. Guarantee it."

"Thanks for the wisdom," I said, and Elizabeth added, "And thanks for the ride!"

I'd almost forgotten she was still in the back seat, she'd been so quiet.

Mom had saved leftovers for us—it was after 8:00, and they'd already eaten dinner.

"Uh. What is this, exactly?" Elizabeth asked, looking at the bowls of food.

"Quinoa casserole," I said. "It's a Greenfield special. Try it. It's better than it looks."

I took my dinner up to my room—our room—and worked on highlighting my lines in the script while I ate.

Elizabeth joined me a few minutes later, curling up beneath the covers with a book. Probably the Bible.

Or maybe not. Maybe Elizabeth was really into, like, nerdy sci-fi. Or trashy romance novels. What did I actually even know about her?

Part of me wanted to ask what she was reading, but another part of me was wary. It had been easier to resent her for taking over my room, my dad, my life, when I thought of her as Little Miss Perfect Catholic Schoolgirl. Now I wasn't sure if that's who she was, or if the real Elizabeth was Pulls-Out-a-Pack-of-Smokes-after-Mass Girl. Or some weird combination of those personas that I totally did not understand.

I racked my brain for a safe topic of conversation.

"So," I said, "are you going to the Fall Ball?"

"Oh, I don't know," Elizabeth said, without looking up from her book.

"Why not?" I said before I could stop myself. "Everyone goes—it'll be fun. You don't have to take a date, really, it's pretty casual."

"Do you have a date?"

"Um . . . yeah, actually." I felt myself blushing.

"Who?"

"Oh, you probably haven't met him yet. His name is Farhan. We're just friends."

"People don't blush that much about their friends," she said, smirking at me.

I couldn't help grinning. "So, are you going or not?"

"Oh, like I said, I don't know. I've never actually been to a dance before."

"You *what*?"

"Yeah, we didn't have dances at St. Joseph. Not a very Catholic school thing. They thought we'd all start, like, heavy petting or something."

"No way. All schools have dances. And, um, 'heavy petting'? What even *is* that?"

We both laughed.

"Well, maybe we had dances," she admitted. "But I was never really interested."

"Liar!" I said, triumphantly. "I knew it. You should go with me and Farhan and Raven and Max. We'll find you a date." Why was I trying so hard to get her to go to the dance? But now that I'd started, I couldn't exactly take it back. "So, do you have anything to wear?"

"Well—I guess it'd be a good idea to go and meet some people." She went to the closet and pulled out a sleeveless blue dress, held it up against her body, and looked in the mirror. "Would this work?"

I shrugged. It was a little boring, but if it suited her, fine. And the color did go nicely with her eyes. "Raven can probably lend you something if you want," I told her. "I think you're about the same size. You'd be swimming in my clothes."

"No, this is fine." She was staring at herself in the mirror. "I was supposed to wear it for my mom's . . ." But she didn't finish the sentence, and when I waited, she just shook her head. "Never mind."

CHAPTER ELEVEN

The next night, I didn't get home from rehearsal until 8:00 again. When I walked in the door, I was surprised to see everyone still sitting at the dinner table. Laughing.

"What's going on?" I asked, dropping my backpack by the door and coming into the kitchen.

"Oh, we're just telling stories," Mom said, wiping her eyes, still chuckling. When was the last time I'd even seen her laugh?

"About the olden days," Dad added. "Stupid stuff we did in college."

Josh's face was flushed, he'd been laughing so hard. "Tell the pineapple story again!"

Elizabeth and Mom dissolved into fits of giggles while Dad shook his head. "I don't think I'd survive the experience."

"The pineapple story?" I said. "What pineapple story?"

Mom coughed. "It was just—a game we used to play. In college. Late nights cleaning at the co-op. If you skipped a chore, you had to do the 'wine shackle challenge' as punishment—strap a bottle of wine to your chest and leave it there until it was empty, but you couldn't drink from it; only other people could, and they couldn't remove it from your body. The whole thing was stupid, of course."

"But I misheard it as the 'pineapple challenge,'" Dad admitted. "In my defense, the acoustics in that kitchen were *terrible*."

Everyone started laughing again.

"Oh," Mom gasped, "the looks on everyone's faces when Dad

strapped that pineapple to his chest! And then he strutted over to Rain and Bow Knowlton and asked them to bite into it!"

"You knew people named Rain and Bow?" Elizabeth asked.

"Twins!" Mom and Dad said at exactly the same time, and went off into peals of laughter again.

"Ha! That's nothing. Didn't your mom ever tell you stories about Ahimsa House?" I said, dropping into the empty seat next to Elizabeth. "Some *really* wacky names there."

The table went quiet.

"What?" I said. "What'd I say?"

"Well," Mom said, "I'd better start loading the dishwasher. Could you hand me that plate, Ross?"

Okay, hang on. *Ross?* Just a moment ago, he'd been back to "Dad" status.

"But I just got here!" I said.

"Yes, but it's getting late," Mom said, taking a stack of dishes to the sink.

I looked at Josh, who was frowning at me as if I'd killed the vibe. As if *I'd* done something wrong.

So. Not. Fair. How was I supposed to know Ahimsa House was off-limits? I'd walked in the door and stumbled right into Mom and Dad's fragile spiderweb of a truce—both a thing of beauty and a trap—and torn it all to pieces.

That was a good image. I repeated it to myself while I gulped down a bowl of soup at the sink and then stomped upstairs. Spiderweb, spiderweb, spiderweb. And Elizabeth at the center of it, spinning the threads around us—no, Mom at the center, trying to ensnare—*Oh, I don't know,* I mumbled, pulling my phone out of my pocket. I dialed Raven. She'd have something snarky to say; she'd know how to make me feel better.

But Mom poked her head into my room as soon as Raven picked up the phone.

"No phone time after eight," she said. "Homework time. Then bed."

No phone time after eight? "Since when?"

"And no talking back, young lady."

"Jeez," I whispered to Raven, going downstairs. "I guess I have to talk to you in the basement."

But Josh was already down there, practicing. "Mom asked me to practice down here so she could go to sleep early."

"Never mind," I sighed to Raven. "I'll just talk to you tomorrow."

"Okay," she said. "Hang in there, National Park." Sometimes it made me laugh when she called me that. Tonight it just reminded me of Rain and Bow and wacky names and killing the conversation.

And Mom and Dad and Josh and Elizabeth, laughing around a dinner table without me.

I did my homework on the couch, then fell asleep reading the introduction to *Much Ado*. When I woke up around midnight, I saw that Dad had come downstairs and fallen asleep in the armchair next to me. Because I'd taken his spot.

What a mess.

· · ·

The next day was rough. I had trouble keeping my eyes open in all my classes, even drama. We were working on our scenes from *The Crucible*, and I'd been paired up with Sam Shotwell— at long last. (Thank Zeus I'd worn something nice today: saddle shoes, paired with my red plaid skirt, purple tights, and a low-cut black sweater.) We were doing the scene where Elizabeth Proctor confronts her husband, John, about sleeping with their former servant, Abigail, who is now accusing Elizabeth of witchcraft—hoping to get Elizabeth sent to the gallows so Abigail can marry John herself. It wasn't exactly the most romantic scene.

We were trying to memorize our lines, to get "off book," because Robin wouldn't let us start working on blocking—stage directions—until the lines themselves were "engraved into our bodies," as he put it. (Which sounded sort of painful.) Sam clearly hadn't worked on his lines over the weekend. Not that I had either—I'd completely forgotten about the assignment, what with dress buying and churchgoing and all—but it was a short scene, and there weren't *that* many lines.

"I'm sorry," Sam finally said, after our sixth attempt to get through the scene without picking up our books. "I'll work on it tonight and be better for next class. Let's just use the script for today." So we read through it again, on book.

"Inevitable and only, people!" Robin kept calling, marching around the room. "Each line must be the inevitable and only continuation of the one before it. Don't *read* your lines. *Listen* to your partner and *respond*. Listen for what makes your next line *inevitable*."

I liked playing Elizabeth Proctor's character. It was a challenge to understand where she was coming from—hard to get into her head. An important plot point was that she couldn't tell a lie. She blamed herself for John's infidelity, saying she'd been a cold woman and her neglect had forced him into Abigail's arms. At the end, she let her husband give himself up to the gallows, because she knew that was the only way he could feel that his soul was cleansed of his sin. And yet, by the end of the play you had respect for this woman, not just pity. She stood by a code of ethics that didn't make sense to me, but you couldn't help admiring the fervor with which she believed in it.

I wondered if I could ever feel that way about Elizabeth's religion—not Proctor, the one who was sleeping in my bedroom every night.

Sam and I stumbled through the scene one last time, then he threw his book down in disgust and said he was going to the bathroom. I sat on the edge of the stage and watched Robin coach Zephyr, who was paired up with a quiet girl named Nina. She always sounded too terrified to speak above a whisper. They were working on the scene at the very end of Act Two, when John Proctor finds out that his new servant girl, Mary Warren, knows about his past with Abigail. He tries to bully her into confessing that all the servant girls are fabricating their stories of witchcraft at Abigail's bidding. Nina, her eyes widening as Zephyr ranted and raved, with his hands buried in his thick hair, was actually sort of perfect for the role. So was he, of course. Zephyr could play any role he wanted to.

"Cut!" Robin yelled, waving his arms. "What does that mean, 'only what we always were, but naked now'?" he asked Nina, quoting a line Zephyr had just spoken.

She bit her lip. "Um. They're, um, they're being uncovered?"

"Not *they*, *we*. You *are* Mary Warren, Nina. Think like Mary Warren. What are you doing to John Proctor here? Not taking his clothes off, obviously. But uncovering him, yes. In what way?"

"Um, uncovering him, like, for who he really is?"

Zephyr frowned down at his hands. "Who he's *always* been. That's what he says. 'Only what we always were.'"

"Right," Robin said, addressing Zephyr now. "You say, 'no great change.' This is not some moment of epiphany, of coming to

118

understand that you're someone totally different from who you thought you were. This is about acknowledging what was buried inside you all along. Who you are even though maybe you'd been masking it, or trying to be someone else."

Zephyr was still staring at his hands, not making eye contact with Robin, but Nina was scribbling notes on her script. I wondered if Zephyr resented the direction. Why? Robin was right.

"Those lines can't be melodramatic or loud," Robin was saying. "They come from somewhere deep in your gut. You're talking to yourself, watching your carefully constructed life crumble. You already know what's under there. You were just hoping you'd never have to face it." Robin almost seemed to be talking to himself now.

Zephyr looked at him for a quick moment, something unreadable in his eyes. Then he nodded and picked up his script, just as the bell rang.

"All right!" Robin shouted, clapping his hands. "Good work again, people, but let's get these scenes off book ASAP."

As everyone else packed up and filed out the door, I lingered. Rehearsing that scene with Sam had made me feel good for the first time all day, and I didn't want the feeling to go away just yet.

Robin was packing up his messenger bag in the front-row seats. I went around to the side of the stage and used the steps to descend instead of jumping off—took more time that way. Then I made my way down the first row.

He looked up. "Acadia! Nice work today."

"Thanks." I felt that glow in my chest, the same glow as when he'd praised me for having my own copy of *Much Ado*. The same way I felt when Dad was proud of me.

I squashed that thought.

"So," he said, studying my face, "what can I do for you?"

"Oh, I was just—" I thought quickly. "Um, I was just wondering, what was your name before you changed it to Robin Goodfellow?"

He let out a surprised bark of laughter. "Well, well. That was the last thing I expected you to ask."

"I'm sorry, if it's too personal—"

"No, no, no. It's not exactly classified information. Are you ready? Hold on to your hat." He paused dramatically. (Can you call it a dramatic pause if it's the drama teacher who's pausing? Isn't it sort of by definition a dramatic pause?) "My birth name was Rubens Pfefferkorn."

Moment of silence.

"Oh, my," I managed.

"Yes, indeed. Rubens was a family name on my mother's side. Pfefferkorn was my father's. And I wanted something entirely my own. I didn't want to be reminded of either of them whenever I wrote or said my own name."

"I get that," I said, without thinking.

Robin narrowed his eyes and gazed at me. "I don't recommend changing your name without careful consideration," he said. "It tends to—send a message to your family. Makes them very upset, causes a lot of pain. Unless, you know, you think they deserve that pain." He smiled, a wry, sad smile. "But of course, you're not eighteen, anyway."

"And I'm not really thinking about changing my name," I said quickly. Then, before I could stop myself, "What did your family do to deserve it?"

"Well, that's—complicated. Maybe we'll talk about that another time."

"I'm so sorry," I said. Do you ever wish there could be a *back* button in real life? I do. All the time. "Of course, that was a totally nosy and inappropriate question for me to ask. I'm sorry."

He laughed. "No, no. You're interested in people, Acadia, and that's a wonderful thing for an actor. You're an observer of human nature; you're thirsty for it. I can see that. Store it all up, everything you observe, and use it onstage." He smiled at me, a real, warm smile this time. It made his face all wrinkly around the corners of his eyes. "You're doing a great job in *Much Ado*, by the way. I'm very pleased with the way you're approaching the character."

He was? How was I approaching the character? I felt a big goofy smile blossom across my face.

"Now, was there anything else you wanted to talk about?"

I shook my head.

"Well, then. I have to get to a meeting, but walk with me—I have some notes for you. In the very first scene, when you're talking about Benedick with Leonato and Hero . . ."

I followed Robin out of the theater without noticing that there was a floor beneath my feet.

. . .

I wasn't called for any scenes on Wednesday evening's *Much Ado* rehearsal schedule, so I decided to see if I could go home with Raven that night. I really didn't need another strained dinner, or another night vying with Dad for the couch. I packed up everything at my locker and slammed it shut, then turned and almost walked into Farhan.

"Hey, Cadie," he said, holding his backpack on his shoulder with one hand. His signature move. Okay, okay, not exactly patented, I know. Probably eighty-five percent of boys hold

121

their backpacks that way. But I loved the way he made it look.

I snapped my gaze away and looked down at my saddle shoes. We were just about the same height. If I'd collided with him any harder, we might've accidentally kissed. He was standing so close I could smell his cologne—or was it laundry detergent? Dryer sheets? Something clean and fresh. And under that, a very faint whiff of male sweat. *Ugh, pheromones*, I could hear Raven saying. I wondered what it would feel like to dance with him . . . to feel his arms around me . . .

"Cadie?"

"Hmm?" I glanced back up.

He wasn't looking at me. "I'm really sorry, this is super awkward—but you mentioned that you wouldn't mind—"

I waited. "Mind what?"

"Oh, just, um. God. I'm so sorry, this is the worst. I'm the worst."

"What?" He couldn't go to the dance. He forgot he'd already asked someone else. His girlfriend. His fiancée.

"I'm so, so sorry," he said, "but I have to take the bus downtown for my internship today and I just realized I'm broke, and you said you wouldn't mind paying for your ticket—"

"Oh my god, I'm so sorry." It was my turn to say that phrase as many times as I could, while I dug my duct-tape wallet out of my purse, which was stuffed into my backpack, and then shuffled through it looking for change. Thanks, gods of not-looking-stupid-in-front-of-your-first-ever-date. Thanks a lot. I finally found a few crumpled one-dollar bills and some quarters. "How much do you need for the bus? I'm so sorry, I'll get you the rest of the money tomorrow. Tickets were ten dollars, right?"

"No, no, don't worry about it, this is fine. Just enough for the bus. I'll pay you back."

"Don't pay me back, this is me paying *you* back, I still owe you—"

But he was gone.

I ran down the hall to Raven's locker, wailing. "Raaavennnn, ohmygod ohmygod—"

It was not my day for staying out of other people's personal spaces. I zoomed around the corner and smacked right into Raven.

And Max.

Making out against her locker, of course.

Everyone made an *oomph* noise as we all slammed against the lockers, and I bounced back, did a one-eighty, and took off the way I'd come.

"What the hell, Cadie?" Max yelled.

He was laughing, thank Isis and Osiris, but Raven was most definitively *not.* The glare she was giving me could've cut a block of granite into itty-bitty pieces. I turned and walked back toward them slowly, regaining my dignity.

"Well, you shouldn't go having private moments in public places if you don't want to get interrupted," I muttered, hitching up my backpack and smoothing out my skirt. "Hey, Fish. What's shakin'?"

Raven intensified her glare, if that was possible. I smiled back sweetly. Sometimes I like pushing her buttons.

Our whole class had been calling Max Frisch "Fish" since first grade. It suited him. He had big brown eyes and pouty-looking lips—pouty *fish* lips, the kind of pout female movie stars do on the covers of magazines—but on him, it just looked like he was

123

always about to laugh, always hiding mischief of some sort. He was still the same old goofball to me, but now that Raven was going out with him, she'd switched to using his proper name and requested that I do the same in her presence.

"How can you get excited about kissing a guy named Fish?" she'd asked, pragmatically. This was back at the beginning of the summer, and we were treading water in the pool in her backyard, to tone our triceps.

"I don't know, but I sure hope you don't get married. How could anyone take you seriously, a couple named Raven and Fish? You'd have to name your kids Otter and Tadpole."

"Who says I'm having kids? Or getting married? I certainly wouldn't change my name, anyhow. The Woodbury name—"

"I know, I know. The Woodbury name represents the sacred sisterhood."

"Amen."

"Hey, ever wonder why it's not a-*women*?"

"Because the world was invented by sexist assholes." That was Raven's standard response when she was getting bored with an argument. It was also a perfect launching-off point into whatever political rant she'd been working herself up about lately. And as such, my cue to change the topic. So I'd dunked her, and we'd spent the next half hour or so chasing each other around the pool.

"So," Max asked, bringing me back to the present, "what're you in such a hurry for?"

"Oh, I just did the most embarrassing thing of my *life*," I moaned. "I almost face-planted into Farhan, and then he asked me for money, and then I gave him money and told him I'll give him the rest tomorrow but he didn't want more tomorrow, just today, and—"

"Cadie, you're not making sense," Raven cut in, "and Max has soccer practice to get to."

"Right," he said, and leaned in to kiss her one more time. "Bye, babe." Then he hefted his soccer bag onto his shoulder (not at *all* the way Farhan would've done it) and took off down the hall. "See ya, Cadie!" he called.

"Bye, babe," I mimicked, and Raven socked me in the stomach. "Hey!" I protested.

"Hey what, you're the one who just barged in on us!"

"You're in a *public hallway*. Anyway, can I come home with you? Everything's weird at home again. Dad and I *both* slept in the living room last night."

Raven was suddenly all sympathy. "I'm so sorry, I have debate team today. Do you want to hang out and wait for me?"

"Debate team! No, that's all right. Elizabeth is on debate, too. So we'll probably have dinner without her tonight." The thought was such sweet relief, I felt my shoulders actually sag, as if I'd been clenching them all day. Which I probably had. "Oh, hey, by the way. I asked her if she was going to the Fall Ball."

"And?"

"And, well, I think I kind of invited her to go with us. With the four of us."

"Won't that be awkward? Fifth-wheel-y?" Raven frowned.

"We can find her a date, right?"

"Sure, I mean, I'm surprised no one's asked her yet. New girl in town, plus that hair, plus that body—"

"*Raven!*"

"What?" she said. "Your sister's hot."

"My sister," I echoed.

"God. That still . . . sounds so strange."

"Yeah." I didn't know what else to say to that. We observed a moment of silence for the demise of my formerly sisterless existence—or, my former existence in which Raven was the closest thing to a sister I'd ever needed.

Huh. I looked at Raven. Was she *jealous* of Elizabeth?

No, Raven would've told me if she felt that way. She never minced words. Besides, how could she possibly be jealous of someone who was causing so much stress in my life? It wasn't like Elizabeth and I were staying up late watching movies and painting our toenails, or having deep conversations, or any of the things Raven and I did together.

I dismissed the thought. "So I'll ask her tonight if she has a date yet. If not, maybe we can—oh."

Elizabeth was coming down the hall toward us, walking next to a tall blond guy in a soccer jersey. Who was holding her books and asking her something that seemed to be making her uncomfortable. She tossed her hair and forced a smile, nodded, said something. He smiled back, handed her the stack of books, touched her on her shoulder, and spun away, walking like he had springs on the bottoms of his shoes.

"Guess she does have a date," Raven said, her eyebrows almost touching her hairline. "That sure didn't take long. And, wow—Sam Shotwell?"

"Yeah, well. As you predicted, right? I'll see ya."

And I went down the hall toward the administrative offices to meet Mom, hoping Elizabeth hadn't seen us standing there watching.

Stop it, I told myself. *You're going to the Fall Ball with Farhan. Your one true love. What more could you ask? And besides, you have no claims on Sam Shotwell; you only did a couple of stupid acting-class exercises together. So what if he grinned at you once or twice? You should be ashamed of yourself, trying to hog all the guys for yourself. Who do you think you are, anyway?*

Sometimes, no matter how hard I pushed "stop," that stupid loop just wouldn't shut off.

. . .

At least I had Friday to look forward to. Friday afternoon, the whole drama class plus the rest of the *Much Ado* cast and crew piled into a school bus and drove down to the Shakespeare Theatre in DC.

None of us ever got to ride on real school buses, the cheddar-colored kind. We did have a small Fern Grove bus (white with the school insignia painted in green) that picked up some students who lived farther away, but almost all the younger kids got dropped off and picked up by their parents, and the older kids took city buses—or drove themselves. I sat with Micayla near the back, and we exhausted ourselves singing stupid school bus songs for a while—"The Wheels on the Bus," "Ninety-Nine Bottles of Beer" (which we changed to mead, then Red Bull, then Gatorade, and then it wasn't funny anymore). Finally Robin stood up at the front of the bus, clapped his hands, and said, "People. Don't make me throw any students out the window. It's against the code of ethics in my contract."

So we stopped singing and watched the Beltway creep by outside the window. There's no such thing as speeding, or even driving *at* the speed limit, during rush hour—which, in the Baltimore-DC metro area, is actually four hours.

"How are the costumes coming along?" I asked.

Micayla sighed. "I don't know. Peg wants us to do a cross between Shakespearean and contemporary—like, contemporary outfits with period pieces thrown in here and there. She said it's a simple comedy, not a political play, so there's no reason to try to say anything political using the costumes. She hates when people overpoliticize the comedies."

"'Does this *say* anything?'" I murmured.

"What's that?"

"Oh, just a quote. The first play Dad and I ever saw together, years ago—*A Man for All Seasons*. There's this Everyman character, and he wears all black, and he comes onstage by himself to talk to the audience and complains about his costume. 'Is this a costume? Does this *say* anything? It barely covers one man's nakedness! A bit of black material to reduce Old Adam to the Common Man.' Isn't that fantastic? We've been quoting that line ever since."

Micayla stared at me. "You remember lines from a play you saw *years* ago?"

I shrugged. "Well, like I said, we've been quoting it at each other."

"Girl, no wonder you're on stage and I'm not. I can barely remember how to get dressed some mornings."

I checked out her outfit today—she was dressed up for the field trip, which for Micayla just meant regular clothes with minimal amounts of paint spilled on them. But instead of tying her hair back with a scarf or bandana like she usually did, she'd swept her long braids into a pile on the top of her head, stuck through with a couple of thin paintbrushes.

"Anyway," she continued, "Peg wants us to sew as much as we can from scratch, so at least it'll be good experience for me. And maybe I can use some of the clothes for my portfolio.

Not that I want to do textiles or fashion, but it can't hurt to be well-rounded."

"Man. College." It seemed like Micayla didn't have time to think about anything else these days.

"Yeah . . . let's talk about something else."

"Oh! Guess what—I found out Robin's birth name. Before he changed it to Robin Goodfellow."

"Oh, yeah?"

"You won't believe this: *Rubens Pfefferkorn*."

Micayla's eyebrows shot up. "Whoa. So he had more than one good reason to change it, huh?"

"More than one?"

"Yeah, I'd heard that he changed it after his parents kicked him out—they disowned him or something."

"*What?*"

"Yep. Small-town, small-minded family couldn't deal with their fabulous son who loved Broadway and Shakespeare. And other boys."

"But—that's ridiculous! He's so talented. They should've been proud of him."

"'Course they should've. Therefore, the name change, I suppose."

We lapsed into silence. *Wow.* Poor Robin. If I thought my family situation was tough . . .

A loud cheer went up from the front of the bus. We'd finally pulled up in front of the Shakespeare Theatre.

"People! Please wait outside the bus in some semblance of order so we can count and tag you like cattle." Robin sounded a little stressed. He was wearing his usual black turtleneck and tight black jeans, but he'd added a black blazer on top for the occasion. I looked at him and tried to imagine what it must've been like for him to make his own way at eighteen. Just a few years older than I was.

We waited outside the bus for Robin and Peg to take roll, then filed into the theater. It was only 6:00—we'd arrived early enough to hear the preshow lecture. As Micayla and I walked through the lobby, Heron ran over to join us. "Hey, Mic, let's see if we can check out the costume room before it starts!"

"Do you think they'd let us?" said Micayla.

Heron shrugged. "Can't hurt to ask, right?"

"Save us seats," Micayla told me, and they took off.

I went into the theater and plunked myself down at the end of a row. Then Sam Shotwell came down the other aisle, waved at me, and started to make his way down the row from the other side.

I jumped up as if I'd been sitting on porcupine quills and looked around, pretending I was trying to find someone I'd been waiting for. I walked back a few rows, a safe distance from Sam, and this time I picked a seat in the middle of the row, right next to the person who was already sitting there. Zephyr.

"Hey," I said. "Mind if I sit here?"

I draped my coat over the empty seats to my left, to save them for Micayla and Heron.

"Hey," he said.

I took that to mean *Sure, go ahead.*

Zephyr didn't say much off stage, when he didn't have lines written out for him. Maybe that was smart. Sometimes I thought my life would be much smoother if I could hire a scriptwriter to dictate it all for me.

We hadn't talked to each other at all, in fact, except for the words we'd spoken as Beatrice and Benedick in the audition and the read-through. I wasn't sure what to make of him. He was two grades ahead of me, a senior, and he'd only started at Fern Grove three years ago. Which, in Friends terms, made him a newbie. No one seemed to know him very well. He wasn't involved in any activities besides drama and he didn't belong to any particular group—jocks, art kids, nerds.

"So," I said, "have you been here before?"

"Couple of times."

"Me, too. My dad and I already saw this production, actually. We don't usually come all the way to DC for anything except Shakespeare. We have season tickets to Center Stage in Baltimore."

He nodded.

I nodded.

We were like two bobbleheads on a dashboard.

"They're doing *Who's Afraid of Virginia Woolf?* this season," he offered. "At Center Stage. You seen it yet?"

"No, never heard of it."

"Oh, my god. Edward Albee. Possibly the greatest play written in the last century. Besides *Arcadia* of course." He was still speaking quietly, but much faster. "I saw it on Broadway this summer, with my—with some friends. Tracy Letts was playing George, if you can believe it. Saw a few things at the Booth while I was in New York, but we all agreed that was by far the winner."

I had no idea what he was talking about. "Wow. So, what were you doing in New York?"

"Oh, I just went to a summer program. You know. Drama camp."

Drama camp. I pictured a roomful of Zephyr-like guys, with twisted hair and leather jackets, sitting in a circle on stage and meditating. Reading through the best plays of the last century. Going to see shows on Broadway. And girls, too, of course. Girls wearing lipstick and big earrings and tight, low-cut dresses like Rina Crane and Tori Lopez, who were now sitting on either side of Sam Shotwell and giggling like parakeets. Not that parakeets giggle. But the noises they were making sounded that ridiculous.

Micayla and Heron came in and looked around for me, and I waved and called their names. They made their way to our row and slid in.

"They let us backstage!" Micayla reported, breathless. "We saw *everything*—the costume room, the props closet, the scenery."

"They have an internship we could apply for," said Heron, as if she were saying, *They have a roomful of gold coins that they don't want anymore and they gave us garbage bags to fill.*

"Wow, that's great!" I said. "Zephyr was just telling me about a drama camp in New York. Have you guys ever considered drama camp?"

"Oh, I went to the summer program here every year in junior high," said Heron. "That's how I pulled strings to get us backstage."

Micayla nodded. "I did the program at Center Stage two summers ago. I was too busy with my art classes at MICA this past summer, but the Center Stage thing was fun. You should definitely consider it."

I had no idea I was so behind. Or so inexperienced. Had everyone else in this class been on stage since they were in diapers?

Someone came out to the podium then to start the preshow

lecture, and I pulled out my notebook to take notes. I needed all the help I could get.

Robin had warned us not to see this as an opportunity to copy the professional actors, but rather to collect ideas on what we liked and didn't like about the production. We were supposed to write a one-page review for homework and another page of new ideas about our own character, or for the lights, costumes, and scenery, if you were on crew.

The curtain finally went up to reveal Leonato, Hero, and Beatrice sitting on the stoop outside an apartment building, with Leonato's messenger hovering at his elbow. The Shakespeare Theatre's set designers had definitely tried to "say something" with the costumes and scenery, contrary to Peg's views—they'd set the play in mid-twentieth-century Chicago, with Leonato, Don John, and Don Pedro all dressed like Italian mafiosos. Oh, and for some reason, there was half a grand piano hanging from the rafters. After seeing the production once already, I still wasn't sure if the set and costumes made any sense to me. I put it all down on my "Don't Like" list.

It was amazing how much more I saw the second time through. Beatrice talks about Benedick from the very first scene—she's already crazy about him, she just doesn't realize it. Or maybe she won't admit it to herself. She's fiercely intelligent and independent and doesn't have the patience for any man who can't match her wit. When Beatrice and Benedick finally do start to fall for each other, it's partly because their friends trick each of them into thinking the other one is secretly in love with them. But it's also partly through words, through a meeting of minds—they barely mention each other's physical appearance. It's the anti-Romeo-and-Juliet play. Beatrice visibly lights up in their scenes of verbal

133

sparring. And Benedick dissects her sarcastic comments and manages to interpret them as cleverly disguised words of love. *He's the stereotypical teenage girl,* I thought, and had to stifle a laugh.

Halfway through the first act, I decided I did like the costumes after all. Hero was wearing a poodle skirt and her hair was styled in a perfect '50s flip—you could practically see her salivating at the chance to cook and vacuum for Claudio, happily, in high heels, without Prozac, for the rest of her life. Beatrice, on the other hand, was costumed in pants and a no-frills oxford shirt, a sweater tied around her shoulders, her hair pulled back in a loose braid. She looked pretty but comfortable. *Dressed for no one but herself,* I jotted in my notes.

Micayla and Heron were scribbling away, too. Zephyr wasn't. He was slouched in his seat, his eyes half-closed. I thought he was falling asleep until I realized he was mouthing along silently with some of the lines. His eyes were narrowed in concentration, not boredom.

At intermission, the lights came back up and Heron and Micayla started discussing their notes, talking at breakneck speed. Zephyr pulled his phone out of his pocket and frowned. It was buzzing. He got out of his seat as he answered it and made his way to the aisle. As he went, I heard him say, "Ava, I can't talk right now, I'm at a play—no, with my *class*—"

Hmm.

"Hey," I said, interrupting Micayla and Heron, "is there anyone who goes to Fern Grove named Ava?"

"Nope," said Heron. "Why?"

"Nothing. Just wondering. How are you so sure?"

"I used to work in the cafeteria swiping meal cards. If there's an Ava, she'd have to be in the primary school. I know all the names in the high school and the junior high. Anyway, what'd you think about the first half?"

Maybe Zephyr had a sister.

Or friends outside of school. *What a concept,* I heard Raven's dry voice say in my head. Maybe Ava was a friend from his old school, or from drama camp. I didn't know why I cared, anyway. Except that he was such an enigma.

Micayla and Heron and I went out to the lobby for hot chocolate, which of course meant that as soon as we took our first sips, the lights blinked, signaling the end of intermission. You couldn't bring beverages into the theater, so we gulped them down and went back in with burnt tongues.

Zephyr slid into his seat just before the curtain went up again. He was still frowning.

None. Of. Your. Business, my brain reminded me. *Nosypants Greenfield.*

In the second half of the play, Beatrice and Benedick finally confess their love to each other. Which means, of course, since it's a romantic comedy, they kiss.

I didn't remember the actors holding it nearly this long the first time I'd seen the play with Dad. Benedick swept Beatrice off her feet and carried her to a couch upstage to continue the embrace more horizontally, not letting his lips leave hers all the way across the stage. The audience let out a collective sigh of satisfaction.

Beatrice and Benedick immediately started to argue again, this time about Hero and Claudio, but the rest of the lines in that scene went right over my head. I felt my face burn, trying as hard

135

as I could *not* to visualize myself on that stage, not to imagine how it would feel to play that kiss with the leather-jacketed guy in the seat next to me. I let my eyes slide in his direction without moving my head. He was very carefully staring straight ahead, still whispering Benedick's lines along with the actor. I couldn't tell in the dark theater whether he was blushing, too.

CHAPTER TWELVE

I went back to church with Elizabeth that weekend, because I'd said I would. I told myself I just wouldn't think about Sam Shotwell. She hadn't mentioned him or the dance, and I hadn't asked. *Besides,* I reminded myself, *you don't have dibs on every boy in your school. In fact, you only have dibs on one of them, because you put on your big-girl pants and asked him to the Fall Ball. And that does give you dibs. But Sam Shotwell can take whoever he wants to the dance.*

We started walking down Keswick, and she asked how play rehearsals were going. I told her a little about the Shakespeare Theatre field trip, and asked about debate team. She said she liked the advisor and the other students. Then the conversation flagged, and I started thinking about the play again and worrying. Was Robin going to ask Zephyr and me to kiss onstage? My first kiss couldn't be a stage kiss. That would just be *wrong.* My first kiss was supposed to be with Farhan, my one true love. But if Robin did ask, I couldn't very well tell him I'd never kissed anyone. I couldn't say that in front of the cast, or Zephyr. I was probably the only person in the whole cast who'd never kissed anyone. From what Micayla had told me, they'd all had plenty of practice kissing each *other.* And according to Raven, it took a while to get it right. It was sloppy and awkward at first. If I had to kiss Zephyr onstage, he'd know immediately that I'd never done it before.

To distract myself, I blurted, "So, what about the Fall Ball? Do you have a date yet?"

Elizabeth waved a hand in front of her face, as if brushing away a fly. "Oh, that. Yeah."

"You do? That's great! Who is it?"

"Just a guy from my math class. You probably don't know him."

I forced a laugh. "It's Fern Grove—I know everyone and their cousins and their dogs."

"Oh. Well, his name is Sam."

"Sam Shotwell!" I said, acting surprised and overshooting the mark by about twenty yards.

She looked startled at my enthusiasm.

"That's great. He's a great guy. You'll have a great time." I was going to get fined for excessive *great*-ing.

"And this topic is starting to *grate* on my nerves," Elizabeth said, grinning.

I laughed, despite myself. She knew how to pull out the sarcasm when you were least expecting it. And she did have Dad's way with words, his talent for dumb puns.

When we entered the church, Elizabeth dipped her fingertips into a little sconce in the wall filled with water, and crossed herself.

"What's that, holy water?" I whispered.

She nodded.

I let her walk ahead of me, so she wouldn't see me dip my fingertips in, too. It just felt like normal lukewarm water, though. I wondered if my Communist grandparents and all my Jewish ancestors were rolling over in their graves.

Mass was a little more intelligible this week—I remembered some of the places I was supposed to stand, or sit, or kneel. I liked that the calls and responses were the same every time. It was like a very elaborate weekly rehearsal. Or maybe it was more like a play, and the congregation was the devoted audience who went to see every single show.

I hesitated when it was time for Communion. I didn't want to go face the priest again with my arms folded, but I also didn't really want to sit in the pew all by myself while everyone else went up. At least if I stood in line, I wouldn't stick out like such a . . . well, like such an atheist Jew at a Catholic Mass. So I got up with Elizabeth and we made our way slowly to the front together.

When it was my turn, I folded my arms across my chest and then—I couldn't help it—whispered to the priest, "I'm not Catholic. I'm just, um, trying it out." He smiled at me and nodded, then bowed his head, made the sign of the cross, and said the blessing over me. Were you supposed to thank a priest for a blessing? I nodded back to him when he was done, and that felt like the right thing to do.

I turned to tell Elizabeth, but she was in front of the priest now, receiving Communion.

Only she wasn't receiving Communion, either—the priest was saying the blessing over her, too, because her arms were also folded across her chest.

It didn't seem like the sort of thing you could ask about. I felt like I'd invaded her privacy just by watching. So I didn't mention it. But I couldn't help wondering, as we started walking home. Elizabeth took out her pack of cigarettes and held it out to me. I hesitated, then shook my head. "Good choice," she muttered.

We were both quiet for a few minutes, and I remembered our conversation from last week, how much she'd opened up to me about her mother.

"Could I ask you something else about—Ohio?" I ventured.

"Sure."

"Well, I was just wondering. I mean, I don't know how to put this, but I'm assuming—when your mom lived at Ahimsa House—she wasn't Catholic then, was she? So, I was just wondering—how did you become—"

"How come I'm so religious if my mom was a hippie?" she interrupted.

"Well, yeah."

She breathed out a long, smoky exhale. "My mom was raised Catholic. But she rebelled and ran away from home when she was sixteen, changed her name to Sunshine, and hitchhiked up and down the East Coast, lived on a couple of communes, finally ended up in Takoma Park. When she got pregnant with me, she freaked out and went home—my grandparents still lived in Ohio."

"Wow. And they took her back in?"

"Of course. They were amazing people. Gram died when I was five, and Grandpa went downhill quickly after that. Mom said he just couldn't face life without Gram. But I do remember them."

"So your mom went back to religion when she came home?"

"Yeah, Mom figured God had punished her for turning her back on Him, and it was time to return to His good graces."

"Elizabeth. You don't really believe that you were sent to your mom as a *punishment*?"

She grimaced. "Well, no. That was what Mom thought back then, though. She was in rough shape for a while. But Gram and Grandpa helped her get her GED, find a job. They had enough money to put me into St. Joe, and they left us enough to live on after they were gone."

"Wow," I said again. "You were really lucky."

"We were," Elizabeth agreed. "And God was very good to us."

140

"Until the end," I muttered, before I could stop myself.

She shook her head. "He calls us all back to Him someday. I just have to be grateful for the time we had together."

How did Elizabeth manage to say things that sounded both pathetic and pompous at the same time? She made me want to put my arms around her and also put my hands around her throat.

"And I have to trust that He has a plan," she added.

"I don't get it," I said, against my better judgment. "I like the ritual. I like the prayers. I like peace and love and treating thy neighbor as thyself, but how can you still believe in a God who would do that to you? What kind of benevolent power would take a mother away from her child?"

She paused for a long time, long enough that I thought she wasn't going to answer me. Finally she said, "We're all given crosses to bear. Some of us have more strength than others. And the rest of us just have to find that strength. Somehow."

. . .

I had rehearsal Monday, Tuesday, and Wednesday after school that week. So far, so good—we'd discussed the Shakespeare Theatre production, but Robin hadn't mentioned any stage kissing. We started working on our blocking, even though we were still on book. He said it would help us internalize our stage directions along with the words we were speaking. "Your movements must be inevitable, people," he said, "just like every line you speak. Remember, every line is the *inevitable* and *only* continuation of the line that came before it. Every response to a cue is the inevitable and only response."

In class, too, we were working on blocking for our *Crucible* scenes. Robin had moved us from Meisner repetitions to Uta Hagen's "object exercise." And, thankfully, we were working on

141

whole scenes now, not just partner exercises. I kept telling my-self there was no reason to be awkward around Sam, but couldn't seem to convince myself that "awkward" wasn't the inevitable and only way to behave around him.

"What are the given circumstances?" Robin kept saying, walking from group to group. "Don't just move aimlessly around the room and flail your arms when you speak because that's what actors do. Think, people, don't act. Think *given circumstances*. Where are you, what time is it, what surrounds you? What do you want, what's in the way of getting what you want? What is your *objective*?"

He paused to watch my group run through our scene, but we didn't get more than five lines in before he waved his arms and yelled, "Cut! What did I say? We're *doing*, not *acting*. Rina, what are you *doing* in this scene? What's your objective?"

Rina was playing Abigail in the scene where she and John argue in front of the court. "Um," she said. "I'm—trying to make John feel—"

"No!" Robin cut her off. "Making someone feel something is not an action. It's not a *doing*. Unless you're literally taking his hand and running it over something to make him feel a texture."

Rina rolled her eyes. "And if I'm doing that," she muttered to Sam, "then I'd hope we were in the back seat of your car, not in drama class." A few students standing nearby snickered.

Robin raised his eyebrows. "Next time you try to imbue my innocent words with innuendo, please remember that I am not hard of hearing," he said mildly. "Now, what is your *action* in this scene?"

So drama was good, school was good, but every night when I climbed into Micayla's car after rehearsal, I wished I could go

142

home with her or Heron. Monday, Tuesday, and Wednesday were all the same—either everyone was still sitting around the table when I got home, savoring dessert and telling funny stories, or else Dad and Elizabeth would be reading next to each other on the couch, while Josh practiced and Mom worked at the kitchen table. The house felt full, complete, before I even walked in.

Thursday, since I didn't have rehearsal, I took the bus to Fine Print. I should've waited for Elizabeth, but I just didn't feel like it.

"Hey, Dad," I said, dropping my backpack by the front door. He was behind the front counter today, for a change. "Where's Cassandra?"

"Where's Elizabeth?" he countered.

"I don't know. We're not joined at the hip."

"Defensive: adjective, derived from the verb 'to defend'; behaving in a way that shows you feel people are criticizing you," Dad intoned in Dry Professor Voice.

"So where's Cassandra?" I repeated, ignoring him.

"Persistent: adjective, derived from the verb 'to persist'; continuing along a path of inquiry even after it has been discouraged."

"Annoying: adjective, meaning Ross Greenfield."

Dad grinned. "That's my girl."

Despite myself, a bubble of happiness expanded in my chest.

"So, for real," he said. "Where's Elizabeth? I just got a complete leather-bound set of Tolstoy, published 1927. I promised I'd let her sniff it and maybe even touch the covers when it came in."

The bubble burst. "I don't know, Dad. I guess she went home with Mom and Josh."

"Oh. All right, then."

Pause.

"Well, Cassandra's taking her driving test this afternoon, so I'm covering the desk for her."

"Cassandra doesn't have a license? She's, like, thirty years old!"

"And no one gets a driver's license in New York City till they turn forty-five and move to Connecticut."

"But this is Baltimore. People drive places here."

"Unless you've been trying to time-travel back to the 1400s for the past twenty years of your life."

"Poor Cassandra. I guess she finally gave up on that."

"Or else this is but the next step of her complex and difficult journey. Perhaps she'll find a time-traveling device for her car. Speaking of cars . . ."

"No," I groaned. "Do we have to?"

"Well, I know Elizabeth is quite eager to get her practice hours out of the way. You don't have to come along if you don't want to."

I pictured Elizabeth and Dad doing driving lessons without me, having more quality one-on-one father-daughter bonding time. The thought made my teeth itch.

"It's fine," I grumbled. "I don't want to fall further behind." How come I couldn't even spend ten minutes with Dad without talking or thinking about Elizabeth?

"So, how are rehearsals coming along?" Dad asked.

"They're fine. I better get home, I've got lines to memorize. Plus a ton of homework."

"Oh, and I've been meaning to ask you . . ." He leaned over the counter and lowered his voice, even though there were only a few customers at the back of the shop. "How is the whole, uh, church thing going? Want me to take church duty next Sunday?"

144

I thought about Elizabeth smoking on the way home. About our conversation last weekend, about her mom and her grandparents. "It's fine. I don't mind."

"I can't tell you how much I appreciate it, honey," Dad said, visibly relieved. "You know religion makes my scalp crawl. It's been one of the toughest things for me to accept about—this whole situation."

Screw that. I was *not* going to have a heart-to-heart with Dad, of all people, about how tough "this whole situation" was.

"I have to go," I repeated.

"All right, then. Dad-daughter driving lesson after dinner? We're on?"

"Sure." I picked up my backpack and banged out the door, just in time to see the bus pulling away from the curb. My luck. And it had started to rain, a heavy, cold, Baltimore autumn rain. I trudged down to the bus shelter, pulled the hood of my jacket up over my already-frizzing hair, and plunked myself down on the bench to wait.

The bench was stamped with big white letters: *Baltimore— The Greatest City in America*. Dad and I always made fun of those benches. For a while, the city's motto was *Baltimore: The City That Reads*. Dad loved that one, of course, although I didn't think it made any sense. As Raven was always quick to remind me whenever we'd pass one of those benches, "Thirty-eight percent of this city cannot read well enough to complete a job application. That's almost *twice* the illiteracy rate in the rest of Maryland." But Baltimore seemed to think that if all its benches shouted one thing long and loud enough, they could make it come true.

Maybe I should paint my own bench.

The problem was, I didn't even know what I'd want it to say.

145

. . .

And then it was the second week of October, the week of Fall Festival, and the whole school went crazy decorating. There was an open house all day on Saturday and the school-wide Pumpkin Picnic on Saturday afternoon, followed by the Fall Ball that night. Oh, and parent-teacher conferences were slated for Monday. That was the administration's brilliant idea to make sure students behaved themselves Saturday night. Mom's idea, probably.

On Friday afternoon, all the teachers made us set up special displays in their classrooms for the open house. In biology, my last class of the day, we built scale models of the parts of a cell, strung DNA streamers around the room, and decorated each corner to represent one of the kingdoms of living creatures: bacteria, fungi, plants, and animals. We drew Protista all over the whiteboard because we'd run out of corners and DJ Derry said it would be against school safety policy to have us decorate the ceiling.

DJ Derry was actually Becca Derry, and she was another teacher who'd told us to use her first name—but ever since someone found out she moonlighted as a folk radio deejay, we hadn't called her anything except DJ Derry. She was also going to deejay the Fall Ball, and students had been putting in requests for weeks.

"Guys, enough already," she sighed, holding up a list three pages long. "Who added Metallica? Seriously? Plus, we're going to be there till Sunday morning if I play all these songs."

"Exactly!" someone yelled. "Dance all night!"

"Dance till dawn!"

"Daaaaance!"

. . .

On Saturday, it was hard to enjoy the Open House or the picnic, my stomach was such a tight-wound ball of yarn. Or maybe a ball of frayed cables, shooting out little sparks of excitement every time I thought about the dance that night. Raven promised she'd bring the dresses over to my house after the picnic with plenty of time to get ready before dinner.

We were supposed to meet Max, Farhan, and Sam at Tamber's at six o'clock—Dad was going to drop us off. Mom had stayed at school, so she could help set up for the dance. Elizabeth vanished into the bathroom for one of her endless showers at quarter of five, and fifteen minutes later, Raven texted me *Running late! Leaving now!*

I hadn't even seen my dress since Ruby had worked her magic on it. What if I'd gained weight and it didn't fit anymore? What if she hadn't had time to sew on all the lace and beads, and I showed up to the Fall Ball in a plain cream-colored dress like a nervous bride? Oh god, what if Farhan thought I was trying to prepare for our wedding day?

The doorbell rang at 5:09 and I flew down the stairs.

"*Raven Woodbury,*" I said, opening the door.

"Sorry, sorry, sorry." She pushed past me with a garment bag draped over each arm. "Ruby was putting the finishing touches on yours. Wait till you see it."

She laid the bags out side by side on my bed, and I unzipped mine.

Ruby had transformed the dress completely. Black lace all down the sides framed an hourglass-shaped cream silhouette. The lace was edged with tiny midnight-blue beads that shone iridescent when the fabric moved. And the central panel was crisscrossed by swirls of cream-colored beads that blended in against the fabric but added texture. The dress was a work of art.

Raven had already stripped down to her underwear and her

147

perfect little red satin B-cup bra, and was standing in front of the mirror with an enormous tote bag full of makeup, combing some sort of product into her curls.

"Oh, hi." Elizabeth shut the door quickly behind her, averting her eyes and pulling her baby-blue terry-cloth robe around herself more tightly.

"Hey!" Raven looked over at her. "Got any hair shimmer?"

"Any . . . what?" Elizabeth looked mystified.

"Never mind, found it," Raven said, pulling a hot-pink bottle out of her bag.

"Should I go get dressed in the bathroom?" said Elizabeth.

"No, no, there's plenty of room in here for all of us. If that's okay with you," I added quickly.

"Sure." But I noticed that Elizabeth kept her gaze away from Raven and stepped into her dress with her back to us, practically standing in the closet. "I'll be right back," she said. "I left all my makeup in the bathroom."

"Makeup *before* clothes," Raven lectured me as Elizabeth closed the door behind her. "So you don't accidentally stain anything."

I threw her a T-shirt. "Then put this on, you're offending Mother Teresa."

She looked amused. "Am I?" But she pulled on the shirt.

I handed Raven my sparkly blue eyeliner and she did cat-eyes for me, her specialty. Then she handed me the black and gray eye shadow and I did smoky eyes for her, my specialty. I sifted through my rainbow lipsticks and found a purple one for me and a classic red one for her.

Elizabeth came back then, her hair pulled into a ponytail, wearing a little lip gloss. "Okay, I'm ready."

"You're done?" Raven said. "Just like that?"

Elizabeth nodded. Raven eyed her.

The blue dress brought out the color of her eyes, and although the cut was modest, it showed off her slim figure. Even pulled back in a simple ponytail, her strawberry-blond hair was gorgeous. She looked like she'd stepped out of the pages of a catalogue. I knew what Raven was thinking, though. She never went out on a date without at least half an hour of prep time (or primp time, as I called it).

"At least let us do something with your hair," Raven said finally.

So Elizabeth sat in front of the vanity while I twisted strands into tiny braids and gathered them back into a half-bun, and then Raven curled the rest into long soft waves while I got dressed. My stomach fluttered a little as Elizabeth zipped up the back of my dress and I stared at myself in the mirror. No B-cups for me. I'd invested in a strapless bra that looked like it could hold a pair of grapefruits just for this occasion. I pressed my hands to my chest and tried to squeeze it into submission.

"That dress looks incredible, Cadie," said Raven, from behind me, and Elizabeth murmured her agreement.

It did. Ruby had outdone herself. The beads glittered when I moved and the pale color set off the brown tone of my skin perfectly. The pink, purple, and blue tips of my hair brushed the top of the dress. "It's just so *low-cut.*"

"That's called cleavage, my friend," said Raven. "Some of us have only heard rumors of this legendary blessing."

"Affliction, you mean," I muttered.

"Oh, please. Farhan won't be able to take his eyes off you."

I'd just zipped Raven into her teal mermaid dress when Dad

149

knocked, then poked his head in. "Girls? Are we ready to—oh. Oh, my." He adjusted his glasses.

"Dad, this is not the moment to weep," I said.

"I'm not. I'm not. I just—something in my eye." He blinked rapidly and beamed at us.

Raven, Elizabeth, and I barefooted it down the stairs, then strapped on our shoes. It felt strange to be getting ready for my first dance in a group of three. It had always been just me and Raven, doing our first everythings together. Our first time going to a concert by ourselves. Our first sleep-away summer camp—two weeks out on the Eastern Shore, learning to rock climb and sea-kayak. Our first airplane ride, even. Ruby and Renata had invited me to come along with the Sisterhood for a weeklong vacation to Kennebunkport, Maine, two summers ago. They even rented a car and drove us up to Acadia National Park for a day trip to pay our respects to my namesake.

"Pictures," I reminded everyone. "Ruby will kill me if I don't get pictures of this dress for her." So Raven pulled out her phone and Dad lined us up in front of the piano and took photos. Then he made us wait while he got out his digital camera, which he barely ever used, and took more photos.

"Dad, we can take pictures once we get to the restaurant. And they're going to have a photographer at the dance, too." My stomach was rumbling, and not with hunger. This wasn't just my first dance—it was my first date, too. And Farhan, my one true love, was about to see me in the most beautiful dress I'd ever worn.

I felt like throwing up.

As it turned out, though, dinner was less terrifying than I'd thought it would be. Max and Raven were so relaxed around each other, it made sitting across from Farhan seem almost normal. The boys were all wearing suits, but they acted just like their usual selves. Boys. They made everything look simple.

I barely ate anything, I was so worried about spilling food on my dress in front of Farhan. I don't remember what we talked about—mostly the boys talked, while our side of the table gazed lovingly (Raven) or stared down at our plates (me and Elizabeth). Afterward, we all piled into Sam's SUV. Mom and Dad had agreed, reluctantly, to let us ride to the dance with him, as long as Mom brought us home at the end of the night. Elizabeth didn't argue—in fact, she seemed relieved. I couldn't figure it out. Half the girls in the high school would've traded places with her to be Sam's date, and yet she seemed eager to spend as little time as possible with him.

When we arrived at the dance, we paused and smiled for the photographer on the steps leading up to the gym, and then Farhan took my arm and steered me inside. A disco ball spun slowly on the ceiling, throwing bits of light like confetti all around the room. Long tables full of desserts and drinks lined the back wall, and chairs were clustered around small round tables at the other end of the room.

The six of us stood in an awkward circle and bobbed our heads for a few songs. Then DJ Derry shifted into something slower, and Max and Raven split off to dance by themselves.

Elizabeth said she was going to the bathroom, so Sam wandered over to the dessert table. Which left me and Farhan by ourselves.

We escaped to one of the small tables, where I saw Micayla and Troy sitting with Heron and her date, a senior named Aimee.

They had covered the table with an assortment of petits fours, fruit tarts, and cupcakes, and were ranking all the desserts on a complicated chart scribbled on the paper tablecloth.

That took up about twenty minutes or so. Then a guy I didn't know came over and asked Micayla to dance, and Tori Lopez asked Troy to dance. Another slow song came on, and Heron and Aimee got up, too. Suddenly I was terrified that someone else was going to come ask Farhan for a dance if I didn't do it.

"Well, guess we should dance," I managed. *Ten points, Cadie, for making it sound like a chore to dance with your one true love.*

He nodded and we got up, moved toward the dance floor. He put one hand on my waist. I let the fingertips of my left hand brush his shoulder. He took my right hand with his left. We swayed back and forth. I was sure he could see my heart pounding, exposed as my chest was. Oh god. Was he looking at my chest? I sneaked a peek at his eyes, but he seemed to be looking over my shoulder. Probably making sure we weren't going to crash into another couple. Good. Except no one was really moving very much. It seemed that slow dancing was more like slow standing.

"Cadie," he said, bringing his face closer to mine. Any breath remaining in my body went *whoosh*, vacuumed out as if I'd just taken a volleyball to the sternum. The music faded out as my ears started ringing, a telltale sign that my face was turning the color of a Hawaiian sunset.

I tried looking into his eyes again. His dark hair fell low over his eyebrows, those thick eyelashes batting nervously. Could he possibly be as nervous as I was?

His face was so close.

I closed my eyes and tried to remember all of Raven's advice. *Don't rush it, but don't hang on if he starts to pull away, either.*

*Let your lips relax, let your jaw relax. If all else fails, pay atten-
tion to what he's doing and just copy him.*

"Cadie," he whispered again. "We're friends, right?"

My eyes flew open. Was that what he was supposed to say?
"Yeah, of course."

"Okay, good. So, can I ask you something?"

*He might ask first, or he might just make meaningful eye
contact, or touch your face. If you want to jump-start things, you
can do that, too, you know. Any of those things.* Ha. Like I'd have
the courage.

"The answer's yes," I said, in what I hoped was a suave and
sultry voice. Except it came out as more of a quiver. Almost a
question.

He raised an eyebrow. "I didn't ask yet."

"Ha! Right." My heart thudded. "So, what is it?"

He leaned in even closer, if that was possible, so that his lips
brushed my ear. "It's, um, about Elizabeth. I was just wondering.
Is she dating Sam, do you know? Or are they just friends?"

. . .

Raven found me in the bathroom—I didn't know how, since I'd
fled to the single-stall one all the way up by the front office. She
locked the door behind her. "Cadie! What happened?"

"She's ruined everything," I sobbed, not caring that my
sparkly blue cat-eyes were running down my cheeks. "*Everything.* First Mom and Dad, and my room, and books, and driving,
and then Sam, who didn't even matter, but that wasn't enough,
because now *this.*"

I may have mentioned that I don't do crying. Which was why
Raven's eyes were as round as the holes Elizabeth had punched
right through my life.

"Cadie. Slower. You're not making sense."

I told her about my dance with Farhan. The kiss that wasn't. The anti-kiss. "It's not fair! Why can't she just leave my life *alone*?"

Raven spread a double layer of toilet paper over the closed toilet seat, tucked her dress around her legs, and sat. Gingerly. Raven hates public bathrooms, even the ones at school. "It's not exactly her fault, you know."

"Raven!"

"Well, it's not."

"That's not what you're supposed to say."

"Best friends don't say things they're supposed to say, they say true things. And it's not going to do you any good to be mad at Elizabeth. Be mad at *Farhan*. Fart-on. That's what we're going to call him from now on, okay?"

I snorted through my tears, despite myself. "Gross."

"He's the one with the thick head," she continued. "I mean, look at you. You're a catch, Cadie. The best catch in this school. You're smart, funny, talented at everything you try. And smoking hot, especially in that dress. Cut your losses and move on before he knows what hit him."

"That's not really helping, either," I sniffled.

Raven sighed. "What do you want me to say? Your date's a loser? He is. He had us very cleverly deceived all these years. So let him run after the Virgin Mary. He'll be sorry when he realizes what an ice princess she is."

I thought about walking home from Mass with Elizabeth and her smoking. Virgin Mary? Maybe not, after all. I took a deep breath. "She's actually . . . more complicated than that. And you're right. It's not her fault."

"That's the wrong attitude, missy." Raven was the president of the 180-degree club. She could change her opinion at the speed of light. "You have the right to be mad at anyone you choose tonight."

"'Heaven has no rage like love to hatred turned, nor hell a fury like a woman scorned.'"

"What?"

"It's a quote. From some play Dad hates." I couldn't believe even in this moment thoughts of Dad were sneaking in. Like he and Elizabeth just couldn't leave any minute of my life alone.

"You know, you quote the strangest things in times of crisis, have I ever told you that? Well, good. I'm glad your brain is still functioning, even if your eyes are behaving very oddly. Are you done crying yet? It's seriously freaking me out."

I wiped my eyes. Blue glitter all over the paper towels.

Raven stood. "Now, what's the plan?"

"What plan?"

"I'm bored of this shindig. Want to cut out?"

I knew that couldn't possibly be true. She and Max had danced almost every dance together. She looked ravishing in her dress, and she loved being the center of attention. She was practically glowing with contentment right now. And yet, she was willing to lie about all that and leave, just to save me from my misery. This was why I loved her.

I couldn't say all that, though. For one thing, my tear ducts were threatening to start leaking again, just from thinking it. And Raven would deny it all, anyway. So I said, "Mom's expecting to take us home at the end of the night . . ."

"I'll go find her and tell her you're not feeling well. And then I'll call Renata and she'll drive us to the Charmery for emergency ice cream and then we can drop you off. Okay?"

"I think I'd rather just go straight home. You should stay here and have fun."

Raven gave me a long look, then nodded. "Ice cream rain check. Let me just go find your mom. Wait at the office for me; no one will bother you there."

Five minutes later, she was back, and fifteen minutes after that, Renata called to say she was outside the school.

Raven came along for the short ride, although she promised me she'd go back to the dance afterward. I didn't know if Raven had told her what happened, but Renata didn't ask me any questions. Raven got in the back seat with me and put her arm around me. I was grateful for her bony shoulder to lean on. I closed my eyes and tried to just not think.

When we reached my house, Renata only said, "Good night, kiddo. You look stunning."

"Thanks," I managed. "Sorry to put you to trouble."

She shook her head. "Nonsense. You're my other daughter. You know that."

Raven got out of the car to give me a hug. "That's still a killer dress, National Park Greenfield. The next time you wear it you'll be with someone who's not a total douche."

I hugged her back, not trusting my voice to thank her. Anyway, she knew.

Inside, I crept up the stairs, hoping not to have to face Dad. I didn't want to talk to him. I didn't want to talk to anyone.

Someone was waiting at the top of the stairs, though. Josh. He took one look at my tearstained face and went to get his cello.

When was the last time I'd spent more than ten minutes

156

with Josh, other than mealtimes? As I changed into my pajamas, I tried to remember. We'd barely talked since Elizabeth had moved in. Not that he ever talked much, but we used to spend time together, at least. I'd been too busy with my own problems lately to make time for him. And one of Josh's talents was blending into the background. Like a little chameleon. His competition was coming up in mid-December, and I had no idea how he was feeling about it. Barely any idea what he was playing. Popper something? Requiem? Rhapsody?

"You're a chameleon," I told him when he brought the cello into my room. He perched on the bed and raised an eyebrow at me.

"It made sense in my head," I mumbled, suddenly exhausted. My words were slurred, as if I'd been drinking. I was dehydrated from crying. Tipsy on tears. "Oh, Josh," I said. "Why can't we just move back to Ahimsa House? Maybe that would fix everything. I know you don't remember it. But you'd love it, trust me. Things were so different there. Mom and Dad were . . . so much happier. Sometimes I wish we could go back."

He looked at me thoughtfully and drew the bow across the strings. I felt every tight muscle in my shoulders soften at the sound. When Josh played his cello, I could forget anything that was bothering me and relax into the music.

"Was it really that different?" he asked.

"Ahimsa House?"

He nodded.

"Mom was like—another person. Trust me."

Josh played a few more open strings. "Did you know she wants to send me to Michigan?"

"*What?*"

"For high school. Interlochen. She mentioned it to Olga last week."

"Well . . . high school's still pretty far off for you. Don't worry about it yet."

He shrugged, plucked a chord. "What do you want to hear?"

"Anything you want to play."

So I curled up under the covers while my little brother played the tender, poignant Prelude from the second Bach cello suite over and over until I fell asleep. I didn't even hear Mom and Elizabeth come home.

. . .

Sunday morning, Mom and Dad were already gone by the time I woke up—Mom had to prepare for parent-teacher conferences, and Dad must've gone in early to the bookshop. There was a note on the table with three lines in Mom's neat handwriting—

C: hope you're feeling better! please remember to take E to church.

J: don't forget to practice your Popper.

C: make sure J practices his Popper.

I wasn't hungry, so I stuck a granola bar in my pocket while Elizabeth got ready for church. Josh was already practicing his scales and arpeggios, so I left a note outside his door that said *At church—Mom says to practice Popper—sorry. Thanks for the music last night. Love you.*

Elizabeth protested that she knew the way and didn't need me to walk with her. I sure would've liked to stay home—in fact, I didn't feel like talking to Elizabeth ever again—but I knew how angry Mom would be if she found out that I'd let Elizabeth walk by herself. *Not that she cares if her precious ten-year-old son is home alone, because she knows he'll lock himself up all day with his cello and not come out until someone reminds him it's time to eat. Little Miss Perfect, though, needs all the protection she can get on these big bad streets.*

"Look," I told Elizabeth, as we left the house, "I think I'll just wait for you at the Daily Grind today and meet you after Mass. I have tons of lines to memorize."

"Okay."

There was silence for a few blocks. Then, "Cadie, what happened last night? Something happened at the dance. Right?"

"It's not a big deal."

"Oh."

More silence.

"Is it—was it—did I do something? Or say something?"

"No."

"Oh."

I sighed. "Fine. It's really not a big deal, okay? But my friend Farhan kind of likes you. So do me a favor, and if he asks you out, feel free to say yes. If you want to, I mean. He's a great guy. I'm sure you'd like him, too."

Elizabeth stopped walking. "Wait. Your *boyfriend* Farhan, you mean?"

"He's not my boyfriend!" I said over my shoulder, without slowing down, and it came out louder than I'd intended. Elizabeth had to run a few steps to catch up with me. "We're just friends. We went to the dance as friends. And he told me that he has a crush on you. He asked if you were dating Sam. You're not, right?"

She shook her head. "No, no, I'm not."

"Why not?" I couldn't help it, I was curious. "I mean, half the girls in our school are in love with Sam Shotwell."

159

"Oh, he's just not my type."

"Okay. Well, if nerdy guys with great taste in music are your type"—I felt a burning sensation behind my eyes and blinked angrily—"then you and Farhan would get along really well."

"Cadie, I don't—are you sure? I could've sworn you said you liked him. I mean, as more than friends."

"Nope. I thought so, maybe, for like two minutes. But he's not my type," I said, echoing her without meaning to. The words felt strange in my mouth. I wondered if they'd felt equally strange in hers.

We were across the street from Saints Philip and James now.

"All right, I'll meet you back here when Mass is over." I was more than ready to end this conversation.

"Bye," she said, and hesitated, as if wondering whether she should say something else.

I walked away before she could decide, and I didn't look back.

Instead of going to the Daily Grind, though, I wandered over to the Baltimore Museum of Art. It's right next to the Hopkins campus, and admission is free. Micayla had introduced me to the museum. She brought her homework there sometimes and worked sprawled out on a bench in front of her favorite paintings. "Osmosis and all that. Can't hurt to try," she said.

After talking about Farhan, I felt too restless to sit and memorize lines. I decided to go to the Matisse and Van Gogh room instead. All those wild colors seemed like the right medicine for my mood.

"Hey, Cadie."

I looked up. Heron Lang was standing behind the front desk in the lobby.

"Heron! I didn't know you worked here."

"Just a weekend gig. Gets me free admission."

"But admission is already free . . ."

"I know. Joke. Ha?"

I shook my head. "Ha. Sorry, I had kind of a rough night. And a rough morning."

Heron nodded sympathetically. "Dance drama?"

"Yeah, why? Please don't tell me you've already heard about it." At a school as small as Fern Grove, rumors spread like maple syrup across a hot pancake . . . My stomach started grumbling, and I realized I still hadn't eaten my granola bar.

"Heard nothing," she said. "I could see it in your face."

I studied Heron. She had dark circles under her eyes. "Did you have dance drama, too?"

"Bingo." She hunched her shoulders. "I think me and Aimee are over for good this time."

"Oh, Heron, I'm sorry. I didn't even know you were dating her."

"Ehh. We were on-again, off-again all last year. I thought going to the Fall Ball together might help us feel like more of a couple, but she said it just showed her that she'll never feel that way about me."

"Well, turns out my date didn't feel the same way about me, either." Somehow It was easier to talk to Heron, whom I barely knew, about what had happened with Farhan. The whole story came spilling out. "You know what? I realized I don't even know him. Like, we've gone to school together since forever, but I've barely ever even said a word to him. Until this whole dance thing. So why the hell am I so upset?"

Heron came around the desk to give me a hug. "I'm sorry, Cadie. It still sucks. You deserve better than that. And what's Elizabeth's deal, anyway? I thought I saw her there with Sam Shotwell."

"Yeah, but apparently she's not interested in him."

"Whoa. Not sure if Sam's ego can take that; he's used to getting any chick he wants. Well, good for her. Showing him that he can't automatically snap up the new hot pick of the week."

"Heron!"

"I mean, no offense, I know she's your sister and all, but— *wow*. She's kind of smokin'."

I laughed. "Don't even. Know where she is right now? At church. That's why I'm here. I'm waiting for Mass to be over so I can escort her home. My mother thinks she'll get kidnapped or something if we let her wander around Baltimore on her own."

Heron raised her eyebrows. "I thought your family was Jewish?"

"We are. She's my half sister, through my dad. Her mom was a super-religious Catholic."

"I could set a world record," Heron said, "in the category of Falling for the Most Unavailable Girls. Any roomful of people, I can instantly pick out the girl who is least likely to ever want to date me. And of course that's the one I won't be able to stop thinking about."

I sighed. "I know that feeling."

"Guess we're both screwed." But Heron grinned. "Thanks for listening to me complain. It helps a little."

"No, thank *you*. I'm the one who started it."

"Hey—I get off at three, and Micayla's meeting me to drown

162

our sorrows in milk shakes at the Charmery. Her date with Troy didn't go so great either. Want to come?"

"Sure. Mind if I invite Raven, too? She wanted to go last night, but I wasn't feeling up to it."

"Of course."

"Great. See you later, then."

I started up the stairs, then turned around and found a table in the museum café instead. I ordered a grilled cheese sandwich with extra cheese and cracked open my *Much Ado* script to page one. I was starving, and I really did have a lot of lines to learn.

CHAPTER THIRTEEN

At Monday night's rehearsal, we were supposed to be off book.

Ha.

Actually, I didn't do too badly. We ran a few of the Beatrice-Benedick scenes, and Zephyr had his lines down perfectly. But I was only one or two cues short.

"Seven weeks!" Robin moaned. "Seven weeks until tech week, people. I know that sounds like a long time, but remember that time is an *illusion*. And that's not the Bard, it's Einstein, so don't argue. Please, please, please. Do whatever it takes this week to get these lines down. Consider this me begging and groveling."

The play was the first weekend in December—the weekend before Josh's competition. Last night at dinner, Mom had told me she'd probably have to come to the Sunday matinee of *Much Ado*, since Josh had an important rehearsal with his pianist on Friday evening and couldn't stay out too late on Saturday. Dad said he wouldn't miss opening night for the world.

"Josh, are you sure you don't want to change your rehearsal so you and Mom can come to Cadie's opening night?" he asked. "I'm sure you can move it to a different day."

"He cannot move it," Mom snapped. "The pianist had *very* limited availability; we're lucky to have squeezed in any rehearsals with her at all."

Then Dad said, "Let Josh speak for himself, Melissa," and Mom was about to respond, but Elizabeth interrupted to say,

"May I be excused?" That seemed to remind Mom and Dad that there were other people in the room, and they stopped arguing, although the air was still so charged it felt like static was crackling between them. Josh toyed with his food. I put my arm around him.

"Hey," I said, "how about some after-dinner music?"

But he shook his head no.

"Okay. A game of Spit?"

His eyes lit up. "We haven't played that in forever!"

So I went up to Josh's room with him, since Elizabeth had gone into our room and closed the door, and we played a break-neck game of cards, and then another, and another. Just like we used to in the olden days. B.E.—Before Elizabeth.

I was done trying to be friends with her, and I was done trying to forgive Dad for bringing her into our lives, too. It was time for *him* to figure out how to make things right again—right with Mom, with me, with all of us. Maybe I wasn't exactly on Mom's side either, but I was sick of picking sides. I was on my own side.

. . .

Zephyr and I sat silently in the back of the theater and watched Rina rehearse one of her Dogberry scenes. We had a Beatrice/Benedick scene scheduled for this time slot, but Rina's rehearsal was running behind. She was still overacting all her lines, killing the comedy of them, and Robin kept making her start over.

"So, um." I tried to think of something to say to Zephyr. "Did you have fun at the Fall Ball this weekend? I don't think I saw you there."

He shrugged. "Yeah, didn't go. Long story."

"Oh." Why was it so hard to make conversation with Zephyr? When we were on stage, our lines flew back and forth like the ball in a tennis match. Off stage, we were more like a game of golf—I'd hit the ball, watch it roll far away from where it was supposed to go, and then wait while he teed up. Was that what golf was like? I'd never actually played.

"What're you thinking about?" Zephyr asked.

"Golf," I said, before I could stop myself. *Brilliant.*

Zephyr raised an eyebrow. "Oh?"

"Just kidding. Um, I was thinking about the *Who's Afraid of Virginia Woolf?* production at Center Stage. It opens this weekend; we just got a postcard in the mail. Actually, we have an extra ticket. Want to go see it?"

Wait a minute. *What* had my brain just told my mouth to say?

Zephyr raised his other eyebrow, so his amber-gold eyes widened. "Okay. Sure. I'd like that."

"Great! I'll, um, I'll get the ticket and bring it tomorrow and—"

"People!" Robin roared, facing the back of the theater and shading his eyes with one hand. "I can't see who that is back there, so count yourselves lucky. I shall *flay* anyone who disrupts this rehearsal one more time with that infernal chatter!"

Zephyr and I ducked our heads and tried not to look at each other. I knew I'd break into an uncontrollable giggle fit if we made eye contact, and he must've felt the same way, because when I sneaked a glance at him out of the corner of my eye, his jaw was twitching. So was the dimple in his cheek.

Zephyr had a dimple? I'd never noticed before. I wondered if he had one on the other side to match. I'd have to remember to check next time we were facing each other. Sometime when I wasn't trying to remember lines of Shakespeare, of course.

.   .   .

That night, I found everyone still eating dinner when Micayla dropped me off.

"Mushroom-kale casserole," Dad said, handing me a plate. "Took longer than I thought, so you get it fresh from the oven tonight."

"Lucky me," I muttered.

Mom looked at me sharply, but didn't say anything.

"So!" Dad said. "How was rehearsal?"

"Fine. Hey, by the way, you weren't planning on going to Center Stage this weekend to see *Who's Afraid of Virginia Woolf?*, right?"

Dad blinked.

I barreled on. "I figured, since we only have two tickets, it wouldn't really be fair if I stole you for the whole evening. And I didn't think you'd want to leave everyone else out."

By *everyone else*, of course, I meant Elizabeth. Mom had never expressed any interest in joining our father-daughter theater outings, and Josh wasn't allowed to stay out late unless it was for a concert—Mom worried that a late night would interfere with his practicing schedule.

"So," I continued, "I invited someone from the play to go with me. As long as it's okay if he uses your ticket?"

Dad cleared his throat.

Say no. Say I'm wrong. Say you'd love nothing more than to spend an evening at Center Stage with your daughter just like old times. Your first daughter—well, technically your second daughter, but your real *daughter.*

But all he said was, "Okay, then, if that's what you want to do."

"He?" Mom said.

167

I raised my eyebrows.

"You said 'he.' You asked if it was okay if 'he' used Dad's ticket. Who's 'he'?"

"Oh, just a guy from the play. He's Benedick."

Mom looked shocked. "Then why are you asking him out?"

"What? I'm not asking him out!"

"It sounds like you are, and you just said he'd been a dick. By the way, I don't appreciate that kind of language at the dinner table."

Dad and I burst out laughing at the same time. I hated how this felt like we were somehow on the same team again, as if I hadn't just wounded him. I didn't want to be on Dad's team anymore.

"*Benedick*," I said to Mom. "It's the name of the main character in *Much Ado About Nothing*."

"Beatrice's, aka Cadie's, love interest," Dad added, winking. He was pretending that I hadn't just hurt him by asking for his ticket. Or maybe he wasn't hurt. Did he care? I *wanted* him to care.

"Only in the play," I said, pushing my chair back. "Which reminds me, I have to go work on my lines. Can I bring my plate upstairs?"

"Cadie, we need to talk more about this!" Mom called after me. "What night are you going? How will you get there? Will anyone else be with—"

I slammed my door to cut off the rest.

No one came up to try to talk to me until Elizabeth came in a while later to do her homework.

I ignored her, too.

· · ·

168

The next morning, I dodged the hordes of students moving far too slowly, trying to make my way to Raven's locker. I had to catch her before first period and tell her what had happened.

Then I turned the corner and saw Farhan. Leaning against Elizabeth's locker, an idiotic smile splitting his stupid face. He noticed me before I could look away and pretend I hadn't seen them. Elizabeth turned and smiled at me, too, a hesitant smile. Farhan wiggled his eyebrows and gave me a quick thumbs-up while Elizabeth was still turned, looking at me. Both of them looking at me. I waved, then ducked my head and kept going.

Forget about Farhan, he's an infant, I told myself. *Zephyr's a senior. You asked out a senior. Did you ask him out? I think you asked him out. He said yes. I think you're going on a date with a senior.*

I had to find Raven, or I was going to progress to full-scale endless looping arguments with myself in my head. I scanned the wall of lockers and spotted her curly red head. Pushed my way through the crowd.

"Raven! You'll never guess what happened."

She looked up at me, her arms full of books and her eyes brimming with concern. "I know. I saw."

"Wait—what?"

"Farhan. Fart-on. And—"

"Oh, don't worry about it. And you don't have to call him that. I'm fine, really."

"No, you're not," she said sensibly, slamming her locker door. "You're very good at *pretending* you're fine. We both know it's one of your best skills. But that's not the same as *being* fine. And you don't have to pretend with me."

"Okay, maybe I'm not fine with it, but I'm distracted right now. Listen." I told her about the *Much Ado* rehearsal last night, about asking Zephyr to the play.

"But—I don't get it, how did you have an extra ticket? I thought you had season tickets with your dad, so wasn't that your dad's ticket?"

"Well, *yes*, but I don't know, my mouth just moved faster than my brain and made up things, and then I couldn't exactly go back and tell him I didn't have an extra ticket after all. What was I supposed to say?"

"You could say you thought your dad couldn't go, but it turns out now he can."

"Dad doesn't want to go anyway. I asked him if Zephyr could use his ticket and he agreed right away."

"Huh. That's weird. I thought he really loved going to see plays with you."

I felt myself getting annoyed at Raven for taking Dad's side. "He did, before he had another, better daughter to spend time with."

Raven snorted. "That's just melodramatic."

"Well, melodrama is another one of my best skills."

"And that's why you're the star in the school play." Raven grinned at me and, thankfully, changed the subject. "Renata and Ruby are *so* excited to see you make your debut. They keep talking about it. I'm just warning you—I think they're both going to throw bouquets of flowers at you when you take your curtain call."

It was my turn to snort. "Yeah . . . if I actually finish learning my lines."

"Want to come over and run lines with me after school? And then you can quiz me on my debate points."

It was hard to stay annoyed at Raven for long.

.   .   .

Our *Who's Afraid of Virginia Woolf?* tickets were for Friday night, opening night. I gave Zephyr his ticket while we packed up our bags after drama class on Friday.

"Sweet, thanks!" he said. "If it's really good, maybe I can get tickets for us to see it again tomorrow. I love seeing the same show two nights in a row, don't you?"

"Really? I've never done that before." *He might want to spend two evenings in a row with me?*

"Oh, it's the best! You get to see all kinds of things about the production's consistency, which parts the actors were improvising. Sometimes you get to see the B cast and compare. In New York, we used to get rush tickets for *three* performances in one weekend sometimes, if we could get them cheap enough."

In New York . . . with his theater camp friends? Who was "we"?

I tried to keep my head in the conversation. "So, do you want to meet there?"

"Nah, I can come pick you up. Where do you live?"

"Hampden."

"Perfect, I'm just over in Waverly. I'll come get you at seven thirty; that should give us plenty of time."

I took out my phone. "I'll text you my address."

"No, my phone's dead," he said. "Here, just tell it to me." He was holding a pen poised over his arm.

So I told Zephyr Daniels my address, and he wrote it on his skin. In ink.

171

Oh, the melodrama! I heard Raven's voice say in my head. *Oh, swoon!*

Stop it, I told the voice. *He just forgot to charge his phone.*

Zephyr capped his pen and scooped up his bag. "Great, see you later."

See? Definitely nothing romantic in that tone of voice.

Robin was standing by the door, frowning at us. "Zephyr. Hold on a minute. I have a few notes for you from rehearsal last night."

Zephyr looked at him, surprised. "Okay . . ."

I was surprised, too. I'd barely heard Robin address two words to Zephyr so far. I assumed it was because he was doing such a great job, Robin didn't have much to tell him. And Robin was always busy correcting something much more urgent, like someone who was flailing around (cough, cough, Rina) or missing their cues (Sam), or else arguing with Peg about the costume and lighting budget (pretty much nonexistent, from what I'd overheard).

Zephyr shrugged a shoulder at me and said, "Ciao."

"Ciao, ciao, ciao!" I repeated, like an idiot, and walked promptly into the left side of the double doors, the side that was always locked.

"Are you okay?" I heard Zephyr asking behind me, but I pulled open the right side of the door and fled.

Well, it was official. I'd definitely asked Zephyr on a date. Those seemed to be the telltale signs: when I started babbling and walking into things.

Zeus almighty.

. . .

I mentioned to Mom on the way home from school that Zephyr would be picking me up at seven thirty.

"In his car?"

"I didn't ask. Maybe he has a motorcycle?"

"Acadia!"

"Just kidding, Mom. Yes, in his car."

"Well, we don't know this boy at all."

"*Mom.* You're the *head of school,* you know every student. You could've pulled his file to look up his grades and behavior record, if you'd wanted to."

"No comment," said Mom, crisply.

I glanced into the rearview mirror. Elizabeth and Josh, in the back seat, were hanging on to every word with identical expressions of shock mixed with glee on their faces. They really did look like siblings.

"She sighed heavily," I said, copying Dad's Shakespearean Tragic Voice before I could stop myself. Good lord. *Yes, universe, I recognize that we're all related. Big whoop. You can stop now.*

"Cadie?" said Mom.

"Sorry, I was conversing with the universe in my head."

She frowned at me. "I was saying that I would like to meet this boy before he whisks you off in his car. I'd like to at least feel that I've done my duty as a mother to determine whether he's a reliable driver. I try to keep my work life and my home life separate, you know."

"All right, Mom, fine. We'll pretend you've never met him before, and I'll invite him in to say hello before we leave."

"*Gracias.*" Mom managed to slather that one word with sarcasm, letting me know that I hadn't won any ground.

173

Dad called and said he was going to work late tonight, and we should have dinner without him. So Mom went and picked up Thai food.

I ate in a hurry and then went upstairs to get dressed. I'd picked out three options the night before, but now none of them seemed right. Finally I settled on an olive-green sweater-dress with a wide brown belt and rust-colored cable-knit tights, since it was chilly at night now.

"Do you mind if I come in?" Elizabeth asked, poking her head in the door as I was brushing my hair in front of the vanity.

"Of course not, it's your room, too." The words came out sounding abrupt and rude.

"Um," she said, hesitating in the doorway, as if she might need to make a quick escape, "I wanted to ask you something."

"Shoot."

"It's, um, it's about Farhan."

"I said, shoot."

"He asked if I wanted to go see a movie next weekend."

"Great." I brushed faster.

"So—you're okay with that?"

I slammed the brush down on the vanity table harder than I meant to. "Yes, I told you I'm fine with you going out with Farhan. You don't have to ask permission."

"Okay, I just thought—never mind." She disappeared and closed the door behind her.

Farhan was an idiot. I no longer liked him. I'd relinquished any claim on him. So why did my stomach twist when I thought about them, Elizabeth and Farhan, going to the movies together? Holding hands, sitting shoulder-to-shoulder. His warm lips near her ear, whispering to her the way he'd whispered to me at the dance . . .

The doorbell rang, and I flew down the stairs. "I'll get it!"

I opened the door, and Zephyr was on my doorstep, in his usual brown leather jacket and jeans.

"Hey," I said, trying to catch my breath, "I'm so sorry, but my mom wants you to come in for a minute before we leave. She's nervous about letting me drive somewhere with someone she doesn't know."

"Your mom's Head Laredo-Levy, right?"

"Yeah. Just—would you mind coming in?"

"No, of course not." He stepped in, swept his gaze over the living room. I took in what he was seeing: the upright piano against one wall, its keys coated in a fine layer of dust. The saggy red couch and threadbare ottoman. The exposed brick wall that Mom's friends always get so excited about: "Oh, Melissa, you have exposed brick! I *love* exposed brick!"

Mom came bustling down the stairs.

Zephyr adjusted his jacket and rubbed his chin. "Hi, Head Laredo-Levy."

"Hello, Zephyr. Thank you so much for picking up Cadie." Mom was using her honey-sweet voice, reserved for people we didn't know very well. But she had a real smile on her face, not the pasted-on one. Maybe she really was glad that I was going to the play without Dad. *Why do you have to make everything be about the war between Mom and Dad?*

Because everything is, I answered myself. And was Dad really working late? Or had he just stayed at the bookshop so he wouldn't think about missing opening night at Center Stage?

A twinge of guilt tightened the twist in my stomach, but I forced myself not to pay attention to it.

Mom asked Zephyr a few questions—how long he'd had his license, where we were planning to park—and I thanked him a million times in my head for answering patiently. Finally she nodded and said, "Well, have a good time," and I zipped out the door before she could change her mind.

Zephyr followed me, slid into the driver's seat of his orange Volkswagen Beetle, and twisted the key in the ignition. The car coughed to life as I climbed in. Raven would flip when I told her about it—owning a Beetle was one of her life goals.

"Thank you so, so, so much for doing that," I said.

He laughed. "No problem. Kind of fun to see another side of Dr. Double-Hockey-Sticks."

I blinked. I knew kids called her that, but no one ever said it in front of me. I decided I liked how Zephyr didn't treat me like The Head of School's Daughter.

"So," I said, "is your mom that overprotective?"

"Uh, no. I don't have a mom, actually."

"Oh."

He didn't explain further, and I searched for a new topic. "So, nice car!"

"Thanks, a buddy of mine works at an auto shop and cut me a sweet deal on it."

He had buddies who worked at auto shops? Who cut sweet deals? So this was what it was like to go out with a senior. Or maybe be friends with a senior. Zephyr wasn't acting like this was a date. He hadn't opened the car door for me, or tried to hold my hand, or anything like that. Of course, I could open a car door perfectly well myself, and it wouldn't be safe for him to hold my hand while he was driving.

I tried to make a little conversation about play rehearsals, but it was a quick drive, and before long we were at Center Stage. He only had to circle the block once to find a parking spot. Dad always parked in the garage.

I felt older walking into the theater with someone other than Dad. It was a rush, like I'd been cut free from a tether. Like anything could happen.

Our seats weren't great—in the first row of the balcony at stage left, so we had a skewed view of the stage. But at least we didn't have to worry about seeing over anyone's heads. And Zephyr didn't seem to mind. "These are great seats!" he said.

In fact, Zephyr was enthusiastic about everything from the time we walked into the theater. "I love this play," he kept saying. "I can't wait to see what you think. I promise not to nudge you at all the good parts. I'll try, anyway." I didn't think I'd ever seen him this animated, except on stage.

Watching Zephyr watch the play was like a whole show in itself. His mouth never stopped moving—either whispering lines along with the actors or grinning a huge cheesy grin at the funny parts, and sometimes at the sad parts, too. His eyebrows shot up and down. Even his ears wiggled a little, he was moving his face so much. I realized, watching him, that I'd never actually seen him *smile*. I'd certainly never seen him do this many facial expressions, not even on stage. I couldn't tell if he was aware of what he was doing or not—he certainly wasn't aware of me watching him. It was like he was in his own private bubble. But every once in a while, when his delight overpowered him, he'd turn the grin on me, as if to say, *Look! Are you seeing this, too?*

"You know," I commented, as we made our way out to the lobby at intermission, "some people might find you incredibly annoying to sit next to at an event like this." His goofiness seemed to have unlocked my tongue—I had my powers of speech back. Hallelujah.

Zephyr stared at me. "What did you say?"

"Oh, come on. You seriously don't know you're doing it?"

"Doing what?"

"The silent cackling! Whispering lines along with the actors! The absolutely psychotic glee you're manifesting out of every pore!"

He smiled uncertainly. "Is that a good thing?"

Oh my god. He really didn't know he was doing it. "It's a joy to watch."

"You should be watching the stage, not me." Now he was grinning, a lopsided smirk, and I felt my face flush.

"So," I said, trying to change the subject, "you said you had a long story to tell me."

He frowned. "What long story?"

"Why you didn't go to the Fall Ball—you said it was a long story?"

"Ah." He shoved his hands into his pockets and looked around, as if searching for an emergency exit. "Cadie, that's what people say when they don't want to talk about something."

"Of course." My face burned hotter. "I'm sorry, forget it."

"No, no. It's okay. It's not a big deal. Oh, look, brownies."

He made a beeline for the snack table, and I excused myself to go to the bathroom. There was a long line, of course, and by the time I got back, the lights were flickering.

"Here," he said, holding out something folded up in a paper napkin, "I got you a brownie, too."

"Oh! Thanks," I said, slipping it into my purse, where I was sure it would shed crumbs all over everything. I couldn't very well cram it into my mouth in the two seconds we had left before going back in for the second half, though. Why was everything so much more complicated on a date? *Were we on a date?* I still wasn't sure. How were you supposed to know whether it was a date or not?

Zephyr took my elbow to steer me back toward the theater. A jolt of static electricity zapped my arm, and he snatched his hand back. "Ow!"

"That was your fault!"

"Was not!"

We both laughed.

Maybe it was a date?

"So anyway," he continued, as we found our seats, "about the Fall Ball. It's not a big deal. It's just that my girlfriend lives in New York, and she didn't want me to go without her."

The lights went down over the audience, and a spotlight illuminated the actors already on the stage.

A good thing, because my face was burning again, and I didn't want Zephyr to notice.

Of course. His girlfriend. *Ava,* I remembered suddenly. The girl whose call he'd answered at the Shakespeare Theatre.

What kind of an idiot was I, asking out a senior who already had a *girlfriend*?

179

And yet, he'd said yes. So what if it wasn't a date? I didn't have tons of guy friends, but maybe this was totally normal for Zephyr. I'd just play it cool. Of course he had a girlfriend. Maybe he assumed I had a boyfriend, too.

And we were having a good time. A great time. His face was about to crack open with joy again, watching the stage, and I was having fun for what felt like the first time in ages.

So just take this for what it is, Acadia Greenfield, and be content for once. Stop always wanting more.

· · ·

Who's Afraid of Virginia Woolf? was unlike any play I'd ever seen before. There were only four characters: a middle-aged couple, George and Martha, and a younger couple, Nick and Honey. Only one setting—George and Martha's living room. The whole thing took place over the course of one evening. The way the characters manipulated each other, and the audience, had my head spinning—every time you finally figured out whose side you were supposed to be on, someone would reveal a new horrible secret and turn the tables. George and Martha were more complicated and intense than any characters I'd ever seen on stage, more honest and deceitful and humble and arrogant. They were larger than life. They were hilarious and excruciating and mind-bogglingly *real*. I fell in love. So hard that I said yes instantly, without even pausing to think, when Zephyr asked if I wanted to see it with him again the next night.

Dad was surprised when I came home that night and told him I was going to see the play a second time, and even more surprised when I still didn't ask him to go with me. He mentioned that *Who's Afraid of Virginia Woolf?* was his favorite Edward Albee play, that he hadn't seen it performed since college. I ignored him.

On Saturday, I slept late and then lolled around in bed, filling up the hours before going back to Center Stage by working on my *Much Ado* lines. I had them almost all down. What I wouldn't give to run them with Dad . . . but he was out somewhere with Elizabeth. They were probably off exploring Baltimore, or going into raptures over dusty old books. Mom and Josh and I ordered takeout for dinner again, and just as we were finishing, the doorbell rang and Zephyr was there with his Beetle to pick me up.

At Center Stage, we sat on the opposite side of the theater this time, but otherwise we did a repeat of the previous night: me trying to figure out how these four actors were causing such a tornado of emotion on stage, and Zephyr drinking it all in next to me and whispering, nodding, chortling silently. We were both in a daze afterward as we stumbled out into the lobby.

"I think they did an even better job tonight," I said.

"You just picked up more this time, probably. You knew what was coming."

"No, I liked not knowing what was going to happen next last night, the freshness of all the surprises. But tonight—I don't know, it seemed like they dug *deeper*—"

"Twisted the knife," he said, miming it.

"Makes *Much Ado* seem a little boring."

"Yeah, it's not my favorite Shakespeare, to be honest. Hey, want to walk around the block a couple times? I don't think I can focus on driving yet."

He was right. He was giddy, stumbling, drunk on Albee.

So we walked around the block a couple times and then a couple more times, and then a couple *more*, talking about George and Martha and Nick and Honey, and which Shakespeare play we liked best, and I realized afterward I hadn't thought about

181

Elizabeth or Farhan or Mom or Dad once all night. I thought I heard Zephyr's phone buzz in his pocket, twice, but he didn't answer it.

"This was a great weekend," he said, as we finally buckled ourselves into our seats in the Beetle. "Thanks again for inviting me."

"Thanks for inviting *me* to see it again. I don't know how I'll ever settle for seeing a play just once after this."

He grinned. "It's a slippery slope."

"So," I said, trying to keep my voice casual, "does your girlfriend like theater, too?"

He shifted in his seat and didn't look at me. Then again, he was driving, so it was good that he kept his gaze on the road. "Yeah. We met at theater camp this summer. She's a killer actor, but she's more into film, wants to direct. Move out to LA and all that."

How sophisticated.

"What about you?" he said. "You dating anyone? Seems like the whole cast is already going out with each other."

I was surprised he'd noticed. It didn't seem like the sort of thing Zephyr paid attention to.

"No, I'm just"—I remembered one of Renata's phrases, whenever Mom asked her whether she was seeing anyone—"I'm just doing me right now."

He nodded.

That seemed to kill the conversation, to burst the bubble of excitement we'd both been glowing in after the play. We rode in silence, and soon we were back in Hampden.

"Well, thanks again," he said, pulling up at my house. "See you on Monday."

"See you," I said, and wondered what Monday would be like. Would we act any differently around each other now that we'd spent time together outside of school, outside of *Much Ado*? Now that we'd exchanged more than pre-written words, and now that I'd witnessed the manic dynamo that was Zephyr at a play? What did it mean that he'd allowed me to see that side of him?

It just means you're friends now, I told myself. *Friends who can walk in circles around the same block for forty-five minutes talking about acting technique and authentic emotion and the merits of* Hamlet *versus* Macbeth. *As friends do.*

. . .

I couldn't sleep until the wee hours on Saturday night—too much energy still zooming around inside me. I crept downstairs and was surprised not to see Dad sleeping on the couch. Then I went into the kitchen for a glass of water and found him there instead, slumped over at the table with his cheek resting on an open book, as if he'd fallen asleep while reading. I poked his shoulder and he grunted, so at least I knew he was still breathing. I left him there, drank my water, and went back up to bed.

Sunday morning, what felt like only a few hours later, I walked Elizabeth to church, wearing my headphones and listening to Red Hot Chili Peppers so we wouldn't have to talk. I knew it was rude, but I was too groggy from lack of sleep to care. While she was at Mass, I went to the BMA to hang out with Heron again. I told her about the Center Stage production, but I didn't mention that I'd seen it twice. Or that I'd seen it with Zephyr. Both times.

I didn't tell Raven, either. Somehow I worried the magic would drain out of the memory if I told it too many times. And I didn't want her to jump all over it and analyze everything Zephyr had said. He had a girlfriend, I had a broken heart. I was probably rebounding. What I'd said to him was true: I needed to "just do me" for a while right now. Raven would agree. It felt strange not to tell her about it, though. All day Sunday, I kept taking out my phone to call her and then putting it away again.

That night, as we were getting ready for bed, Elizabeth said, "Cadie—you know him a lot better than I do, of course, but—do you think Josh is okay?"

"What do you mean?"

"Well, when I was in the bathroom brushing my teeth just now, he was going downstairs with his cello. I don't think he realized that I saw him."

I checked the time—10:04. Huh. It was well past Josh's bedtime, let alone his practice time. "I'm sure he's fine," I said, annoyed that Elizabeth had noticed and I hadn't. A few minutes later, though, I made a big show of pretending I couldn't find my script, and crept down the stairs.

I didn't see or hear anything at first—Dad wasn't even on the couch or in the kitchen. Then I went to the basement stairs and pushed the door open a crack. Soft music floated up. Well, soft sounds—Josh was practicing something with a mute on down there, and it didn't exactly sound like music. I listened for a few more minutes and caught snatches of melody here and there, but couldn't figure out what he was trying to play. It sounded like he was hitting a lot of wrong notes. Judging by that and how frequently he stopped and muttered to himself, he was trying to learn something new.

I closed the door gently and turned to find Mom standing behind me, her whole face creased into a frown. "He's got seven weeks until the competition, and his Popper is a *wreck*."

184

"He'll be fine, Mom," I said.

"He's not fine, listen to that!" Mom took a deep breath, then continued more quietly. "I didn't know he was sneaking out of bed to practice. Has he been doing it for a long time?"

"I have no idea." I felt as miserable as she looked. How long had Josh been practicing in the basement in the middle of the night? How could I not have noticed before?

"I'll talk to him about it in the morning," Mom said. "I don't want him to think I'm spying on him."

The music stopped for a moment, and we both jumped as we heard something crash downstairs. It sounded like Josh had thrown his rock stop across the room. "Mom, why can't he just play one of his Bach suites for the competition? He sounds fantastic on those, and he practices them all the time. He loves them."

She shook her head. "Those aren't competition pieces. There are certain pieces assigned to each age category, and we're trying to show how far above his age level Josh is. That's why we picked the Hungarian Rhapsody."

"We?"

"Yes, me and Olga. If he wins this competition, or even if he places well, that would open all sorts of doors for him for high school—Interlochen, or—"

That sounded familiar. Josh had told me something about Michigan last weekend, hadn't he? "You'd send him all the way to *Interlochen*? Mom, that's in Michigan, right?"

"We'll have to do what's best for your brother's career," Mom said, and turned to go up the stairs.

"He's just a kid, Mom, he doesn't have a *career*!"

"Not yet. But you wait and see, Cadie, that boy is going to be something special."

And what about me, Mom? I thought. *Why is it always about Josh, Josh, Josh with you?*

．　．　．

Monday morning, I woke up with a fluttering stomach. It took me a few minutes to remember why. Ah, yes. Drama class.

Zephyr smiled at me when I walked into the Shed, but other than that, he didn't treat me any differently than he had pre–Center Stage binge weekend. Which meant he didn't go out of his way to talk to me at all, unless we were working on a scripted scene together. *So much for having a new friend?*

"Cadie," Robin called, snapping me out of my reverie. "What are you *doing* in this scene? What's your objective? What do you *want?*"

We were still working on our *Crucible* scenes in class.

"Sorry," I said, "I forgot how I did it last time."

Robin waved his arms as if hailing help from a sinking ship. "No, no, no! How many times have I said this? We don't 're-member' anything on stage. *Conscious forgetting*, people. Every time you step into a scene, your reactions should be new and real. Forget, forget, forget!"

"Then I'm doing a great job," Sam muttered. He'd forgotten three of his lines and missed two cues already.

"Wipe the slate clean." Robin clapped his hands. "Try again."

I took a deep breath and tried to forget the blocking, the cues I was expecting, to relax my body enough that all of that would come naturally. Inevitably. Trying to make it look like I wasn't doing any work at all. Easy peasy my ass.

Robin had us run the scene two more times, and then we sat down and watched the next group. He stopped them even more

186

frequently, with more arm waving and even some Shakespearean cursing thrown in.

After class, I lingered over my backpack, just to see if Zephyr would come over to talk. He didn't. In fact, it seemed like he packed up and left extra quickly, ignoring the fact that Robin was trying to wave him over. Robin looked extremely annoyed. He flagged me down by the door instead and said, "Cadie, if you happen to see Zephyr before tonight's *Much Ado* rehearsal, would you please remind him that he has been running late for his scenes? Actors are expected fifteen minutes *before* their call times."

"Um, I don't really see him outside of class. But sure." My face was burning, and, although I told myself I was imagining it, it felt like Robin could see right through my lie. Why would he care, anyway, that I'd spent the weekend at Center Stage with Zephyr? It wasn't like we were dating. And anyway, even if we were, plenty of the cast was already going out with each other.

He muttered something that sounded like, "Too much talent to waste," as I walked away. "Not you," he said quickly, as I turned back to look at him, "you're doing a wonderful job, Cadie. Making lots of progress. Sorry I snapped at you today."

My mood soared. "I am? Making progress?"

"Oh, yes, most definitely. Actually, if you have a few minutes before your next class, let's talk about that scene we're going to rehearse tomorrow night—I have an idea I'd like to run past you."

CHAPTER FOURTEEN

"I *knew* this would happen," I moaned, collapsing on Raven's bedroom carpet. "Ever since we saw the Shakespeare Theatre production with my class."

I wasn't called for any scenes tonight, so I'd gone home with Raven after school and told her about Robin's "idea," and then I'd finally told her everything about my weekend, too—"All the beans," she'd said, snapping her fingers, "spill 'em."

"Having your first kiss on stage is not the end of the world," she said, but the way she said it, she could've been pronouncing the imminent demise of mankind.

"I could say no," I said, for the hundredth time. "Robin said to think about it and let him know if I was comfortable with it or not. He said I don't have to do it if I don't want to. He can re-block the scene instead. And it won't *really* be kissing. He's going to show us how to stage it so it's just an illusion."

"You said all that already," Raven said. "But I still don't understand how it works. How will the audience not notice that Zephyr's kissing his thumb instead of your mouth?"

"He'll have his downstage hand on the side of my head, and—"

"Okay, whatever," Raven interrupted. "The point is, do you want to do it or not?"

"I think the scene will work a lot better if we do it," I admitted. "As long as it's not horribly awkward."

"Zephyr's been in lots of plays, I'm sure he's done plenty of stage kisses before."

"And it doesn't count as my first kiss?"

"Definitely not," Raven said.

"Okay. So why do you have that look on your face?"

"Because you went on two dates with this guy over the weekend, and you didn't tell me about it until today."

"They weren't dates! I told you, he has a girlfriend. And I'm still in mourning for Farhan. Or something."

Raven shook her head. "It's just weird, dude. We always tell each other everything."

"Well, I told you about the Friday night plan, *dude*. The Saturday night one was kind of last-minute."

"And?"

"And . . . nothing. Everything's so intense right now at home. It was nice to have a distraction."

Raven nodded. "Okay, okay, fine, I forgive you. Now, speaking of distractions, I have to study for my history test tomorrow, my math test on Friday, and my debate tournament in two weeks. Pick one and quiz me." She plunked a stack of notebooks down on the carpet next to me.

"Right. What's a friend for?" I rolled my eyes at her and let out a Dramatic Groan. But I did feel a little better.

Maybe my dad had a secret past I'd never known about and my parents weren't speaking to each other or sleeping in the same bed. Maybe my surprise sister was stealing my dad and the boy who'd been my one true love since forever. Maybe my brother was sneaking around and even more withdrawn than he'd ever been, which meant he was basically turning into a human snail.

Maybe I wasn't a senior, or a New Yorker planning to move to LA to direct movies, but Raven thought I was sophisticated enough to handle a stage kiss.

Sure. A stage kiss? No big deal.

. . .

Zephyr certainly didn't act like it was a big deal. Robin had us come to rehearsal early Tuesday night to practice before everyone else got there, so we wouldn't have to try it for the first time with an audience of teenagers. In my head, I flapped my arms wildly to make sure the gods were watching, so they'd reward Robin appropriately in the afterlife.

Although, Robin was the one who was making things awkward. He was describing how Zephyr should hold his hand, and the exact angle we should stand from the audience to create the illusion. But he was doing all this from the first row of seats. Ordinarily he didn't hesitate to get up on stage with us during rehearsals, sometimes physically moving us around like chess pieces or giant dolls if we were struggling with the blocking and he got fed up with verbal instruction. Tonight, though, he was simply waving his hands in the air to explain what he meant.

Finally Zephyr said, politely, "Mind if we just try it? I remember how. I've done this before."

Robin said, "Yes, yes, of course," and waved his hands again, as if to clear away all the instructions he'd just given. "Of course you have. Take it away." He folded his arms. I couldn't figure out why he seemed so uncomfortable.

Zephyr placed his hand on the downstage side of my head, just like Robin had explained, slid his thumb over my mouth, and leaned in to touch his lips to his thumb.

I closed my eyes. It wasn't a kiss. It didn't even feel like a kiss.

It felt like a boy putting his hand on the side of my head and kissing his thumb in front of my face.

But Zephyr's hand was pleasantly cool against my warm face, and it smelled like cocoa butter and soap, and the touch of his thumb made my lips feel like they were swelling. I didn't want it to end.

"Hold—and—yes, that's it. That's very good," said Robin, clapping his hands twice, all businesslike. "Excellent. Let's break until the others arrive."

And that was it. My first stage kiss. Zephyr stepped away from me and picked up his script, slouched into the wings to practice his lines. I wandered into the audience seats and, with my back to Robin, touched my own thumb to my lips. It didn't feel the same.

Rehearsal that night was glorious. We were mostly off book, at last, and the scene picked up a rhythm it hadn't had before. It was the wedding scene—the first wedding scene, where Claudio and Hero are supposed to get married, halfway through the play. But Claudio has been tricked by Don John, the villain, aka Sam Shotwell, into thinking Hero is dillydallying with other men behind his back. At the altar, in front of everyone, Claudio accuses her of cheating. Then he storms off, Hero faints, and Beatrice and Benedick are left to figure out how to fix the whole mess, with Beatrice furious at Claudio for humiliating her beloved, innocent cousin.

Benedick finally declares his love to Beatrice and tells her he'd do anything for her. Cue stage kiss. Then she tells him if he really loves her, he should go kill Claudio.

Raven would love this part.

Tori Lopez was doing a great job as Claudio, storming around

191

and preening like a male peacock, and Priya Pashari, playing Hero, did a very credible swoon. But our stage kiss took the cake—everyone hooted and whooped from the wings, and even Zephyr was blushing when he pulled away.

"People!" Robin yelled, clapping his hands for quiet. "All right, all right. Benedick, Beatrice, please proceed."

We ran through the rest of the scene, on fire from all the excitement in the room. Everyone was watching us, holding their breath, it felt like, to see if we'd do it again. We didn't—Robin had only blocked in the one stage kiss—and everyone stopped making a big deal about it by the end of the night, after we'd run the scene two more times.

"That's a wrap for tonight," Robin said, at last. "Go home, sleep, run your lines. Simultaneously if need be."

"Hey," I said to Zephyr, as we packed up our bags, "good job tonight."

"Yeah, you too." He smiled at me. "That wasn't too awkward, right?"

"Nope, not at all. Hey, I was wondering if you, um, wanted to go get ice cream?"

"Right now?"

"Yeah, it's on the way to my place, if you don't mind driving. Unless you have to be home by a certain time—"

"Oh, no, I don't." Zephyr seemed flustered. I'd never seen him flustered before. "It's just—I didn't drive tonight, and my ride is leaving—what about tomorrow night instead?"

"Sure, sounds good." Who had he driven to rehearsal with? I didn't remember him coming in with anyone. And we'd both gotten to rehearsal early—Micayla had agreed to drive me over early, since she had extra work to do on the costumes.

"Oh my god," she groaned, coming up behind me at that moment.

I spun around. "Oh, hey."

"Sorry," she said, "was I interrupting?"

"No, it's fine." I turned back to Zephyr, but he'd slipped away. I scanned the room but didn't see him. He and his ride, whoever it was, must've scooted right out the door.

"Anyway," Micayla said, "I screwed up Priya's dress and I have to start all over again. Can you help me carry some stuff out to the car? I want to take this dress home and work on it more."

"Sure," I said, and filed the Zephyr mystery away to think about another time.

. . .

That night, there was another giant bouquet of flowers on the table—peonies, this time. Mom's other favorite.

So she and Dad were still fighting. Or whatever they were doing. Or not doing. They'd waited for me to have dinner, which meant that everyone was grumpy and starving when I got home. Mom and Dad sat at opposite ends of the table and bowed their heads while Elizabeth said grace. Mom was clasping her hands together so hard her knuckles went white. The peonies were perched in the middle of the table like an awkward grin. Once the meal started, Mom didn't say anything except for asking me or Josh or Elizabeth to pass things to her. Dad tried floating a few conversation openers her way, but she managed to avoid responding directly to him. How much longer could this go on?

"So!" Dad said, in Forced Good Cheer Voice. "Elizabeth, have you and your, uh, *fellow* decided what you're going to see on Friday night? I hear *The Super Duper Swamp Monster Blood and Guts IV* is very good."

"That's not a real movie, Dad," said Josh, while my stomach churned. Elizabeth and Farhan's date—I'd completely forgotten.

Mom's eyes narrowed. "What *fellow?*"

Dad looked at Elizabeth. "Ah. Sorry, didn't realize we were keeping this under wraps."

"No, it's fine." Elizabeth shook her head. "Sorry, Melissa, I didn't tell you yet. I asked Ross if it was okay."

"Well, of course it's okay," Mom said, with a tight smile. "I'm very glad that you're getting out and meeting people. So, who is it?"

"Just someone from school," Elizabeth said.

"I know everyone from school," Mom said. "Who is it?"

"It's Farhan," I said, "she's going out with Farhan."

Mom raised her eyebrows at me. "You mean, Farhan who was *your*—"

"My friend, right," I said, cutting across her words. "Yeah, I set them up together. Sort of."

Now Dad was giving Elizabeth a funny look. I wondered how much she'd told him. If she'd said anything about what happened at the Fall Ball.

Mom was still staring at me. "So you and Farhan are just friends? I thought . . . ?"

"*Yes*, we're just friends." It came out more aggressively than I'd meant it to. This conversation was making my stomach hurt worse. To change the subject, I said, "So, I had my first stage kiss tonight."

Mom and Dad both froze.

Josh, to my surprise, cracked up.

"What's so funny?" I asked, annoyed.

He kept laughing, and said, "Ewwwww. You have to *kiss?*"

Boys.

Elizabeth, on the other hand, looked equal parts shocked and impressed. "Wow," she said. "Was it—weird?"

"No, not at all. Zephyr has a lot of experience on stage. He's really good at it."

Dad wrinkled his nose. "Cadie, I'm happy for you, but I have to say, it makes a father queasy to think about his daughter's first kiss."

"It's not a *real* kiss, Dad, it's just a stage kiss. He's kissing his thumb, over my mouth, not—"

Dad waved a hand as if to clear the air, in a way that reminded me of Robin. "No, no, that's enough detail. Great. Good for you."

Mom actually smirked. "Yes, good for you." *Good for you for making your father uncomfortable,* she meant.

The image of Elizabeth and Farhan was still swirling around in my head. And the image of Elizabeth telling Dad about her first date here in Baltimore, asking his permission. Not even bothering to tell Mom, because she wasn't related to Mom, so why should she make an effort?

"Mom," I said, and I heard myself use a Voice, just like Dad. Innocent Lamb Voice. "Do you have a lot of work tonight?"

Mom frowned. "No, actually. Why?"

"I know it's late, but would you take me out for a quick driving lesson? Just us. You know, some mother-daughter time?"

It was like I got hit with three javelins to the stomach at once: Dad's face, falling so hard you could hear it *thump.* Mom's, lighting up with such a hopeful expression she looked like a golden retriever begging for treats. And Elizabeth's, crumpling, although she looked down quickly at her plate to hide it. *Because she doesn't have* any *mother-daughter time anymore, you idiot.* My stomach twisted with guilt. I hadn't meant to rub salt in *that* wound.

I couldn't see Josh's face, since he was sitting right next to me, but that was fine. I didn't need to know whether I could've possibly hurt him, too.

"Absolutely, *mija*," Mom purred. "I'd love to see the progress you're making."

Uh-oh. "Well, don't get too optimistic," I said, trying to sound as jolly as Dad had a few minutes ago. "I'm definitely still a beginner."

"I'll just go grab my coat, and then we can take a spin," said Mom, pushing her chair back from the table. Half of her tempeh Reuben was still on her plate. "I'll save this for later," she added, whisking her plate off to the kitchen.

So I took my half-eaten dinner to the kitchen, too, since my stomach was hurting too much to eat anyway. I pulled out two Tupperware containers—but Mom scraped her plate into the trash instead, giving me a conspiratorial smile. She hated tempeh and sauerkraut. Dad knew that. He must've forgotten.

It was nice, for once, to share something with Mom, to know that I'd made her happy. She was actually humming as she went to the closet for her coat. I just couldn't believe how much both of us were willing to hurt Dad.

When we got into the car, Mom said, "I'm glad to have some time alone together. We really haven't talked, just the two of us, since—everything happened. How are you—"

"I'm fine," I said, cutting her off and forcing a smile. "You know what? For tonight, I'd rather not talk about it. I just want to focus on my driving."

She smiled back at me—a warm smile, a real one. "You're my big girl," she said softly. "I'm proud of you."

I'd thought it would somehow help me feel better, making Mom happy, but my stomach was tied in tighter knots than ever.

. . .

I was only called for one scene at rehearsal the next night, and Zephyr wasn't called at all. So much for our ice cream plan. *Oh well,* I told myself, *it didn't seem like he really wanted to go anyway.*

But when I jumped off the edge of the stage after my scene, there he was, waiting by my backpack.

"Hey," he said, "that was fantastic."

"Oh! Thanks!" I said, flustered. "Have you been watching this whole time?"

He nodded.

"But—you're not called tonight."

"I know, but I had to blow you off last night, so I owe you a rain check."

"Nah, you don't owe me anything. Don't worry about it."

Zephyr rubbed his chin, a gesture I was starting to recognize as something he did when he felt self-conscious. "I thought we had plans. That's why I came to pick you up."

"Oh!" I couldn't think of anything else to say, and Robin was glaring daggers at us for talking during rehearsal, so I slung my backpack over my shoulder and we ducked up the aisle.

"Still want ice cream?" Zephyr said, once we were outside the Shed. "Or . . . would you consider something else?"

"Like what?"

He spun his car keys around one finger. "I haven't had dinner yet, I'm starving. Do you like sushi?"

"Ugh. I've never had it. I'm a vegetarian."

He grinned. "Oh-ho, one of those. Well, you can get avocado rolls, or soup, or noodles. Or we can go somewhere else."

Adrenaline zinged through me. Zephyr Daniels wanted to have dinner with me? Before I could second-guess myself, I said, "No, you know what? I want to try sushi. It sounds fun." And by *fun*, I meant *sophisticated* and *New York*. Aka *perfect*.

I called home and checked in with Mom, who said it was fine as long as I was home by 9:30. So we climbed into the orange Beetle and zoomed down St. Paul Street. Zephyr parked on 33rd and led me toward a set of stairs right off the street, next to a sign that said Sushi Below. The restaurant was in a basement, apparently. I followed him down the stairs, and when he pushed open the door, I was startled by a burst of blue light. The foyer was decked out with fish ponds and colorful floodlights, rock sculptures and pink flamingos and fake palm trees. The waitresses all wore neon pink-and-green or yellow-and-blue kimonos, which clashed with their beehive hairdos and cat-eye glasses, and the soundtrack to *Hairspray* was playing quietly in the background.

Zephyr swept a hand out in front of us, encompassing the whole scene. "What do you think?"

"Very Baltimore," I said, nodding in approval.

The hostess seated us in the back corner—perfect for people watching. I noticed Zephyr glancing around the room, too.

"Do you like people watching?" I asked.

"Oh, I'm incurable." Zephyr sounded like a book sometimes.

198

As if he hadn't played with other kids much when he was little. Maybe he was an only child.

I decided to ask. "Do you have brothers or sisters?"

He hesitated for the briefest second, then shook his head. "What about you?"

"One brother." I hesitated, too. "And—one half sister. She just moved here. My parents didn't even know she existed until a couple months ago. Things have been kind of rough lately." Once I'd started talking about it, the words tumbled out. "My dad and I were always super close, but now it's like we're on opposite teams, because he has this giant secret I never knew about, and somehow I'm getting closer with my mom even though I can't stand her most of the time, and she and my dad aren't talking to each other at all." I made myself stop before I blabbed my entire life story.

Zephyr didn't look freaked out, though, just concerned. "Wow, 'rough' sounds like an understatement."

I felt my face heating up, so I picked up a menu. "Yeah. Well. Time to drown my sorrows in sushi."

I ordered an avocado roll and a bowl of miso soup. Zephyr ordered a spicy tuna roll, a yellowtail roll, and something called *unagi* sashimi.

"What's that?" I said, after the waitress had taken our order. "That last thing you said."

"Eel," he said, grinning.

"Seriously? *Ugh.*"

"Hey, you don't have to eat any of it. But I'm warning you, it's possibly the most delicious thing on this planet."

"Yeah . . . I'll pass." I looked down, fiddling with my napkin. "Sorry I spilled all that on you. About my family stuff."

199

He shook his head. "Not at all. I'm sorry you're going through it."

"Thanks."

"Anyway, sounds like great stuff to use on stage."

I smiled. "I guess that's a good way to think about it. It's just all so weird. How about you? Are you close with your parents? What are they like?" I knew I was prying, but I desperately wanted to stop talking about myself. And right as I said that I remembered—he didn't have a mother. He'd told me that on our way to Center Stage the first time. *Crap.*

Before I could try to dig myself out of that one, though, he cleared his throat and answered my question. "I don't know much at all about my parents—my birth parents. I'm adopted."

"Oh! Cool."

"I have two dads, actually."

"Very cool!"

"We've been fighting about college stuff lately, but usually we get along pretty well."

I nodded, and then, thank Poseidon, our food arrived before I could say "cool" one more time. Zephyr didn't seem to mind my blunders, though. Or else he was just a very good actor. *Which you already know,* I reminded myself. Oh well. Either way, my stomach wasn't churning the way it usually did when I got nervous or upset.

Dealing with the food kept us busy for a while. I knew how to use chopsticks, sort of, but there was a whole thing to do with mixing the wasabi and soy sauce, which came separately on a little white dish with two compartments. Zephyr showed me how to take a smidge of wasabi on the end of one chopstick and mash it into the soy sauce compartment, taste it, then repeat until it was as hot as I wanted. I mixed in too much wasabi right away, though, and coughed until my eyes watered. Zephyr laughed at me, and I swatted him with my napkin, which knocked his teacup onto the floor. It didn't shatter, but tea splashed everywhere.

Ordinarily, I would've been mortified for all that to happen in front of a boy, but he was laughing so hard that I couldn't help laughing, too. When we finally calmed ourselves down and the waitress had brought him a new teacup, I dipped one of my avocado roll slices into the wasabi–soy sauce mixture and, mimicking Zephyr, popped it into my mouth whole.

"Tha's de-*lishoush*," I mumbled around the mouthful of spicy rice, seaweed, and avocado. He beamed as if he'd cooked it himself.

We ate for a little while in silence. Then I said, "So, you're in the middle of college applications now?"

He grimaced. "Yeah, it's pretty much taken over my life outside of school."

"You're applying to drama programs, right?"

"Nope. Astrophysics."

I almost dropped my chopsticks. "Are you serious?"

Zephyr prodded one of his rolls toward me. "Are you sure you don't want to try some of the real stuff?"

"Maybe just one bite. I *do* eat fish every once in a while. Mostly when I'm mad at my parents."

I took a nibble of his raw tuna roll gingerly and almost spat it back out. "Ew! It's so—*fishy*."

"Uh, yeah," he said, drawling the words. "It's, like, *fish*."

This set us off into another round of laughter. What was I so giddy about? Was it something in the food?

"We're high on wasabi," he said, as if he'd read my mind.

201

"Clears up your nasal passages and makes you all light-headed."

"Airheaded," I said.

"Speak for yourself!" He jabbed his chopsticks toward me and I jabbed mine right back.

"So," I said. "Why aren't you applying for a theater degree? You're the best actor in this whole school."

"I don't want to be, like, working at McDonald's the rest of my life. Most theater majors don't just waltz out of school and make it big-time on Broadway."

"I bet you could."

He was shaking his head.

"Well, then you could teach! Like Robin."

He sighed. "Okay, okay. That's not the real reason. That's just what I tell people. It's a long story."

"A long story?" I remembered what he'd said at Center Stage: *Cadie, that's what people say when they don't want to talk about something.* "Does that mean I should stop asking questions?"

He smiled. "No, I don't mind talking about it. If I'm not boring you."

"Of course not." I motioned toward the two sushi rolls still sitting in front of him, untouched. "And maybe I'll get brave enough to try that eel, if you distract me."

He narrowed his eyes at me and ate another piece of sushi. Then he set his chopsticks down. "Okay. It's like this. Imagine this is Earth." He picked a grain of rice off his sushi and set it on the tablecloth. Then he added ten more next to it. "Now, Jupiter is about eleven times wider than Earth—you could fit, like, thirteen hundred Earths inside the volume of Jupiter. So imagine how enormous Jupiter is." He put another piece of rice halfway down the table. "Here's our moon. See how huge Jupiter is? Well, you could fit Jupiter plus all the rest of the planets in our solar system into the space between Earth and our moon. So that gives you a tiny sense of how much space is out there."

He paused to let that sink in, then gestured with his chopsticks at the space between the grains of rice. "And that distance, from us to the moon? Is only like a third of the diameter of our sun. But the sun is just a star. The largest star we know of in the Milky Way galaxy is *one billion* times bigger than the sun. And yet, if you shrank the sun down to the size of a human white blood cell and shrank the galaxy along with it proportionately, the whole galaxy would be the size of the United States compared to that blood cell. That's how huge our galaxy is."

My head was beginning to spin.

"And *then* . . . try to imagine this: in just one photo taken by the Hubble space telescope, you can see thousands of galaxies. Each with millions of stars. Each star with its own planets."

"Wow," I breathed. I'd forgotten I was still holding chopsticks; they quivered as my hand hovered over my plate. I set them down carefully, as if I might disrupt the universe he'd just laid out on the table.

"Yeah. And that's just the beginning. Makes you feel less depressed about only getting the chance to live one life, right?"

I frowned. "How do you get there?"

"Well, on the one hand, if we're really that tiny and insignificant, what does anything matter?"

"Do you really believe that?"

"Nah, it's just the easy answer." He smiled. "On the other hand, when I think about the universe—it gives me this colossal sense of wonder that life exists at all, that all the things that matter to us really *do* matter to us, somehow. That we can think

203

and create and destroy and feel emotional about art, even though we're smaller than specks of specks of specks. And it seems incredibly unfair that we only get to do it once. *Once.*" He took a deep breath. "So, that's why I love the stage. That's why I act— to experience something outside myself. To get to *be* someone besides myself."

We sat there for a moment without speaking, letting those words hang between us.

"Why do you act?" he asked, finally.

I wasn't sure what to say after that speech. "To escape myself, I think." The words came out before I had time to think about them. Almost as if I were saying a line I'd memorized—as if it were my inevitable and only response to his question.

He raised an eyebrow.

"You know, to get out of my own head. To pretend I'm someone else, someone without all my problems." Was it true? Sure, I'd originally signed up for drama because of Dad. But the rush I felt on stage, when I was speaking someone else's words instead of my own, diving into the authentic reactions of my character— it was a relief to press *pause* on my own thoughts for a while, to "consciously forget" and block out everything else and focus all my energy on being Beatrice, or Elizabeth Proctor, or whoever.

"Really? You'd rather be someone else? You, Acadia Greenfield?" He was teasing, but something about the way he said it made my face warm up. As if he thought Acadia Greenfield was a pretty okay person to be. Or maybe it was just the wasabi.

While Zephyr went to the bathroom, I thought more about what he'd said. About how it wasn't fair that we only got this one chance at life, and how acting can give you the chance to try being all kinds of other people. I loved that. And then I remembered something Robin had said to me, back at the beginning of the year: *You're interested in people, Acadia, and that's a wonderful thing for an actor. You're an observer of human nature; you're thirsty for it.*

Maybe that was the real reason I loved the stage. Or maybe it was okay for both reasons to be true.

Zephyr came back just as the waitress brought our check, and we pulled out our wallets to figure out who owed what.

"Oh, I never tried the eel!" I said, looking at his empty plates.

Zephyr grinned. "Part of my master plan. Now we have to come back."

We rode home in contented quiet, our stomachs full, the car warm.

"Thanks," I said, when he dropped me off at my door. "I'm glad you owed me a rain check. That was a lot of fun."

All he said was, "Yeah," but he smiled and waved as I closed the car door.

CHAPTER FIFTEEN

The next few weeks flew by, what with play rehearsals, midterms, and the occasional driving lesson. And then, just to make things worse, Elizabeth passed her driving test. On her first try. I still had six months until I'd be old enough to take the test, but now I had *that* to live up to. I'd never pass on my first try.

Dad took Elizabeth out for ice cream to celebrate. I declined his invitation to join them. Instead, I stayed home with Josh and pulled out all our old favorite board games, Clue and Battleship and this weird communists-vs.-capitalists game from the 1970s Grandma Ruth had given us called Class Struggle. For a little while, I forgot about everything else going on. Until I made the mistake of asking Josh how his competition piece was going. Then he shrugged and said he was tired of playing games, and went downstairs for a snack, leaving me to clean everything up.

Elizabeth and Farhan went on a few more dates: to the movies, the ice-skating rink in the Inner Harbor, the Charmery. I tried to pretend they were just characters in a TV show I didn't really care about watching. I still walked Elizabeth to church every Sunday, as per Mom's orders, but we each listened to our own music instead of talking on the way, and I hung out with Heron at the BMA instead of going to Mass. More than once, I lost track of time, and we ended up walking home separately. She didn't say anything about it.

That was the thing about Elizabeth. I could tell she was

unhappy about the tension between us, but she never said a word. And I didn't have the energy to figure out what to do about it. I had enough to worry about, between school and *Much Ado.*

Besides, I told myself, *she's Dad's problem. He should help fix things.* But Dad was spending more and more time at Fine Print. He and Mom were still feuding, obviously, and he'd even started avoiding dinner at home—in the olden days, B.E., a total *no-no* in Mom's book. (Messenger: *"I see, lady, the gentleman is not in your books."* Beatrice: *"No; an' he were, I would burn my study."*)

I'd started quoting lines in my head all the time. Robin was right; once I had the lines memorized, the character of Beatrice felt like my second skin. When I put myself into the "given circumstances" of the play on stage, her words came out of my mouth as easily as my own.

If only it were that easy in real life to morph into someone else, to know the right words to say in every situation, to—

To stop thinking about kissing a gorgeous, brilliant, talented senior who happened to already have a girlfriend. *Really* kissing him, not his thumb.

I'd never thought about Farhan like this. Thought about him randomly a million times throughout the day, like in the middle of doing my homework, or when I was on the bus, or when I was trying to fall asleep at night. Every little thing reminded me of Zephyr—something he'd said, or the way he smelled, or how he smiled.

Sushi Below became our regular hangout for the next few weeks. We never ran out of things to talk about over sushi, although he was still quiet at rehearsals, focused, intent on his role.

207

But in mid-November, he told me that his dads said he couldn't go out at night anymore, except for rehearsals, until all his college applications were turned in.

"When are they due?" I asked.

He sighed. "January, although I'm trying to finish them before Christmas."

January. By then, the play would be over. Without sushi nights, I wouldn't see him outside of class anymore. I didn't know what that meant—what did I want from him, anyway? We weren't dating. Obviously. But still, it felt like he was putting a lid on—something.

"He can't possibly still have a girlfriend," Raven kept insisting. "There's no way she'd be okay with him going on dates with you all the time."

"They're not dates," I argued. "We never hold hands or even hug. We just eat dinner together and talk."

"Yeah, *and talk*. You talk about him all the time, Cadie. It's Zephyr this and Zephyr that. Face it, you have a colossal crush on him. And he is *totally* into you."

"It's not like that, I swear." But I couldn't convince her.

. . .

Friday, November 18 was my sixteenth birthday. I'd been dreading it for weeks. Dad always made a special three-course dinner for birthdays—with double-chocolate ganache cake for mine, and caramel-frosted carrot cake for Josh's. But this year I'd insisted I didn't want a family celebration at all.

Elizabeth was in the bathroom when I woke up, so I pulled on a sweatshirt and brushed my hair at the vanity mirror. There were dark circles under my eyes, and the colorful streaks in my hair were fading a little—I'd have to redo them soon. Did I look any older? I quirked an eyebrow, pouted my lips, tried to smirk. Nope. I just looked tired. I wished I knew how to make myself look cooler, more sophisticated. More, well, *sixteen*. I touched the edge of one eyebrow, tried to imagine a ring there.

"Girls!" Mom called. "Ten minutes!"

I sighed and went downstairs.

Something smelled amazing. Dad was at the kitchen counter, piling pumpkin waffles onto two paper plates. Josh was already eating his at the table.

"*Voilà*, ze gourmet birthday breakfast," Dad said in Parisian Chef Voice, grinning at me.

"Thanks," I mumbled.

Mom was bustling around by the door, ignoring the sizzling waffle iron and the cloud of cinnamon and nutmeg in the air. My stomach growled despite myself.

"So," Dad said, in his usual Weatherman Voice, "are you sure about tonight? I can't even tempt you with five-cheese mac 'n' cheese?"

I shook my head.

"I mean, *sixteen*. It's a big year. We should celebrate!"

"I can't. Raven and Micayla are taking me out to dinner at Papermoon."

Dad frowned. "Now, wait a—"

"It's fine, Ross," Mom called. "Cadie and I already discussed it."

He blinked and looked like he was going to say something else, but just then Elizabeth came downstairs. "Mmm, that smells amazing, what's—oh! Happy birthday, Cadie." She smiled awkwardly.

"Thanks," I said. *This*. This was why I didn't want a family birthday party. I didn't want to watch Josh shrink into his chair and force Mom and Dad to sit at the same table. I didn't want to listen to Elizabeth trying to be cheerful, and spend the whole night avoiding talking to Dad.

I ducked my head, took a paper plate of waffles, and said to Mom, "I'll meet you at the car."

. . .

The school day dragged on forever, but I was only called for one short scene at rehearsal that night, and at least I had dinner with Micayla and Raven to look forward to.

Papermoon is this quirky Hampden diner decorated with decapitated dolls and broken knickknacks and glitter and beads glued all over the rainbow-painted walls. It's creepy and weird and, most important, serves breakfast all day and all night. "Like any self-respecting diner should," Micayla said as we walked in.

Raven agreed. "I am *so* ready for second breakfast."

We ordered pancakes, French toast, and milk shakes. Raven or Micayla must've told the waitress it was my birthday, because she stuck candles in everything and brought the food out with three other waitresses, dancing and singing a loud, cheesy "Happy Birthday." The whole diner clapped.

"You guys!" I groaned, pulling my sweatshirt hood up over my head.

"... are the best?" Raven prompted, and even though my face was burning, I grinned.

But as we ate, I kept wondering what everyone was doing at home. Were they eating dinner together without me? Or was Dad working late at Fine Print? Maybe Elizabeth was out with Farhan. Josh was probably practicing in his room. If I'd stayed home, we'd be eating five-cheese mac 'n' cheese together right now. Maybe Mom would've made an effort to be nice to Dad, for my sake. Elizabeth would've tried extra hard to be friendly, and Dad—well, Dad would've pulled out all the stops for a sweet-sixteen birthday dinner. Maybe we would've all gone out to the movies afterward. Birthdays were the only time all year that Mom ever agreed to go to the movies.

My stomach twisted a little, and I set down my half-finished milk shake.

"Presents!" said Micayla, reaching into her giant tote bag and pulling out a wrapped package.

I blocked out thoughts of the family celebration I'd refused, and ripped the paper off Micayla's present. It was a new thrift store painting—this one was a scene with three little blond-haired, blue-eyed girls at a ballet lesson. She'd painted in a T. rex, also in a pink tutu, trying to do a pirouette.

Raven pulled out two smaller packages. One was a gorgeous pair of turquoise earrings she'd found at a craft fair, and the other was a T-shirt that said, *A world without adjectives would be*, which made me laugh.

"You *are* the best," I told them. "Thank you. I really, really needed this."

Raven put an arm around my shoulders, and Micayla reached across the table to squeeze my hands.

"Of course," said Raven, "we're just getting started. Tomorrow, we're taking you downtown."

I tried to protest. "I have to work on my lines this weekend."

But Micayla said, "Dude, you only turn sixteen once," and Raven said, "Seriously. Plus, you need to stop thinking about that play for a few hours."

A distraction did sound great. And it probably wouldn't hurt to take my mind off sushi nights, too—or the lack thereof.

I hadn't told Zephyr it was my birthday. I didn't want him to feel like he had to do something special. Besides, what would I even want him to do?

When Raven and Micayla dropped me off at home, the house smelled like chocolate.

"How was your dinner?" Mom asked, her voice a little higher than usual. "So nice of your friends to take you out."

"It was fun," I said.

"Fun? Just fun?" said Dad, coming in from the kitchen.

I shrugged.

"Well, I seem to have found a cake in the oven—still hungry?"

"Dad . . . I *said* I didn't want to do anything."

"I know, but I like baking," he said. Then, switching to Robot Voice: "Besides—programmed I am—to bake a cake—on birth date of daughter."

I gave him a weak smile. "Okay . . . well, I'll have some tomorrow. I'm pretty full right now."

Dad's face sagged. Just for a moment. Then he squared his shoulders and said, "All right, but we aren't going to let you get away without some birthday presents!"

So we all sat in the living room, and I opened presents. Mom gave me a matching knitted hat-and-scarf set that I couldn't imagine ever wearing, but she'd helped Josh with his present, too—an awesome new pair of noise-canceling headphones. Elizabeth gave me a gift card for a clothing store at the mall. "I didn't know what you'd like," she said. "I hope you can use it."

"I shop there all the time," I lied. "It's perfect."

Dad presented me with his gift last, a heavy book-shaped

package. I peeled the paper away slowly. It was a brand-new, leather-bound *Complete Works of William Shakespeare*. The pages were onion-skin thin and edged in gold, and there were two silk ribbon bookmarks sewn into the binding. I traced the engraved lettering on the cover, remembering how I still hadn't even made it through the introduction in the paperback *Much Ado* he'd given me.

"Thanks, Dad," I managed. "It's beautiful."

Mom was already cleaning up the wrapping paper and Josh was yawning, so I said, "Well, I'm pretty tired. I think I'll get ready for bed."

Elizabeth followed me up to our room, and Mom poked her head in to say good night a while later.

I lay awake for what felt like hours, but I didn't hear Dad come upstairs—he must've gone to sleep on the couch again.

I closed my eyes and imagined playing my future self on a dark stage, with a single spotlight shining on me. Doing a dramatic monologue about my stressful teenage years.

So that was my sixteenth birthday, my character told the dark theater. *I lay in bed and said to myself, "At least it was finally over."*

. . .

The next day, Raven and Micayla and I wandered around the Inner Harbor. It was sunny and windy out, warm enough that I only needed a denim jacket—but that's not unusual for November in Baltimore. We did a little shopping, listened to a few street musicians, watched an impromptu poetry slam. Then Micayla convinced us to go to the American Visionary Art Museum.

I'd never been there before, and my first thought was that whoever ran this place probably designed Papermoon, too. The walls were filled with enormous mosaics created by street people; psychedelic paintings by mental hospital patients; trash sculptures, life-size statues of invented saints, and intricate carvings on the tips of lead pencils so tiny you had to use a magnifying glass to see them. Artwork by factory workers and grandmothers and hermits.

"Visionary art," Micayla lectured us, "means artwork produced by self-taught artists. No training. No schools of thought. Raw, spontaneous, outside the rules. Anti-academic." She groaned. "Maybe I shouldn't be applying to art school. Maybe I should go work in—in a steel factory, or—"

"Working in a steel factory," said Raven, "would be very hipster."

I wandered off to look at an exhibit called *Madonna*. Paintings of the Virgin Mary hung side by side with photo montages of the singer Madonna. The way the pieces were arranged showed "the way our pop culture conflates or contrasts the divine with the deeply flawed, immortality with fame, purity with desire"— or at least, that's what the exhibit placard said. I wondered what Elizabeth would think of it.

On an impulse, I went to the gift shop to look for a postcard of one of the Mary paintings. Maybe I'd give it to Elizabeth, if we ever said anything besides "Excuse me" or "Could you pass the almond butter" to each other again.

But instead, I got sidetracked just inside the gift shop by a small print. It was one of those scratchboard drawings, where you paint swirls of colors on a piece of card stock, color over it with black crayon, and then scrape an image into the crayon layer, revealing the colors beneath. This one showed a woman at a keyboard, leaning back, her arms straight out in front of her as her fingers danced over the keys. Her hair floated behind her as if she were underwater. Sitting on the piano bench next to her, but facing the other way, a man cradled a cello between his knees. He was hunched over his instrument, so the curve of his body was the inverse of hers. The paint beneath the black crayon was all metallic colors, golds and silvers and bronzes, so that the scraped-out figures seemed to shimmer and glow against the inky background.

It reminded me of Mom and Josh, of course, but also of Mom and Dad. The way they used to complement each other, how their personalities fit together—Mom's organization and drive balanced by Dad's humor and sensitivity. The way they were both so creative, Dad with his cooking and his books, Mom with her music. The way Mom used to look playing the piano when we lived at Ahimsa House. I couldn't even remember the last time she'd sat down at the piano. Was there any hope of things going back to the way they used to be? Or would we have to move back to Takoma Park—go back in time—to make that happen?

I bought the print and tucked it carefully into my backpack.

. . .

We always celebrated Thanksgiving with the Woodburys. When Raven and I had become friends in second grade, I'd told her about the Ahimsa House version of social-justice-themed Thanksgiving, which we called Anti-Colonial Thanksgiving—ACT. We prepared a feast using only local vegetarian food, and everyone shared a poem, story, or song about colonization somewhere in the world today. Then we talked about nonviolent decolonization strategies and what we could do on an individual level to help. It was very Ahimsa and very Quaker. Even at the age of seven, Raven thought it was the coolest thing she'd ever heard. She went home and told Renata and Ruby about it, who also loved the idea and asked Mom and Dad to celebrate with them. Every year after that, we took turns hosting.

It was our turn this year. School let out early the day before Thanksgiving, and when we got home, Mom changed out of her business suit into an old ratty pair of overalls—the first time I'd seen her wear them in recent memory. She tied a bandana around her head, turned on Beethoven's Seventh Symphony at top volume, and attacked the floors and furniture with a spray bottle of tea tree oil and lemon juice. Pretty soon, the whole house smelled clean and lemony. Dad, who had closed Fine Print early as well, sorted through farmers' market produce on the kitchen counter while I helped Mom haul the center leaf for the table up from the basement. We squeezed two extra folding chairs plus Josh's cello chair between the other chairs around the table.

Josh was practicing down in the basement, sitting on an overturned box since we'd taken his chair. I thought one reason Mom was blasting music was to cover up the faint sounds of his Popper Hungarian Rhapsody. He clearly still didn't know the piece, although it was improving. But I could tell that Mom was nervous about his competition. She'd been scheduling extra lessons for him all month. She wouldn't even let him help with the cooking. Josh and I always made the cranberry sauce together. This year, though, she told him to keep practicing, so I made the cranberry sauce myself.

It was weird, sharing kitchen space with Dad, helping him make the same dishes we always made together for ACT. I didn't feel like talking, so I put my headphones on and listened to music while I mashed sweet potatoes and chopped vegetables.

And where was Elizabeth? Volunteering at a soup kitchen with a group from church.

I told Raven about that the next afternoon, after the Woodburys arrived for our ACT celebration. Raven and I escaped up to my room while Renata and Ruby were still taking their coats off and unpacking the salads, desserts, and drinks they'd brought. They kept exclaiming over Elizabeth, how much she looked like Dad and Josh, and I just couldn't stand it.

"I mean, she acts like she's the dictionary definition of the word 'perfect.' Seriously, going off to a soup kitchen while Mom and Dad and I were slaving away cooking and cleaning here? What's she trying to prove?" I collapsed onto my bed. "I am so sick of sharing a room. So sick of *her*. And you know what? She's not even as perfect as she pretends to be. Did you know she smokes?"

Raven's eyebrows shot up. "Elizabeth? No way."

"So like, what else don't we know about her? What other secrets does she have? I mean, I feel like I can't trust *anyone* in my family anymore." I groaned. "Ugh, I shouldn't have told you that. About Elizabeth smoking. I promised her I wouldn't tell anyone."

Raven shrugged. "So what? I'm your BFF. You're supposed to tell me everything. Besides, she's kicking my butt on debate team right now. And even more besides, I'm on your side, girl. She stole your family, then she stole your true love, even though he turned out to be a—"

"Ready to go back downstairs?" I interrupted loudly, and Raven turned to see that Elizabeth had just walked into the room. Raven stretched her face into a big, fake grin and said, "Hi, Elizabeth!"

Elizabeth said, "Ross wanted me to tell you that we're all ready for dinner." I wished I believed in a god, so I could pray that she hadn't overheard us. It didn't seem like she had. Still, Raven and I exchanged glances as we hurried down the stairs.

Once we'd all gathered around the table, Ruby filled our glasses—Josh, Elizabeth, Raven, and I got sparkling cranberry-apple cider—and we toasted.

"To *ahimsa*," Ruby said, and we all echoed. As the eldest woman present, Ruby was supposed to give the toast, but this year she asked Dad to do it. "You have such a way with words, dear," she told him.

So Dad led us off, no particular Voice, just Serious Dad: "The word *ahimsa*, as you all know, is Sanskrit for *nonviolence*. To do no injury. To cause no harm. This Anti-Colonial Thanksgiving, we will meditate on this truth: that the violence we inflict on others is a manifestation of the violence within ourselves. Guilt, shame, disappointment—these are all forms of self-violence. When we cannot forgive ourselves, we inflict self-violence. And it is only by learning true unconditional love, compassion, and reconciliation for ourselves that we can learn to live truthfully and compassionately with others."

I snuck a peek at Mom, expecting her to be glaring daggers at Dad. She wasn't. The expression on her face looked like the way I feel when I'm reminding myself that I don't *do* crying. Which, like I said, is something I inherited from Mom in the first place, so she's supposed to be the master of it.

Huh. I hadn't seen her look at Dad like that in a long, long time.

"To paraphrase Gandhi as Keats would've put it," Dad

continued, "truth is ahimsa; and ahimsa, truth. Let us join hands and hold each other in the Light."

"Thank you, Ross," murmured Ruby, and we all bowed our heads. The brussels sprouts, sweet potatoes, carrot-beet fritters, vegan pumpkin lasagna, and apple pie were all keeping warm in the oven, and their scents mingled and swirled around the table, making my mouth water and my stomach rumble.

After a few minutes of silence, someone usually spoke up. That's how a Quaker prayer service works. This time, it was Mom.

"Would you say grace for us before we eat, Elizabeth?" she asked, surprising everyone.

Elizabeth looked especially startled. "Oh, I wouldn't want to disrupt the—I mean, I don't know how to say a Quaker grace. Or a, um, Sanskrit one."

"We like the one you usually say just fine," Mom said, and I had to take another look at her face to make sure she was being sincere.

So we all bowed our heads again, and Elizabeth began the words of her usual prayer. "Bless us, O Lord, and these your gifts—" She stopped, cleared her throat, started again. "Bless us, O Lord—" She broke off and I heard a chair scrape back from the table, and opened my eyes just in time to see her running out of the room.

Everyone started talking at once. "What's going on?" said Raven, and Renata said, "I don't know, I think she went upstairs."

I pushed back my own chair and went up to our room.

Elizabeth was curled up in a ball on her bed, her shoulders heaving. I hadn't seen her cry since that first day we'd walked back from church together. Which, now that I thought about it, was kind of odd. I mean, she'd lost her *mother*. The only parent she'd ever known. Unless she was having private breakdowns with her guidance counselor, she must've been keeping everything incredibly corked up for the past few months.

"Hey," I said, sitting down next to her and putting a hand on her shoulder.

She slapped at my hand, hard, shocking me.

"Go away!" she said, and if my heart had skipped a beat a moment earlier when I'd walked into the room, now it threatened to jump right out of my throat. She sat up, her voice rising. "I don't need you, any of you, your stupid forgiveness and self-love and blah blah blah. You don't really believe in any of that, you don't *know* what sacrifice is, what *penance* is, you don't know anything you're talking about." Her voice broke off on a sob.

"Elizabeth, what—"

"And don't think I don't know you're talking about me!" she screamed. "You and Raven, I'm not deaf! I don't care what you think about me! I'm *trying* to live a good life—trying to do what's right—it's not easy, not easy when—" She broke off again, covering her face with her hands, crying so hard her whole body shook. Harsh, ugly, hacking sounds. I was afraid she was going to throw up.

I realized I was holding my breath, as if by doing so I could erase all the things Raven and I had said about her earlier. "Elizabeth, I'm so sorry," I started, but she cut me off.

"You don't get it, do you?" I could barely understand what she was saying through the thick tears clogging her voice. "You just *don't get it*." And she picked up her pillow and threw it across the room as hard as she could. It hit the vanity table.

Brushes, combs, bottles of perfume and nail polish went flying. She threw a book from her bedside table next. The pages fluttered as the book flew across the room, hitting the mirror, which cracked right down the middle. Then the mirror began to topple forward, as if in slow motion. I jumped up and caught it right before it hit the floor.

"*Get out!*" she screamed, and I set the mirror down and started to back out of the room, just as Dad came rushing in.

He took in the scene with one sweeping glance—the broken mirror, the book and pillow and bottles lying all over the floor. "Sweetie," he said, "I'm here. Shhh. I'm here." He went to her, where she was hunched on her bed, her face contorted and streaked with tears. She reached out for him and he wrapped his arms around her. "Shhhh," he said, "shhhhh. Daddy's here."

I crept slowly back downstairs.

"What's going on?" Mom said, meeting me at the bottom, her face pale.

"I think they need some time," I said. My ears were ringing, my voice sounded like it was coming from someone else.

"Okay," Mom said, nodding. "We'll keep the food warm and . . . we'll . . ."

I waited. We looked at each other.

"Josh!" she said, turning toward the kitchen. "What about some music?"

Everyone at the table was looking up at the ceiling, their eyes wide. They must've heard the crashing from down here.

Josh shook his head.

"Come on," Mom coaxed. "How about your Bach?" To Ruby, Renata, and Raven, she said, "Wait till you hear Josh's Bach. He's way above his grade level, playing like a high schooler. We're very excited to see the results of his competition in a couple weeks . . ." As she went on, talking faster and faster, I saw Josh shrivel in his chair.

"Hey, Mom," I said, "that reminds me." I went to the front hallway and fished in my backpack, which I'd dropped by the door after school. "I got this for you the other day." I handed her the print from the American Visionary Art Museum. I hadn't realized I was going to give it to her, but in the moment, it felt right.

Mom looked at the picture and her eyes softened. "Oh, *mjia*. Thank you. This is beautiful."

"It reminded me of you," I mumbled. "You and Josh." I didn't say, *And you and Dad.*

"Melissa!" Renata said brightly. "Why don't you play us something?"

Ruby clapped her hands. "Yes, yes! Brilliant idea. We haven't heard you play in *ages*, Melissa."

"Oh, now," Mom said. "That's because I haven't practiced in ages. I'm sure I'm as rusty as a bicycle left out in the rain."

Renata and Ruby laughed.

"Mom, go ahead," I said. "I'll watch the food in the oven and make sure nothing burns."

"Well . . ." She propped up my print against the vase of flowers in the middle of the table and went into the living room. We heard her moving milk crates around, shuffling through her sheet music. "How about some Mozart?" she called.

"Lovely!" said Ruby, and she and Renata, Raven, and Josh followed Mom into the living room. Mom warmed up with a few scales, then launched into a piece I remembered her playing a long time ago. She stumbled a few times, laughed, tried again a little slower. Soon she was picking up steam, and when she finished the Mozart she transitioned into something jazzier. I checked on the food and turned the oven temperature down, and then I went into the living room to listen, too.

By the time Dad and Elizabeth came back down, Mom was tearing up and down the keyboard. Raven and I were sitting on the couch, but Renata and Ruby had pushed the coffee table to the wall and were taking turns dancing with Josh, who was flushed but seemed to be enjoying himself.

Elizabeth's face was puffy and swollen, and she didn't make eye contact with anyone, but she appeared calmer. Dad stood still for a few moments, watching Mom from the bottom of the stairs, where she couldn't see him. Then he walked to the piano and laid his hands gently on her shoulders. Mom jumped a little and laughed, tilting her face up to look at him.

"I think we're ready to eat, although I'm sorry to interrupt this delightful concert," he said. "Would you do us the honor of more music after dinner?"

Mom smiled at him—a real smile. "Seems my fingers still remember a thing or two."

"I'll say," he said, then bent and—tentatively, I thought— dropped a kiss on her forehead. She didn't kiss him back, but she didn't push him away, either.

We filed into the kitchen and Dad served the food, and the rest of our Anti-Colonial Thanksgiving was pretty normal. As normal as an Anti-Colonial Thanksgiving can be, anyway. Afterward, Mom played more piano, and Dad danced with Ruby, Renata danced with Josh, and I danced with Raven. Elizabeth disappeared back upstairs, and Dad shook his head when I started to ask if someone should go check on her. "She needs some alone time," he said quietly. But he didn't scold me and Raven for talking about Elizabeth behind her back, so I had to assume that she hadn't told him that part.

Mom played the piano for hours that night, even after the Woodburys left, and Dad sat on the living room couch and listened. The way she kept looking over at him, the way he smiled sometimes when she'd change to a new tune, as if it were an inside joke between them, some old memory—it felt like a private thing, somehow, so I left them alone. I didn't want to go to my room either, with Elizabeth up there. So I took my laptop into the kitchen and watched a movie with my new headphones.

Elizabeth stayed upstairs for the rest of the evening, and when I finally went to bed that night, she was already asleep. Or pretending to be asleep. So I couldn't try to apologize again.

. . .

I woke up early the next morning, hearing noises down in the kitchen. A delicious smell wafted up the stairs. I shoved my feet into my slippers and wandered downstairs to investigate. I noticed that there were no blankets or pillows on the couch, as there had been for the past few months—since Elizabeth had arrived. What was going on?

Dad was making waffles and eggs and fakin' bacon, and Mom was sitting on a stool at the kitchen counter, peeling oranges and arranging the sections on a plate. They were talking quietly and laughing.

"Morning, Cadie!" said Mom, when she saw me standing by the table.

Dad turned from the stove and held his spatula aloft. I recognized the telltale signs: Dramatic Monologue Voice. "But soft! What light through yonder window breaks? It is the east, and Acadia is the sun."

"It's too early for *Romeo and Juliet*," I muttered. "What are you guys doing up so early?"

"It's nearly eight o'clock," Mom said, "and anyway, I always wake up early when I go to bed late. Don't know why." She had dark circles under her eyes, but she was smiling.

"We have something important to talk to you about," Dad added, in his normal voice. "We'll wait till everyone's down." He refused to tell me any more details, so I went upstairs and shook Josh awake, then knocked on the door of my and Elizabeth's room. I had a sinking feeling in my stomach. When parents had been feuding as long as ours had, an "important talk" wasn't usually a good thing—I had enough friends with divorced parents to know that. And yet, it was odd that Mom seemed so happy. Maybe she was just relieved to finally have an end in sight? Or—could I even dare to hope that something had changed?

And was that even what *I* wanted? It was a crappy thing to think, but: Even if Mom somehow managed to forgive Dad . . . how would that change anything between him and me? What if everyone else figured out how to move on, and I got left behind?

We all gathered at the table and Dad doled out generous portions to everyone. "Melissa," he said, "should we make our announcement now? Or after we eat?"

"Now!" I interrupted. "You can't leave us in suspense."

"Very well," said Mom, setting down her fork. "Dad and I had a long talk last night." She wasn't smiling now. My stomach twisted.

"We've had a lot of changes in this house over the past few

225

months," she continued. "Big changes. And we're all so very happy that you're part of our family now, Elizabeth." Elizabeth was looking down at her plate, and Mom reached over to squeeze her hand. Elizabeth looked up, startled.

Dad continued. "But Mom and I have been drifting away from each other, and it's hurting everyone in this family. So, we've decided that we need to take some time—" *Here it comes*, I thought, and I slid my hands under my legs to keep them from shaking. "—some time," Dad was saying, "to heal together. We're going on a vacation."

I sat on my hands, frozen. "So you're *not* getting divorced?" I burst out.

Mom reached over to put her other hand on my shoulder. "I'm so sorry that things have been rough recently. It's been difficult for all of us, and I haven't made it any easier. Dad and I have been together a long time, and we know we can fix things. We just need a chance to start over again."

Elizabeth looked like she was about to cry. "It's all my fault," she said, so quietly I barely heard her. "I'm so sorry. I know I've ruined everything—"

"Elizabeth!" Dad cut her off. "Don't say that, it's not true."

"We love you, and now we can't imagine this family without you, *mija*," Mom said to Elizabeth. My heart squeezed in a fierce and unexpected burst of pride for Mom. That was the first time I'd heard her call Elizabeth *daughter*. "Ross and I were having—relationship difficulties—long before you came to live with us," she continued. "And it's high time we dealt with that. I haven't been myself recently. In many years, in fact." She turned to Josh. "*Mijo*, Dad showed me that I've been pushing you too hard. And

226

I'm so sorry. Can you forgive me?"

Josh said, "I'm fine, Mom."

"No," said Mom, "you're not. I'm going to stop observing your lessons. You and Olga can prepare for this competition better on your own, without my interference, while we're on vacation."

Josh's eyes widened.

"Wait," I said, "when are you leaving?"

"Next week," said Mom. "Right after your play."

"But—that's the week before Josh's competition!"

"Exactly. He doesn't need me around, breathing down his neck. I've already called the Woodburys. They'd be delighted to host you—if that's all right with all of you, of course."

Elizabeth nodded. "So, where will you be going?" she asked.

Mom and Dad beamed at each other.

"A long time ago, we set a goal for ourselves to visit all the major national parks someday," Dad said, "and at this point, we're running very far behind. So, we're going to Yosemite!"

My hand spasmed and knocked over my orange juice.

"Cadie!" said Mom, jumping up to grab paper towels. "What is it? What did we say?"

"Um," I said, trying to cover my rising panic. *Mom deserves to get Dad back. This is a good thing. Stop being selfish, Acadia Rose Greenfield.* I pointed to Josh, then to myself. "Joshua Tree. Acadia Rose. *Yosemite?*"

Mom and Dad burst out laughing.

"Don't worry," Dad said, smiling around the table at all of us, "I think our family is complete just the way it is."

I forced myself to smile back, but inside, I wasn't so sure.

Was I just supposed to pretend that this would fix everything that had gone wrong? I didn't know what I wanted from Dad anymore. But this didn't seem like enough.

. . .

So it was settled. Mom and Dad were leaving right after my Sunday matinee—in fact, they were catching an airport shuttle directly from Fern Grove. Rina Crane overheard me telling Micayla and Heron this news at rehearsal on Monday night.

"Oh, cool!" she said. "So you'll be hosting the cast party, right? Parents out of town, time to party down!" She did raise-the-roof motions and danced around in a little circle.

Micayla, Heron, and I stared at her.

"Um," I said, "I don't think my parents would really—"

But Rina had already run over to Tori, Sam, Kieri, and Priya, and I heard her telling them, "Cadie's parents are going out of town and she's hosting the cast party Sunday night! Spread the news."

I looked at Micayla and Heron, who shrugged helplessly.

"We'll watch out for you," said Micayla. "It'll be fine."

Heron nodded. "Yeah, we'll be the bouncers. Anyone gets too drunk or rowdy, we kick 'em out on their asses."

My eyebrows shot up to my hairline. "You think people will bring *booze*?"

They both burst out laughing.

"Girl," said Micayla, "you are so cute sometimes. I forget you're only a sophomore."

"And a drama virgin," Heron added.

"What the hell is that?" I demanded, feeling grumpy.

"It's your first play," Heron explained. "Your first time treading the boards, as Robin would say."

"Don't remind me," I groaned. Opening night was four days away, and my stomach felt like a volcano getting ready to blow. *Gross,* I told myself. *Never be a poet.*

We had full-cast rehearsal every night that week, which meant I barely had any time at home. But when I was home, I noticed the difference in the air as soon as I opened the front door. Mom wasn't bringing work home with her anymore. She seemed to be humming constantly. And she was playing the piano again—her old favorite Beethoven sonatas, Chopin nocturnes, even Gershwin's *Rhapsody in Blue.* I couldn't believe she remembered all that music after not playing for so long. Dad was coming home early from Fine Print—Cassandra wanted to work some extra hours, he said. He and Mom went out to the grocery store together after work, and then she'd perch on a stool at the counter and sip a glass of wine while he cooked. One night, dinner wasn't ready even by the time I got home, so I went up to my room to start on homework. Ten minutes later, I flew down the stairs because I thought I heard someone shouting, and instead I found Mom and Dad roaring with laughter at the kitchen counter.

It was good to see them getting along again. I couldn't deny it.

But also, it meant I was the only one left who was still mad at Dad. And that made me feel like an island of misery that everyone else had sailed past. I was disappearing on the horizon. I was a speck. Forgotten.

It didn't help that Elizabeth still wasn't speaking to me. Not that anyone else would've noticed. She was very polite, as always, and if I asked her a direct question, she'd answer. She'd just use as few words as possible. As we were getting ready for bed one night, I tried again to apologize for what she'd overheard Raven and me saying about her on Anti-Colonial

Thanksgiving, but she just shrugged and said nothing.

I wanted to ask Dad what to do, but there was an awkward-ness between us anytime we were alone together—which didn't happen very often, since I never went to Fine Print after school anymore, what with my busy rehearsal schedule. Every time I thought about talking to him alone, one-on-one, my stomach twisted a little. I knew it wasn't fair, but I couldn't help feeling like he was a different person than I'd thought he was. And some-how, Mom forgiving him for it made me feel even weirder. What else was there that I didn't know about Dad? About Mom? They'd had lives before they were my parents—strange as that was to imagine. There were things about them I'd never know.

I couldn't tell if it was these thoughts that were keeping me awake every night, or if it was the countdown to Friday.

Opening night.

CHAPTER SIXTEEN

When Tori and Rina tried to sneak a peek at the crowd from behind the curtains, Robin almost had a stroke.

"Get away from there!" he hissed, chasing them back into the wings like they were a pair of errant geese.

He'd gathered us all backstage to do our centering exercise together. Since we were already costumed and couldn't sit on the floor, he had us do a walking meditation. We walked in a clockwise circle at the pace of a snail with our eyes closed, fingertips brushing the shoulder blades of the person in front of us, for five full minutes. Then Robin gave a short speech.

"Remember your lines, remember your cues, but remember this above all," he said. "As the Bard told us, 'All the world's a stage.' This stage you're about to cross for a couple hours tonight—it's only a tiny fragment of the larger stage where we're all playing out our parts. In the grand scheme of things, you could argue that none of it matters. Or you could argue that *since* none of it matters, *all* of it matters. Every last drop."

He pressed the palms of his hands together as if praying, and pointed the tips of his fingers at each of us in turn. "People, I wish this for you on your opening night: that you may discover that the reason why you're doing this, why you're here on a Friday night spouting words you've memorized and wearing funny costumes"—he let his voice drop—"is because every last drop of it matters to you more than anything in the world."

His words sounded oddly familiar, but I didn't have time

to think about it. At that moment, the audience fell silent—the lights must've gone down in the theater. The opening music began to play over the speakers, and Robin mouthed, *"Break a leg!"* and hustled off into the wings. I was in the very first scene. I smoothed my shaking hands over my pants—Micayla had sewn Beatrice a pair of men's trousers and a billowy blouse, instead of a dress—and walked with Priya and Kieri, playing Hero and Leonato, to center stage, where we were supposed to be when the curtain went up.

Opening night was electric. Lines went zinging back and forth. We tossed cues at each other like Frisbees. Sam forgot a few of his lines (shocker), and at one point Jem Mark, playing Don Pedro, completely missed an entrance and there was a moment of panic onstage. But Rina managed to improvise until he came running out of the wings. We were all impressed.

Mostly, though, I was caught up in my scenes with Zephyr. I'd been trembling when the curtain went up, but once I started speaking, I slipped into my Beatrice skin and lost my Acadia nervousness. The play seemed to sling Zephyr and me from one Beatrice-Benedick scene to the next, and each time, we brought something fresh to our dialogue, some new energy we'd never quite reached in rehearsal. Our stage kiss earned us hoots and cheers from the audience, who I'd nearly forgotten about in the intensity of our scene up until that moment. Even with his thumb against my lips, his mouth suddenly felt unnervingly close to mine, and my heart thudded so that the breathlessness of my next lines was entirely real.

After that, I floated on a rush of adrenaline until curtain calls. Renata, Ruby, and Raven did throw flowers at me when I came out to take a bow, and I heard Dad yelling, "Yeahhhhhhh,

Greenfield!" I knew Farhan had asked Elizabeth to go to opening night with him, but I didn't see them in the audience in the brief glimpse I got between bows.

I saw them after the show, though, waiting in the lobby with Dad.

"Cadie!" Dad yelled the minute he saw me, running forward to throw his arms around me. "Oh my god. My little girl. You were *incredible*." Weatherman Voice, but muffled. I finally pulled away, and my throat tightened when I saw the tears streaming down his face.

The Woodburys and Max Frisch were there, too. Mom and Josh were at Josh's dress rehearsal—even after everything that had changed over the past week or so, Dad hadn't been able to convince Mom to move the rehearsal. Farhan had his arm around Elizabeth and was whispering something in her ear. Which . . . actually didn't bother me. I poked at the Elizabeth-stole-Farhan feeling in the pit of my stomach, and nothing happened. Huh.

Then I saw that Max and Raven were holding a giant sign that said *Acadia Rose Greenfield Fan Club*. And they'd made baseball hats, too, with my initials on them. The hats said *ARG*. Something Mom and Dad had not considered when they'd named me, unfortunately.

"You *guys*," I said, "you're so embarrassing." But the afterglow from the show was still pumping through my veins, and there was a warm thrill in my chest at all the attention. "I'm just going to run backstage and change," I said, "and I'll be right back out. Don't go anywhere, Fan Club."

"We made reservations at Tamber's," Raven called after me. "Celebratory masala and milk shakes?"

"Perfect, I'm starving!" I called back.

Almost everyone was still out in the lobby, greeting their families and friends. I didn't expect anyone to be backstage when I turned down the hallways toward the dressing rooms.

So I was startled to see two people standing just outside the dressing room door. Robin and Zephyr. Robin was grinning but his face was streaked with tears, just like Dad's, and he gripped Zephyr's shoulders tightly with both hands.

I must've let out some noise of surprise. They both looked over at me, and Robin quickly wiped his eyes.

"I'm—I'm sorry—," I stammered.

Robin looked at Zephyr, then at me. "You haven't told her, have you?"

Told me what?

Zephyr shook his head. "I'm sorry, Cadie, I'm so sorry. Dad and I didn't want anyone to know—"

"Dad?"

He nodded. "Robin's my dad. We didn't want people—the other kids—to think he was playing favorites or anything, casting me as the lead—"

"And I don't," Robin broke in. "I give each role to the student I think will be able to do it justice, grow in it, bring something new—"

"And I wanted to tell you," Zephyr continued, "but I was worried—"

"Whoa." I held up my hands. "Whoa, whoa, whoa. It's fine. I just need a minute here."

Robin. Was Zephyr's dad. Zephyr Daniels's dad was Robin . . . Goodfellow?

"But he's a Goodfellow and you're a Daniels," I pointed out, feeling thick.

My brain was doing somersaults, trying to wrap itself around this new configuration of reality. And some little voice was going, *Is there one single adult in my life who is who I think they are? Is there* anyone *I can trust?*

"It's my other dad's last name," Zephyr explained.

"I didn't change my name because of stage business," Robin said, "and it took us forever to get legally married, anyhow."

"Oh!" I said, then realized that sounded pretty inadequate. "Congratulations!" I added.

Robin laughed. "Well, thank you." He tousled Zephyr's hair. "Now, if we're past all the awkwardness, I'd like to say officially, on the record, that you two *smashed* it through the park tonight."

I felt my whole face break into a grin. "We kind of did, didn't we?"

Zephyr grinned back. "Indeed, milady Beatrice." He stepped toward me, as if he were going to give me a hug.

But just then, I heard footsteps in the corridor behind me, and I turned to see two people coming toward us—a man with dark skin and hair, dressed in a blue pinstripe suit, and a slim white girl. The man threw himself at Zephyr and Robin, wrapping them both in his arms. "Zeph!" he said. He had a strong British accent. "You *smashed* it! I mean, right through the bloody park!"

Zephyr extricated himself. "Cadie, this is my dad Julian."

Julian turned and noticed me. "Oh, and you! *You!* Perfection, Beatrice, you were *simply* perfection." He grabbed my hand and pumped it up and down. "So pleased to meet you. Robin talks about you all the time, now I know why."

I felt my cheeks grow warm. "Thank you. Pleased to meet you, too."

"And this," said Zephyr, clearing his throat and putting his

235

arm around the girl who'd followed Julian down the hallway, "is my girlfriend. Ava, this is Acadia."

Ava gave me a smile that didn't quite reach her eyes. Her very beautiful large blue eyes, outlined in dark eyeliner. She was pale, even paler than Raven, with dyed-black hair cut stylishly just below her chin, and she was wearing a very low-cut black dress and white go-go boots. She looked like everything I'd imagined her to be: sophisticated, chic, gorgeous. She had *New York* written all over her.

"You did an excellent job," she said to me. "Congratulations." She did not extend a hand to shake.

"Thanks," I said. "Well, I'd better be going. I have to change and then we're all going out to dinner, my family and my fan club. You know, just my friends, but they're calling themselves my fan club tonight. They're being silly." I willed my mouth to stop talking.

Ava turned to Zephyr and flung her arms around his neck. "Baby, you were *amazing*," she purred, and kissed him full on the mouth.

I backed away, then ducked into the dressing room and leaned against the counter. My head was spinning. Probably from low blood sugar. I had to get something to eat. *Robin is Zephyr's dad. Focus on that.*

Micayla banged through the dressing room door. "Cadie! There you are, I'm collecting costumes. Holy Moses, did you see that girl out there wrapped around Zephyr? She step out of *Glamour* magazine?"

I grimaced as I stripped off my costume and grabbed my street clothes. "That's his girlfriend. From New York."

Micayla nodded. "And I guess that's Robin's boyfriend out there with them?"

"His husband." I pressed my lips together. Robin and Zephyr's secret was safe with me.

"*Love* his accent. And that suit!" Micayla continued to chatter away, about the show, her plans with the tech crew that night. "And any word about the party on Sunday?"

I shook my head and groaned. "Don't mention it. Maybe everyone will forget."

· · ·

No one forgot, though. In fact, it seemed like the cast party at my house was all anyone wanted to talk about the next night, after our second performance. People kept asking me what they should bring, where I lived, what time they should come over.

I almost wanted to cancel it—to tell people that my parents had decided to stay home after all, or that I was going out of town too. But by now it seemed too late. Everyone would know that I was lying, that I was chickening out. *Besides,* a tiny part of my brain said, *so what if Mom and Dad find out? What are you so scared of, Acadia Greenfield? So what, if Mom and Dad trust you to be a perfect little daughter—what have they done to deserve your good behavior?*

Friday night, I'd had a nightmare that I was driving down a steep ice-covered hill and the brakes weren't working. The car went faster and faster, and I kept stomping on the brake, but the pedal had turned into a sponge that just squelched under my foot. I'd jerked myself awake, sweating and freezing at the same time, to find that I'd kicked all the covers off the bed.

Ava wasn't at the Saturday performance. I didn't want to

237

ask Zephyr about it, but I felt a little lighter when I saw him standing with only Robin and Julian backstage after the show. "Hey!" I said. "I think a bunch of us are going out to the Charmery tonight, want to come?" I'd addressed the three of them, but Robin and Julian shook their heads.

"Thanks," said Robin, "but I never go out with the cast after a show. Ruins the fun for the students."

"Yes, thanks kindly," said Julian. "You should go, Zeph," he added, giving him a little shove. "Do you good to add on a few pounds. You're turning into a beanstalk this year."

"All right," said Zephyr. "I'm in." He checked to make sure no one was around before giving his dads a quick double hug, then followed me out to the lobby.

"Benediiiick!" Rina yelled. "Over here! Come with us!" She waved wildly, giggling. Sam had one arm around her and one arm around Tori. The three of them were acting so giddy, I wondered if it was really just water in the water bottles they were sipping.

"I'm riding over with Micayla and Heron," I said, "if you want to join us instead."

"I think they might need a driver," Zephyr said, frowning at Rina, Sam, and Tori. "I'll meet you guys there."

The whole cast showed up, which meant we packed the tiny Charmery. Heron and Micayla and I shared an enormous sundae. Priya and Kieri sat with us, too. Priya ordered a double scoop of Fat Elvis (banana, peanut butter, and marshmallow), and Kieri had a cup of Vegan Chai Coconut Cookie. Zephyr just ordered a hot chocolate, which he took to a corner table where Troy and Davis from the tech crew were having a heated discussion about something that sounded like a video game. I caught the words

"battle ninja," "fighter pilot," "super jets," and "donkey tiara."
Or maybe I'd misheard that last part.

Zephyr seemed distracted—I tried to wave him over to our
table, but he didn't see me. He was looking down at his phone
a lot. I wondered if it was Ava texting him. He left early, after
making sure that Rina, Sam, and Tori could get other rides home.
They had stopped drinking from their water bottles and the ice
cream seemed to have sobered them up, which was a good thing—
I didn't want them to get us kicked out of the Charmery.

I felt my stomach twist, and I wasn't sure if it was the lactose
or not. If they'd managed to get that wasted while still on school
property, what was the party at my house going to be like?

· · ·

The Sunday matinee was our best performance yet. I think we
all felt the urgency of the last time, and everyone gave a hundred and ten percent. Rina, as Dogberry, was so perfectly over-
the-top that I got a cramp in my stomach from laughing silently
in the wings. Tori and Priya drew out the Claudio-Hero rejection
scene at the altar a little longer than necessary, but not enough to
make it cheesy—just enough to really milk the audience. I heard
quite a few sniffles as Zephyr and I bent over Priya's limp body
and Friar Francis advised us to pretend that Hero was dead, so
that her father, Leonato, would repent for the terrible way he and
Claudio had treated her. Then Zephyr and I had our big scene
where Benedick reveals his love for Beatrice, and the stage kiss.
I thought Zephyr pulled away a little sooner than usual, oddly.
Everyone else was drawing things out, savoring, trying to make
the show last a little longer before it all evaporated.

Because that's what was happening, and we all knew it. After the curtain came down, we'd never be able to perform this play again. Not even if we gathered all the same people together and wore all the same costumes and recited all the same lines. The momentum came to a halt with that last round of applause, and even if we tried to re-create this production someday, it would never be the same. We would never be the same cast we were today on this stage.

Way to be a faucet-face like Dad, I told myself, trying to keep my eyes dry. Rina was taking her curtain call and the audience was cheering. She bowed, spun around, and did a cartwheel off into the wings. Then it was time for Benedick and Beatrice's curtain call. Zephyr grabbed my hand and we ran out onstage. The audience erupted for us. We took a bow, then another. Then he released my hand and I thought, *Well, now it's really over.*

As I followed him off stage, I wondered if he'd even come to the cast party tonight. He didn't seem to like big groups of people.

I made my way out to the lobby, where all the Woodburys, plus Max, were waiting. Mom, Dad, and Josh were right next to them. I didn't see Elizabeth—maybe she hadn't come.

"That was pretty cool," Josh mumbled, brushing the curls off his forehead and smiling at me. "You kicked butt." And from Josh, that was a full-blast marching band of a compliment. I grinned back and pulled him in for a hug until he squirmed.

"Oh, Cadie," Mom said. "You were *wonderful.* I wish I'd been able to see it more than once." She hesitated. "I wish . . . well, not that it matters now."

I hugged her, too. "It's fine, Mom. Really."

She held me a moment, stroking my hair. I'd forgotten what a great hugger Mom was.

Then she cleared her throat, pulled out a to-do list, and

started spouting last-minute reminders: "Now, let's see. Don't forget to turn down the heat when you all go over to the Woodburys' tonight. But not all the way off, the pipes will freeze."

"Mom!" I said. "I *know*. Go on vacation. Everything will be fine."

Dad looked at his watch. "We were supposed to leave for the airport seven minutes ago, honey."

"Right," she said, and gave me another big hug. "*Mija*, you were incredible, absolutely incredible. Be good. Call us if you need anything. We'll have our cell phones on whenever we have a signal."

She aimed a final hug and kiss at Josh, who ducked.

"We won't call you, Mom," I said. Not making eye contact with Dad. "We'll be fine. You should go forget about the outside world for a while. Besides, I think national parks have a ban on cell phones these days, or something."

"Okay," Mom said, taking a deep breath. "Well, see you next weekend, then." They were flying back just in time for Josh's competition on Sunday afternoon.

Dad finally gave me a hug, too, and slipped something into my hand—a thin envelope. "Read that later," he said, and then before I had a chance to figure out what to say, they were gone.

Ruby and Renata took Josh home with them. I'd told them I wanted to hang out with the cast for a while and Elizabeth would drive us over later—she had her provisional license now, which meant she could drive family members. Mom and Dad had taken a cab to the airport and left us the Comet in case we needed to go somewhere.

"I still can't believe no one's figured this out yet," I whispered to Raven and Max, even though all the parents were already gone.

"Don't sound so fatalistic," said Raven. "It's going to be fine."

She and Max were coming to the cast party—even though they weren't involved in the play. "You *have* to come!" I'd told them. "I don't know how to throw a party! I don't even *want* to be throwing a party! Heron and Micayla already volunteered to be bouncers."

Raven had rolled her eyes at me. "Seriously, Cadie, it's a group of Quaker high school drama nerds. How much trouble can they really cause?"

I went backstage to pack up my makeup and clothes. We were all coming back to strike the set Monday night, but Micayla, who was going to take me home, was still busy collecting and putting away costumes. So I figured I'd clean up my space in the dressing room while I was waiting for her.

First, though, I sat in a chair at the dressing room mirror and opened Dad's note. All the other girls in the cast were still out in the lobby, hugging each other and crying, or talking to their friends and families, so I had the dressing room to myself.

Cadiest, the note began, and I had to swallow a lump that rose suddenly in my throat.

> *Cadiest,*
>
> *First of all, I want to say in writing how
> unbelievably proud of you I am. I cried at every
> single performance. As I'm sure you could've guessed.
> My baby girl has grown into a talented young woman
> who can become anyone she wants on stage, who
> can spout poetry, who can make a grown man weep.
> How did that happen???*
>
> *But that's not why I wrote this note, really. I want*

*to say this in writing, too: I hate the way things have
been between me and you these past few months. I
know you're angry. I understand why. But I still can't
stand it. When Mom and I come back, can we do
something about it? I think we're long overdue for some
quality Dad-Cadie time. We can go down to DC to see
a play, just me and you. Or we can have a day in the
Inner Harbor. Or—anything you want. Just tell me how
to fix things. Please. I miss you.*

 Love,

 Dad

 *P.S. I don't know how much it matters, because
things are the way they are, but I'm so sorry, Cadie. I'm
sorry I let you down. I'm sorry that something I did a
long time ago has turned your world upside down. I'm
sorry I'm not the dad you thought I was.*

I sat there in front of my mirror and stared at it without seeing
my reflection, clutching Dad's note in both hands.

The dressing room door banged open, and Tori, Rina, Kieri,
and Priya came in, talking loudly. It was a good thing everyone
was so emotional after the last show, because no one bothered me
to ask why I had tears running down my face.

. . .

After Micayla dropped me off on her way home, I ran upstairs to
change. It was five o'clock. I had two hours to—well, do whatever
you were supposed to do to get ready for a cast party.

I opened the door to my room, and almost had a heart attack.
The place looked ransacked. "Oh my god, what *happened?*" I said
out loud.

Elizabeth stuck her head out of the closet, which nearly gave me a second coronary arrest. "Hi," she said flatly. "I'm just packing."

I clutched at my chest and crossed the room to sit on my bed. "I didn't realize you were here. Sorry. Wait, packing for what?"

She raised an eyebrow at me. "For our week at the Woodburys' house."

I surveyed the wreckage. "You're bringing *all* these clothes?"

She shrugged. "Figured I'd clean out my side of the closet while I was at it. Reorganize."

"Okay . . ." I realized I hadn't said anything to Elizabeth about the cast party. I'd assumed she'd drive me to Raven's, but hadn't spoken to her about tonight at all. Hadn't even remembered that she'd be here, too. Unless I managed to get her out of the house somehow. "Um," I said. "What are you doing tonight? Are you going out with Farhan or anything?"

"No." She had her back to me, studying the few items left on her side of the closet. Then she ripped everything off the hangers and tossed it all on the bed.

"Okay," I said again. "Well. Um. I'm sort of, um, having some friends over."

"Oh?" She didn't sound interested.

"Yeah. Drama friends. It's sort of, um, a cast party."

Elizabeth spun around to face me, her eyes wide. "A party? Without Ross and Melissa here? They were okay with that?"

I squirmed. "It kind of happened without—I didn't mean to invite—well, Mom and Dad don't know."

She studied my face for a minute. Then she shrugged. "Fine. Whatever. I'll probably just stay up here and clean."

I let out my breath. "Sure, that's fine. If you want. I mean, or

244

feel free to hang out downstairs if you want to."

She nodded, then started folding and sorting the clothes in the heap on her bed.

I sat there for another moment or two, but she didn't look at me or say anything else. So I got up and stuffed a few things into my overnight bag, then changed into a pair of leggings and my unicorn hoodie dress. It made my curves look good—not too wide, not too jiggly—plus it was good luck. And I was going to need all the luck I could get tonight.

Then I went downstairs to cast-party-proof the house.

Micayla and Heron pulled up in Micayla's car, with Raven and Max in the back seat. "We're here early to help you set up!" said Raven, jumping out of the car and hefting two enormous shopping bags of what looked like chips, salsa, and soda bottles out of the trunk. Max followed her and grabbed two more bags. Heron and Micayla had also brought bags of food plus paper plates and red plastic Solo cups.

Great. I was having a Solo-cup party.

And then Sam Shotwell arrived, with Rina, Tori, Kieri, Priya, and an armload of six-packs. Yes, the kind with beer in them. Troy and Davis followed, bearing a bottle of vodka each, and before I knew it there was a full-scale party under way. People were draped over the couches, perched on the kitchen counter, leaning against all the walls. Someone, probably Troy or Davis, had set up a portable speaker in the living room and music was blasting. I heard voices from the basement, so I knew the party had spilled downstairs, too. Where had all these kids come from? Someone must have invited non-cast members. It seemed like every time I turned around, I saw someone new.

Sam Shotwell had set up a beer pong game on the coffee

table, and a couple guys I didn't recognize were playing. How had I ever thought Sam was cute? He was such an *oaf*.

I jumped at the sound of something going *crash* and hurried toward the kitchen.

"Relax, a cooler got knocked over," said Micayla, coming up behind me. "It was empty. No one's broken anything yet." She held out a plate of chips and salsa. "Hungry?"

I took a chip. "Not really."

"Aww, come on," she said. "Have a little fun. It's your party, after all."

"I just want everyone to leave before something horrible happens . . ."

"Here." She shoved a Solo cup under my nose.

I took it, suspiciously. "What's in this?"

She *tsk*ed at me. "Hey, have a little faith. It's a root beer float. I brought three quarts of vanilla, chocolate, and mocha swirl from the Charmery."

"I love you," I said, glugging it.

"Okay, I'm going to hang out with Troy for a bit, see if he's as boring as the last time I actually talked to him."

"Ha," I said.

Micayla sighed. "Go try and have some fun. For real. I've got a plan—I'm hiding the beer can by can, when no one's looking, stashing it all under the kitchen sink. Bet I can dry this crowd out of here in an hour. Ninety minutes tops."

"Godspeed," I said, and drifted out onto the back porch.

Someone was already there. He turned at the sound of the door shutting behind me, and I was surprised to see that it was Zephyr.

"Hey," I said. "Fancy finding you out here."

"What's that supposed to mean?" It was almost dark, but I could see him smiling in the light spilling from the kitchen window.

"Just—you don't seem like the social type."

He shrugged. "Depends who the company is, I guess."

"Oh, so you're a snob? Is that what you're saying?"

He laughed. "It's okay to drop the whole Beatrice thing now, you know."

Somehow I didn't feel like laughing. "Yeah. I wish . . ." I trailed off, not sure how to finish the sentence.

"Hmm?" he prompted. "Wish what?"

I sighed. "That it wasn't over."

He didn't say anything, so I went on. "It all went by so *quick*, you know? Feels like the auditions were just yesterday."

"I know," he said.

I went to the porch railing and leaned my elbows on it, looked up at the sky. A phrase came into my head. "Inevitable and only."

"What?" Zephyr leaned closer to me.

"That thing Robin's always telling us—oh my god, I mean, your dad—Robin, your dad." I laughed a little. "That's still so weird. It's amazing. And it seems, I don't know, *right*. But also very, very weird." I almost felt like I was drunk, too, even though all I'd had was Micayla's root beer float. It was a mixture of the chilly woodsmoke-scented air and the warmth of Zephyr standing so close to me I could feel his body heat. And it was all the feelings tumbling around inside me—feelings about Dad's note, about the play being over, about Elizabeth. Words were tumbling out, and I was too tired to try to stop them.

"Inevitable and only," I repeated. "Remember? How if you're really listening, there's only one true response to each cue, and that's the line that's written for you to say. Maybe that's like life, too."

"That's bullshit," said Zephyr abruptly, and I looked at him, startled out of my trance. "Sorry," he said, "it's just—I know how much you like my dad, and yeah, he's a great teacher, a great director. He's a great dad, too. But he's so *frustrating* sometimes."

"What do you mean?"

"He wants me to go to college for theater. Not astrophysics. Thinks I'm throwing away my talent."

Something stirred in my memory—Robin muttering *Too much talent to waste.*

"He doesn't get it," said Zephyr. "I *love* the stage. I'm just trying to be practical, too. But he gave up everything for the stage—his family, his home—he's devoted his whole life to it. And I think he takes it personally that I don't want to follow in his footsteps."

"But—I heard that he ran away from home for other reasons—"

"Yeah, he did. His family sucked, his whole situation was terrible. But still." Zephyr sighed. "Julian understands. He thinks I'm doing the right thing. I hear them fighting about it sometimes after they think I've gone to bed. I hate that I'm driving a wedge between them."

There was a moment of silence.

"I get that," I said softly.

"I know you do," he said, just as quietly.

"Inevitable and only," I said again, because I wasn't sure what else to say. I felt like I was stuck on repeat. "Do you really think we get just this one life? This is it, our only shot? And yet it's all going to end, that's inevitable—what's that *Macbeth* line? 'Life's but a walking shadow'—"

Zephyr finished the quote for me: "'A poor player that struts and frets his hour upon the stage, and then is heard no more.'"

"Yeah. We get our time, and then we're done. I mean, seriously?"

"No fair," Zephyr agreed. "No fair at all."

"And what about fate?" I said, because I couldn't seem to stop talking, because he was so warm standing there right next to me. "Is everything we *do* inevitable, too? What if every action is the only possible continuation of the things we've already done? I mean, do we really get *any* choices about anything? Ever?"

Zephyr flung his arms up toward the sky, as if gesturing at all the stars and galaxies up there, all the other worlds that weren't this one. "I think we do. Otherwise, I can't wrap my head around it all. My brain feels like it'll explode."

And then somehow when he lowered his arms they ended up around my waist, and my hands crept up to his chest, and we were staring at each other in the faint light from the kitchen window. We'd been this close before, on stage, but this felt completely different.

"I'm glad you came tonight," I said, trying to dilute the tension. He didn't respond, just looked at me.

I tried again. "Zephyr—" But I couldn't think of anything to say next.

There was no inevitable and only next line.

So I kissed him.

It was nothing like the stage kiss. His mouth was warm, warmer than I could've imagined, and it felt alive—not like a thumb, not at all. His lips *moved*, and then I realized I could let my lips move too, and his mouth was so soft—

I pulled away.

He cupped my face with one hand and pulled me back, and we kissed again.

And then I pulled away again, and ran into the house.

He had a girlfriend.

Zephyr had a girlfriend, and I knew that, I'd *met* her, and I'd kissed him anyway. And he'd let me. But I'd started it.

I grabbed a blue can off the kitchen counter, popped the tab, and took a swig. *Ugh.* The warm, bitter beer tore a fizzy path down my esophagus. I chugged more of it. Forced myself to finish the can.

Zephyr didn't follow me in off the porch.

My head spinning, my heart thumping so hard I thought it might crack a rib, I pounded up the stairs to my room. So it turned out I *was* the daughter who was most like Dad after all. Deep down, where it mattered. *You're the one who's indifferent to betrayal. Just like Dad.*

Dizzy and nauseated, I flung open the door of my room.

Elizabeth leaped off her bed with a little scream.

Leaped away from the person lying on the bed next to her, shirt half-unbuttoned. Who'd been holding her when I'd walked in, their limbs intertwined. Who was now sitting up and fumbling with buttons, wiping a hand across her mouth.

Yes, *her* mouth.

The person who had been making out with Elizabeth on her bed was not Farhan. It was Heron Lang.

CHAPTER SEVENTEEN

Micayla was right—after the alcohol disappeared, the party shriveled. She and Raven stayed to help me clean things up. I wasn't sure what had happened to Heron. After I opened the door on her and Elizabeth, I ran back down the stairs and popped the top off a second beer. Micayla raised an eyebrow, but didn't say anything. I curled up on the floor behind the kitchen counter and hid, my face burning, and drank about half of it, until I couldn't tell whether my face was still burning or not. I didn't see Zephyr again—he must've left.

When the house was clean and all the furniture was back in place, Micayla said, "Well, Heron got a ride home with Troy and Davis for some reason. So unless you need anything else . . ."

"No, we're fine," I said, noticing that my tongue felt thick. It was hard to make my lips say words. "Thank you *so* much."

She gave me a hug and took my half-empty can of beer away from me. "Congrats, you survived hosting your first cast party. Drink some water."

"First and last," I said, dully. "I hope." My head felt like a balloon—light and wobbly. I wanted it to stop. I dutifully drank the glass of water Micayla handed me.

"Are you sure you don't want me to stick around?" she asked.

"Nah," I said. "I'll be fine. We have to go. Renata will get worried. Raven, can you go upstairs and tell Elizabeth we need to leave?"

251

"Okay . . . ," she said, giving me a questioning look, but I didn't explain why I couldn't just go talk to Elizabeth myself.

Raven came down a minute later by herself, holding my bag. "Elizabeth said she'd follow us in a few minutes. I guess your parents left her the car keys?"

So Micayla dropped off Raven and me at the Woodburys', and a few minutes later, Elizabeth pulled into their driveway in the Comet. I was just setting down my bag in the spare bedroom when Renata bustled her in.

"You don't mind sharing, do you?" asked Renata. There was a big comfy queen-sized bed with purple satin sheets and about a million throw pillows. Josh was already sleeping downstairs, on the couch.

"I don't mind," I said. By now, my head was starting to feel normal again, and I didn't think I sounded tipsy anymore. I hoped.

Elizabeth was avoiding eye contact. She looked like she'd rather be on the other end of the house from me—or, preferably, in a whole different state. But she didn't say anything.

"Well, then, I think you're all set, girls!" said Renata. "Let me know if you need anything at all. Lovely to have you here."

Raven, who had been hovering by the door, said, "Do you want to go to bed right now, though? They just put *Gilmore Girls* on Netflix, if you want to watch—"

"Raven, it is a *school* night," said Renata. "And very late already. Please let me at least pretend to be a responsible authority figure."

Raven grinned and waved at us. "Fine, nighty-night."

The moment we were alone, Elizabeth said, "I don't want to talk about it."

"Whoa," I said, "I wasn't going to—"

"I said, I *don't* want to *talk* about it," she repeated, her voice rising.

"I don't, either!" I said, holding up both hands. "I'm fine with pretending it never happened, if that's what you want." Okay, now my head was killing me. I dug around in my overnight bag for some Advil.

"Fine," she said.

"Fine."

We unpacked our bags in silence, then took turns changing into our pajamas and brushing our teeth in the bathroom. When we'd both slid under the covers, I closed my eyes and my mind immediately drifted to Zephyr. To the kiss. Kis*es*. What had I been thinking? What was *he* going to think of me?

Elizabeth slipped out of bed and shuffled around in her bag. In the dim light of the room, I saw that she was getting dressed again.

"What are you doing?" I said.

She pulled a sweatshirt over her head and stuck something that looked like a lighter in her pocket. "I'm just—I need some air," she said. "I'm going out for a bit."

"Out? You mean, to smoke?"

She sighed. "Yeah, it helps me, okay? Judge all you want. If you can manage to not blab to any *more* of your friends, that'd be great, but whatever."

I winced, remembering what she'd heard me saying about her to Raven, before Anti-Colonial Thanksgiving. But I took a deep breath and kept my voice steady. "I promise, we do not have to talk about—what happened before. But just in case you want to know . . . I don't care at all."

She looked at me.

253

"I'm sorry," I said quickly. "That's not what I meant. I meant, it's your business, and I don't care who you want to make out with. And I think Heron is awesome, by the way."

Silence. Then, "It's not what you think."

"Uh . . . it's not? Because it seemed pretty clear. Not much interpretation needed, I mean." I was trying to be funny, but it wasn't working.

She shook her head. "I've never done that before. Never. I've dated boys, other boys besides Farhan, and I thought if I just tried hard enough—I thought I could—"

I sat up and looked at her. "Elizabeth, is this a religion thing? Because if you really think God would create you one way and then expect you not to—"

"It's not that," she said, thickly, and I realized she was holding back tears. "It's my *mom*."

"Oh. You mean, your mom didn't approve? And that's why you tried to—change things?"

"She never knew," Elizabeth whispered, sitting back down on the edge of the bed. "I never told her. By the time I'd figured it out—well, I think I always knew, but it took me a long time to admit it to myself—and then it took me a while to work up the courage to tell her. And then she was sick, and it didn't seem like the right time. I thought I'd wait until she was better and things were back to normal. And then she didn't—she didn't get better—" Her voice broke, but she kept going. "And I couldn't tell her, once I knew it was the end. What if it had changed everything? What if she saw me differently, or felt weird about it, and then we never had time to fix things—" She stopped and shoved a fist in her mouth, bit down on it, hard. She was shivering.

I couldn't speak. What she was going through, what she

must've been going through for the past three months, was more horrible than anything I could imagine. I hadn't known the full extent of it, but I'd known enough. And I'd barely given it a thought.

Elizabeth took her hand out of her mouth. "On good days," she said, speaking so quietly and quickly I had to lean in to hear her, "I think, it's fine, she knew me better than anyone. She probably knew, deep down, somehow. And she never said anything, so it was probably fine. But on bad days—" She moaned, and I reached over to take her shaking hands. She let me, so I held them tightly. "Cadie, I never got to ask her if it was okay, if she still loved me. If she thought God still loved me. On the bad days, it feels like I just can't *live* with that."

"Look," I said, just as quietly, "I don't know anything about God and I won't pretend that I do. But your mom loved you no matter what. If you'd told her, it wouldn't have changed *anything*. I swear."

She shook her head. "You have no right to say that. You don't have a clue what any of this is like."

I bit my lip. Fair enough. "I'm sorry," I said. "I know I don't. And I'm—I really am sorry. For what Raven and I said about you, but also for—well, for everything. I know I've—"

"You still don't get it," she interrupted. "*I hate her*. I hate her for leaving me, just when I was finally ready to talk to her about—this. I hate her and I can't forgive her, I feel like I'll *never* forgive her, and that's the worst thing of all. In the eyes of God."

I'd been so focused on my own issues with Dad, and all this time . . . Elizabeth and I were going through something more similar than I'd realized. I couldn't think of anything else to say, so I rubbed her hands some more, and that seemed to be the right thing. Or maybe she felt better just getting all of that out. Her hands, which had been rigid, relaxed slightly in mine, and gradually she stopped sobbing.

After a while, I let go and grabbed a bunch of tissues from the bedside table.

"Thanks." She blew her nose a few times, then attempted to smile. "So, now you know you're welcome to have Farhan back. I couldn't figure out any way to make him leave me alone, especially not with the way you were pretending you didn't care. But now you know."

I had the absurd urge to laugh. "Oh, that doesn't matter anymore. Really and truly."

"What do you mean?" she said, blowing her nose again. "I could tell, you *did* mind, you were so into him."

"Well, yeah. I did, at first. But I'm over him now. Let's talk about you and Heron."

Elizabeth squeaked.

"Come on!" I said. "I told you, I think she's great. So when did you, I mean, how long—"

"*Cadie*. I'm not ready for this yet."

"Right. Sorry." I sat there quietly, while she jiggled the lighter and cigarettes in her pocket. I wished I could do something—say something—fix things, in some small way. But Elizabeth was right. I had no idea what she was going through. I had barely treated her like a sister, much less welcomed her into her new home—into her own family. I'd never met her mom, I knew next to nothing about Sunshine. There was no way I could even begin to help her heal that wound.

"I'm just going to go outside for a few minutes—" she started.

And then an idea hit me. A brilliant, brilliant idea.

"Hey," I said. "Wait. Are you up for an adventure?"

"Umm . . ."

"No, don't think," I said, already out of bed and getting dressed again. "Just grab your license. And your keys."

We tiptoed down the stairs and past Josh, sleeping on the couch. But as we reached the front door, I heard his voice.

"Cadie? Where're you going?"

I turned and put a finger to my lips. "Shhh. We're going on a secret adventure."

He rubbed his eyes. "Can I come?"

Hmm . . . well, why not? "Okay, but hurry. Quietly."

As he slipped on his shoes, I noticed his cello case standing by the door, and I had another idea. "Why don't you bring your cello, too?"

He narrowed his eyes. "Where are we going?"

"I can't tell you yet. Don't you want a surprise?"

Josh is not always a fan of surprises. But then again, he's also not the type of kid to sneak off in the middle of the night. Nothing about this evening was usual.

He looked around, as if making sure Ruby and Renata were nowhere to be seen. Then he strapped his cello onto his back, over his pajamas. "Okay," he stage-whispered, his face breaking into a grin. "I'm ready."

In the car, Elizabeth fiddled with radio stations, while I took out my phone and typed in the address, palms sweaty and heart pounding. I didn't remember these streets, especially not in the dark. Maybe I should've called first. But where was the spontaneity, the spirit of adventure, in that? Josh's eyes shone in the rearview mirror, and I realized I hadn't seen him this happy or excited in a long time. Maybe I wasn't thinking straight. But I didn't care.

In this moment, it was the inevitable and only action.

After I directed Elizabeth onto the highway, I sat back and listened to the radio without actually hearing the music. This was the first time I'd driven anywhere with Elizabeth. I glanced over at her, while she was focused on the road. My throat tightened: her profile was Dad's. The headlights picked up a little misty rain, and the tires hummed on the damp highway. I switched the radio to a pop station and turned up the volume.

"Cadie," Elizabeth said, raising her voice to be heard over the music, "when are you going to tell me where we're going?"

"When we get there," I said, firmly.

She didn't look at me; she kept her eyes on the road. But she grinned.

Forty-five minutes later, we arrived at a huge purple house in a quiet neighborhood with large front yards and plenty of street parking. As Elizabeth pulled up to the curb, doubt settled into the pit of my stomach. The dashboard clock said 11:14. A few lights were still on in the downstairs windows of the house, but what if no one was awake? What if they called Mom and Dad, what if we got Renata and Ruby in trouble?

Well, we were here now. I nudged Elizabeth, who was peering out the windshield with wide eyes. "Hey, let's go."

Elizabeth jumped.

I didn't have to explain where we were. I could tell she'd figured it out, even though she'd never been here. Never seen the place where her life had started, where everything that brought us together had been set in motion.

Where, right under Mom's nose, her mother and Dad had—*Don't think about that now,* I told myself, as she slid out of the car and stood there uncertainly.

Josh took a few steps toward the house and stared at it open-mouthed for a moment. "Wait, is this—"

I nodded.

"Wow," he said softly. And then a huge grin spread across his face. "*Wow!*" He threw his arms around me, catching me completely off-guard. "Just. Wow. Can we go in?"

"Well, that's why we're here!" I said, trying to keep my voice light. "Get your cello and let's go."

I took a deep breath, then walked slowly up the steps to the front porch and rang the bell twice.

A stooped, gray-haired figure opened the door.

"Granny?" I said. "It's me, Acadia."

"Why, is that—Acadia Rose?" she cried. "Come in here and let me look at you. If you aren't all grown up! Oh my, oh my, and this must be little Joshua Tree. *Both* our precious national park babies in one night!"

Then Granny saw Elizabeth on the steps behind us. "Oh my!" she said again. "More guests! Oh, what a delightful surprise." She held the door open wide and made a wafting gesture with her arms, the wide sleeves of her enormous hand-knitted sweater flapping like wings. "Come in, friends, come in!"

Josh stepped inside, but Elizabeth hung back and I lingered next to her, suddenly unsure. What if this was a terrible idea?

"This is it," I said. "Do you want to go in?"

"I don't know . . ." she said. "I mean, are you sure we're not imposing, or—"

Granny interrupted her. "Of course not, dear. And what's your name?"

"Elizabeth," she said, and cleared her throat. "Elizabeth Jennings. I'm—um, I'm Sunshine's daughter."

Granny's jaw dropped. "Well, land sakes! Bless your heart, come in, come in."

As we followed her down the hall, she called out, "Rotem! Come see who's here. Little Acadia and Joshua Greenfield, and a surprise visitor!"

We were quickly surrounded by people, most of them in their pajamas. I remembered some of them. Ravi and Margo, a couple who'd moved in a few years before we left. An older man named Jerry, who'd been in charge of the vegetable garden and who'd built the composting toilet almost singlehandedly. A girl named Lia, who I remembered as a teenager but who was now a young woman holding a baby on her hip.

Rotem, one of the founding members of Ahimsa House and Mom's college roommate, made her way across the living room to greet us with her arms spread wide. Her dark curly hair was still streaked with different colors—pink, blue, purple—just the way I remembered it. I'd modeled my own hair after Rotem's.

"Acadia!" she cried. "What a lovely surprise! Look at you! It's been way too long. How's Ross, how's Missy? How come you guys never visit us?"

I returned her hug, but I didn't know what to say. *Because our lives are totally different now? Because my mom is Dr. Laredo-Levy, not the Missy you remember?*

"And you are . . . ?" Rotem asked, turning to Elizabeth.

"Can you believe it?" Granny said, squeezing Elizabeth's shoulders. "This is *Sunshine's* little girl."

Rotem gasped.

Then I heard Josh tuning his cello.

He had slipped away from all the people and was sitting in the middle of the big yellow couch in the living room, cello

260

between his knees, oblivious to everything else. He started playing Bach. The Prelude to the first suite, the most well-known of all the movements of the Bach suites: a crowd-pleaser. Josh was trying to please the crowd? It certainly seemed to be working. Three little kids—I didn't recognize them—started dancing around on the living room rug. I couldn't believe they were all still up so late at night, but then again, Ahimsa House had never been big on enforcing rules like reasonable bed-times. Six or seven adults gathered around, listening, nodding or swaying along to the music and smiling.

Elizabeth and Rotem were deep in conversation. They looked serious. Probably Rotem was asking about Elizabeth's mom . . . I didn't want to intrude, so I perched on the back of Josh's couch and listened to the music.

So far, no one had asked us about our sudden middle-of-the-night appearance, why we'd arrived unannounced, or where our parents were. Somehow, I didn't think they would. This was Ahimsa House: the doors were always open, the teakettle was always full, there was always an extra bed or pullout couch for someone who needed a place to sleep.

True, it was more chaotic than I'd remembered. There were kids running around, toys and books all over the floor, a sweet-smelling incense mixed with the more acrid smell of a roomful of people who may or may not have been wearing deodorant. But it was still Ahimsa House, the place I'd grown up. Granny was heading toward us with a plate of what looked like oatmeal–carob-chip cookies.

Josh had switched from Bach to folk songs, and then a few pop tunes people requested. I'd never seen Josh take requests before—I didn't even know he knew those songs. People were clapping and

261

singing along and Josh glowed like the varnish on his instrument. He only knew this place from the stories I'd told him. And yet, he looked like he belonged here. As if we'd never left.

I pulled out my phone to take a picture and saw that I'd missed a call. From Zephyr, just a few minutes ago. As I stared at the phone, frowning, it started to buzz again.

I stood up and made my way into the kitchen. It was warm in there, and quieter. I answered the call. "Hello?"

"Cadie! God, I'm so glad you answered. I thought maybe you were ignoring my calls."

I didn't know what to say. Why was he calling me? To tell me how angry he was that I'd kissed him? Or how angry his *girlfriend* was?

"About tonight," I started. "I'm really, really sorry."

"Sorry?"

I wasn't sure if he was just repeating my last word, or if he hadn't heard me, but I kept talking, before I lost my nerve. "Yeah, of course, I don't know what got into me. I was a total idiot. Can we just forget it happened?"

He was quiet for a moment. "Okay, if that's what you'd like. But I think you might want to hear what I have to say first—"

"No, please," I interrupted. "I'm sorry, I know I shouldn't have done it, I just met your girlfriend, I'm a jerk. Please, just forget about it."

"But that's what I want to tell you. Cadie, I broke up with her."

"Because of me? Did she find out? Zephyr, I'm so sorry—"

"Cadie, listen to me. I broke up with her tonight. I called her right after I got home from your place. I didn't want to do it over the phone but—we both knew, we couldn't keep going like that. The long distance wasn't working, we're both too busy. We've been fighting constantly for, like, a month. And besides, Ava already told me she could see that we, I mean me and you, obviously had—you know, chemistry or whatever, on stage. We had a big fight about it last night. And I admitted it, that I had, you know, uh, feelings for you." I'd never heard Zephyr stumble around verbally like this before. "Cadie? You still there?"

Something was soaring in my chest, and I almost thought I wouldn't be able to speak in a normal-pitched voice. "I'm here," I managed.

Chemistry or whatever . . . you know, uh, feelings for you. It wasn't exactly the most romantic or eloquent line ever written. But I'd take it.

And yet—no, I couldn't, I didn't deserve this. "It doesn't feel right. We shouldn't have, you know, done that while you were still—with Ava." Why was it so hard to say *kissed* out loud to Zephyr? "I didn't mean for that to happen. It doesn't feel like the right way to do this."

"Hey. Look. Good people make mistakes, okay? I don't feel good about the way it happened, either. I mean, kissing you was not part of the plan for tonight, believe me. But that doesn't mean I'm not glad it happened." He paused. "Did that make sense? What I'm trying to say is . . . I *am* glad. I wanted it, too."

Good people make mistakes.

Like Dad?

And then, the weirdest thought of all: *Maybe I'm not exactly who I thought I was.*

I cleared my throat. "Well. Technically, I kissed *you*. So it's really my fault."

He laughed. "The first time. But I definitely kissed you back."

I felt myself blushing and was glad he couldn't see. "So. Um. What does this all mean?"

"It means . . ." He took a deep breath. "I'm asking you to give me a fresh start. Because I want to make a plan where kissing you *is* part of the plan."

"Oh!" was my brilliant (inevitable, only) response. "Like what?"

"Well, I was thinking we could begin by catching the last *Virginia Woolf* next weekend. Unless you're sick of it. They're also doing a whole show of ten-minute one-acts down at Single Carrot Theatre that I want to check out, and there's a new musical opening at the Round House called *Improvica!* that sounds so terrible it might be awesome, and—"

"Yes," I said. "All of it. That all sounds great."

He laughed again. "So, Friday night? Pick you up at six?"

"Sure!" I wasn't sure what to say after that. "So, um, I'll see you Friday! And, you know, probably in school this week, since it's such a tiny school and all. Oh, and tomorrow night, for striking the set, of course." I willed my tongue to stick to the roof of my mouth before any more words could escape my throat. Zephyr didn't need to hear a list of every single time we might cross paths before our date on Friday night.

Our date. Our first real *date.*

"See you tomorrow," he said.

"Yes! Right. See ya."

I stared at my phone after he'd hung up, until the screen went dark. Then someone pushed open the door to the kitchen behind me. It was Elizabeth.

"There you are!" she said. "Cadie, this place is *rad*. Is that the right hippie lingo?" Then she saw my face. "What happened?"

I took a deep breath. I *had* to tell someone. "I kissed Zephyr tonight. At the party. And he broke up with his girlfriend, and we're going on a real date."

"Whoa," said Elizabeth. "You. Kissed. Zephyr? Like, Zephyr from the play?"

"And I had a beer, well a beer and a half, and it was *awful*, I don't know why people like it."

Elizabeth grinned, but she didn't interrupt.

So I barreled on. "And—and also it's just like I remembered here. I'm so glad we're all here, I mean except Mom and Dad, but that's all right because they're off fixing things which is good, and—it's just, a lot of stuff is happening—" I couldn't keep going, because tears were clogging my voice.

Elizabeth reached out as if to take my hand, and before I could overthink it, I threw my arms around her. We'd never hugged before. She smelled like shampoo and vanilla and the hug was so warm and comforting I thought I might melt.

She pulled back a little to look at me, and when she smiled, her whole face shone.

"I'm so glad we came here—thank you for bringing me. That woman, Rotem, she knew my mom really well, and she said I'm welcome to come down here anytime I want, just to hang out."

I wiped my eyes. "Oh, good. That's exactly what I was hoping would—" I broke off, as something brushed against my leg. I looked down.

A midnight-black cat gazed up at me and rubbed against my legs again, meowing.

"Sorry, he wants to be fed," said a girl I didn't recognize, bustling into the kitchen and taking a bag out of a cupboard. "Here, Chuz." She rattled some kibble into a dish.

"Chuz?" I echoed.

"Yeah," said the girl, "it's short for Martin Chuzzlewit. I don't know who named the cats around here, but they're all named after Dickens characters. This guy's really old. He's been here forever." She bent and stroked his head. "See the gray whiskers?"

Martin Chuzzlewit. Who else would name a cat Martin Chuzzlewit, except—

I glanced at Elizabeth. She raised her eyebrows, but I wasn't sure if she was thinking what I was thinking.

"Like, how old?" I said.

"Oh, at least ten or twelve. Maybe older." She rubbed his head again. "You're a good old boy, Chuz."

Ten or twelve? Why didn't I remember this cat? I knelt and held out my hand, and the cat stopped eating for a moment to sniff my fingers. Then he flopped over suddenly and stuck his paws in the air, exposing the soft white fur on his belly.

The girl laughed. "He wants tummy rubs. Chuz is a pushover." She put the kibble away and left the room.

I scratched Martin Chuzzlewit's tummy and he purred, and I wiped my eyes with my other hand.

"Elizabeth," I said, "I think the universe or God or somebody has forgiven me for my sins."

"For what?" she said, sitting on the floor next to me and scratching Chuz behind the ears. He closed his eyes and turned his purr up to an audible rumble.

"Never mind," I said. Maybe Elizabeth had forgotten about

my horrible first driving lesson. It was before she moved in with us—before we even knew about her.

Just three months ago.

"Do you think—" she started, then hesitated, staring at Chuz.

"That Dad named this cat?"

"That's exactly what I was thinking."

"Well, I don't remember for sure, but—"

"But *Martin Chuzzlewit?*" she finished for me. She looked like Dad when she grinned.

"I know, right?"

She tucked her hair behind her ears, glanced down at Chuz, and stopped smiling. "Cadie—I know I've sort of ruined everything for you. I know you're mad at Ross, and it feels like it's my fault."

I let that thought sink in for a moment. Elizabeth might be the only person who would truly *get* the way I was feeling . . . "Dad gave me a note today, before they left. He said he wants to fix things, between me and him. But I don't even know where to start. I feel like I don't know who he really is, but also I know that's not fair. I screwed up tonight too, and maybe—maybe I'm not who *he* thinks I am, either."

"Or maybe you shouldn't be so hard on yourself," Elizabeth said. "Or on him."

Good people make mistakes

"He loves you so much, Cadie. If I could go back . . ." She sighed. "If you were being completely honest with him, what would you tell him?"

"Right now?"

"Right now."

I took a deep breath. "I'd tell him—he doesn't have to fix anything."

We sat there quietly together for a few minutes, petting Chuz, whose eyes were slitted shut with contentment. Martin Chuzzlewit. I could almost feel Dad sitting there beside me.

"And I think I'd tell him—that I'd like to go see a play together. Just the two of us. Because I miss him." I bit my lip. "I'd tell him how much I've missed him."

Elizabeth squeezed my hand. "I think that's all you have to say."

"Thank you," I whispered.

"Cadie, do you think maybe . . ."

"Hm?"

"Well, it's pretty late, and I'm not supposed to drive after midnight until I get my full license. So I thought maybe we could spend the night here. If you think that would be okay? I know we have school in the morning, but Melissa said if I ever needed to take personal days off from school, or sick days—the guidance counselor said it was fine too—and Rotem went to look for some pictures of my mom. I'm just not ready to leave yet."

"I think that's a great idea," I said. "I'll text Raven and let her know where we are. So Ruby and Renata don't freak out in the morning when they wake up and we're not there."

"Okay. Good."

My legs were cramping from crouching on the floor. I stood and stretched, then reached down and gave Elizabeth a hand to help her up.

We went back into the living room. It was almost midnight, but Josh was still playing his cello. He was back to Bach now, the playful, cheerful ending of the first suite. The swooping notes of this movement always made me think of butterflies or birds, spiraling back and forth across the sky.

My eyes might've been misting up a little, when Elizabeth put an arm around my shoulders. I don't know what surprised me more: that, or what she said next. "He's really talented," she whispered. "Our little brother."

So I reached out, too, and I put my arm around my sister.

ACKNOWLEDGMENTS

I am indebted to all the people who helped make this book possible. I would especially like to thank:

Linda Epstein, agent extraordinaire, who was the first dream come true.

Rebecca Davis, Cherie Matthews, Barbara Grzeslo, and my whole family at Boyds Mills Press, who believed in Cadie's story and gave her a home with a gorgeous cover.

Bill Loizeaux, without whom I never could've fixed everything that needed fixing.

Kitty Boyan, who encouraged a fourth-grader to keep going until she'd filled a whole marble notebook.

Shalene Gupta, for Friday writing dates.

Elé Veillet-Chowdhury, for *Switched at Birth* and all the big sistering.

John Astin, for Uta Hagan, Sanford Meisner, and the inevitable and only consequence of every action; James Glossman, for teaching me to direct; and Joe Martin, for *Simpatico*.

The Associates of the Boston Public Library, who gave me a room of my own.

Becca Derry, Billie Rinaldi, Clara Brasseur, Danielle Buonaiuto, Karina van Berkum, Mary Greene, Miriam Haviland, Thalia Coombs, and Valerie Caldas, for reading early drafts and telling me which parts made you laugh or cry. You're all gold.

Adi Elbaz, Michael Arnst, and Ouranitsa Abbas for last-minute copyediting help.

Gerard Busnuk and Alison Chaplin, Joe Abrahamson and Danielle Buonaiuto (again!), who made Hampden my home for an incredible year. Thanks, hons.

Naomi Permutt, my Raven and my Elizabeth, forever-friend and sister. The next one's for you.

Carolyn Rosinsky, who screamed in a crowded elevator, and who does with the cello what I try to do with words.

Ned Rosinsky, for raising me on Beethoven sonatas, teaching me to drive, and weeping at all my plays.

Fay Rosinsky, first reader and best reader. I kept going because I knew you were waiting for the next chapter. You're my rock.

Jon Barrows, for living far away, which gave me long car rides to dream up stories, and for saying the magic words that sparked Acadia. I'm very glad we don't live far apart now.